Brothers in Arms

Love's Fortress

Samantha Kane

ELLORA'S CAVE
ROMANTICA PUBLISHING

An Ellora's Cave Romantica Publication

www.ellorascave.com

Love's Fortress

ISBN 9781419961984
ALL RIGHTS RESERVED.
Love's Fortress Copyright © 2010 Samantha Kane
Edited by Raelene Gorlinsky.
Cover art by Syneca.

Electronic book publication July 2010
Trade paperback publication 2010

LOVE'S FORTRESS

Dedication

ॐ

This book is dedicated to today's wounded warriors, service men and women who have been severely injured in the line of duty. May you find as much happiness as my fictional hero. And to those who have dedicated their lives to making that happiness possible for these real-life heroes, I salute you. For more information see the Wounded Warrior Project at http://www.woundedwarriorproject.org/.

This one also goes out to Bernard Cornwell and Sean Bean, whether they want it or not.

Acknowledgements

ℭ

I have to give credit where credit is due. Thanks go out to my siblings, who all helped in the creation of this book. My older brother Will, who first told me about the Forlorn Hope also named this book. My oldest sister Jeri, who named my last Brothers in Arms (Love in Exile) and who helped me figure out how Gideon was injured in a brainstorming session at the beach with our other two siblings. That session included my sister Charlotte, who is an active service member. She told me about the Wounded Warrior Project.

I created a playlist for this book because my three main characters were all so different and setting a mood when I was in each of their heads helped me stay true to each one. But the most important song was The Beatles' "Blackbird", which was Gideon's song. I'd like to think that by the end of the book he'd found his moment to be free.

And to Jules, you were invaluable while I was writing this book. Your encouragement and advice helped get me to The End.

As always, none of it would have happened without the love and support of my number one fan, my husband. Every one is for you, honey.

Chapter One
ഉ

"You did what?" Gideon was very much afraid that he had not misunderstood her at all.

"She will make you a fine wife, North," Anne, Duchess of Ashland, said crisply as she poured a cup of tea.

They were sitting in the gazebo at Blakeley House, Gideon's estate, watching the grooms try to catch the horses in the adjoining pasture. Gideon would have turned his look of horror on the duchess, but he didn't want to take his eyes off the horses. They were his livelihood, after all.

"It isn't as if you didn't advertise for a wife, North," she said with exasperation.

They'd been friends for nearly a year, ever since Gideon had proposed to her. She'd turned him down, of course. She'd been madly in love with Ashland and Brett Haversham, and told him so. He gave her credit for her honesty. Unfortunately she felt his declined proposal gave her the right to interfere in his life.

"You had no right and you know it. I will find myself a wife, thank you." Gideon didn't try to hide his annoyance. She was a very managing female. "I'm going to have to talk to Ashland about keeping you in check," he told her, quite disgruntled by the whole conversation.

The duchess's laughter was hearty and genuinely amused. "Yes, you do that, North. I'm sure that shall curtail my endeavors. Truly. I am chastised."

"Are you sowing the seeds of Gideon's discontent, Anne?"

9

Gideon's back straightened and he gripped the arm of his chair with his good hand as his estate manager Charles Borden took the seat next to Anne at the small table containing the tea service. Gideon didn't look—he didn't have to. He could see the expression of amusement and exasperation on Charles' face in his mind. He'd seen it a thousand times before and surely would see it a thousand times more.

"I suppose you were part of this?" Gideon asked tightly.

"I was not. I heard Her Grace as I was walking up," Charles said, sounding far too superior for Gideon's liking. Charles was worse than the duchess when it came to trying to manage Gideon's life. Charles had been his sergeant in the war. After Gideon's injury Charles had come home with him, nursed him back to health and somehow become Gideon's left hand, replacing the almost useless one he'd brought home from the war. Now he refused to leave. Gideon had dismissed him so many times he'd lost count, and yet every morning to his consternation he found Charles smiling at him over his morning fare. It was damned irritating.

"If I had known it would annoy you so much, however, I would have gladly helped the duchess in any way I could." Charles sounded so happy about the situation it made Gideon grit his teeth and he felt his cheek twitch.

"Splendid," Gideon bit out. "It is my greatest joy in life to amuse you both with my annoyance."

"Well, it pleases us to give you joy, North," the duchess said, "whether you like it or not."

Charles laughed and the sound sent a shiver down Gideon's back. He closed his eyes and took a moment to calm down.

"I will see her," Gideon announced. "But I will make you no promises, Anne. You know my requirements in a wife."

Anne sighed in that long-suffering way of hers. "Yes, Gideon. I have heard it enough to commit it to memory each time you have rejected an applicant." She ticked the items off on her fingers as she began to recite. "She must be practical and hardworking. No ladies with soft hands who've never known a day of work. She must be of a hearty constitution. You do not wish to be met with a case of the vapors every morning over tea. She must not be a talkative woman. You have no use for endless prattle about dresses and such. She must be able to handle the servants and know all about the running of a farm. And she must be self-sufficient, as you need a wife to make your life easier and not to become another burden on your shoulders."

"Like Charles," Gideon added drily.

"Ha," Charles said without rancor. "The burden is mine."

Anne stopped her recitation to nod. "I must agree with Mr. Borden, North. You are a trial."

"I am the very soul of generosity," he argued, reaching for a biscuit. "After all, I put up with you two." He pretended not to see the look that passed between them.

"I have assured her father that this is a splendid opportunity for her." Anne's voice was stern. "Do not make a liar of me. From what Mr. Matthews says, she is a sweet-natured lady who wishes to marry and establish her own home. I cannot say if she meets all your requirements, not having met her myself. But in my experience a man's requirements in a wife rarely coincide with his choices."

Charles snorted beside him.

"She will be here with her father in two weeks' time," Anne continued. "I have agreed to sponsor her introduction and they will stay at Ashton Park. I only ask that you keep an open mind and remember that she is here at your request." Gideon raised a brow. "You did advertise for a wife, North. I merely wrote to the Reverend Whitley and brought your advertisement to his attention."

Gideon sighed in irritation. "I have said I will see her, Anne. That is all I can do."

11

"Hardly," Anne retorted. "That is all you are willing to do."

Gideon blinked innocently at her. "I fail to see the difference."

"You would." Charles spoke drily as he rose from his seat. He tapped his thigh impatiently, as if sitting with them had cost him dearly. Gideon tried to ignore the sight of his tanned hand with its strong, thick fingers patting his perfectly formed, heavily muscled thigh. Charles was the son of a well-to-do farmer, had grown up knowing hard work and enjoyed it still. It showed in his physique. Part of Gideon's discomfort over his obsession with Charles' physical attributes was the jealousy that struck him each time he admired Charles' perfection. He refused to examine the other emotions causing his discomfort.

"As long as you agree to see her, Gideon," Charles told him with a little too much tone of command for Gideon's liking, "and you don't act like an idiot while she is here, I shall be happy."

"Once again," Gideon responded with a bland expression, "your happiness is of the utmost importance to me in this matter."

Charles' grin brought out the fresh-faced boyish charm he hadn't lost, though he was nearing thirty. "I wouldn't have it any other way," he said with a wink in Anne's direction.

Anne's laughter filled the silence as Gideon watched Charles walk away and tried not to think about how important Charles' happiness truly was to him.

Chapter Two

ஒ

She was too bloody quiet.

Sarah Whitley sat across from Gideon, his desk separating them. She wouldn't look at him, had hardly spoken and still wore the most disgusting bonnet he had ever seen. One of those excessively large things women referred to as "poke" or some such nonsense. Apparently because their faces were so hidden within the depths that you couldn't even poke them in the eye. She wasn't a dainty thing at least. She was tall and well built. But he wished she'd take the damn hat off.

"Her Grace assured us that our visit would be welcome, sir," her father said gravely. "Your letter of two weeks past seemed to imply the same. I hope we have not inconvenienced you." Her father, the Reverend Whitley, was a humorless man, although inoffensive Gideon supposed. His demeanor and comment made Gideon realize he'd let his dislike of Miss Whitley's bonnet show.

"You interpreted my correspondence correctly, sir," Gideon reassured him. "I was pleased to receive your inquiry into my advertisement." He looked at his butler. "Anders, please take Miss Whitley's pelisse and hat." He looked at her and caught her flinch. Her father started to reach for her arm, in concern it seemed, but stopped himself. "I hope you will join me for tea," Gideon continued politely.

Miss Whitley sat there, still as a stone. Gideon looked over at Charles, who was standing quietly just inside the study door. Charles gave a small, confused shrug in response to his look. Clearly he did not know what to make of Miss Whitley either.

Perhaps she had not wished to come. Or, more likely, regretted her decision at her first sight of Gideon's face. The burn scars covered the left side from his cheekbone to his neck, and he kept his hair short, not bothering to try to conceal the disfigurement. It would have done no good, and he saw no reason to pretend to be something he wasn't. She hadn't even seen his leg yet. Or what was left of it, anyway.

He deliberately motioned with his scarred left hand for Anders to step forward, watching Miss Whitley. But she wasn't looking at him, of course. She was staring at her lap. Suddenly she rose and turned her back to him. He thought she was going to leave, but instead she started to remove her coat. Her father stood and solicitously helped her. He seemed to care for her, and that allayed Gideon's fears that she had been forced to come.

Anders reached out to take her coat from her father just as Miss Whitley untied and removed that damned bonnet. He gasped and nearly dropped the garment, which was so out of character for the staid butler that Gideon half rose from his chair. He glanced over at Charles and saw a look of shock on his face. Charles took a step toward Miss Whitley just as she turned to Gideon.

Gideon slowly sat back down. Damn. Damn it all to hell.

"We would be happy to stay for tea, Mr. North," she told him in a clear, strong voice, almost challenging him. But who was he to say anything? The dark, strawberry pink birthmark covering most of her right cheek was far less unsightly than his scars.

Gideon cleared his throat. "Very good," he answered. He reached for his crutches and stood, then slowly made his way around the desk. He stopped next to her. "I believe Mrs. Brown has our tea in the drawing room." With a raised brow he indicated she precede him. She smiled wryly and in a swish of skirts and lavender, she did just that.

* * * * *

14

Charles was shaken by this Miss Whitley. She was not what they'd expected. She just might work. And what if she did? What if Gideon married her? Charles had been working toward that goal for over a year now. And yet, now that it might become a reality, he was plagued by doubts. And fears. He couldn't forget the fear. Fear that Gideon would no longer need him. Fear that the next time Gideon dismissed him he'd really mean it, and Charles would have nowhere to go. No life without Gideon.

He took a deep breath and followed them all as they headed for the drawing room. Miss Whitley walked sedately next to Gideon, matching her pace to his effortlessly. She was terribly graceful. And attractive, even with the birthmark. He had been shaken to the core by the birthmark. She understood Gideon right now, after only a brief introduction, better than Charles ever could. She knew. She knew what Gideon went through every day, every time he looked in the mirror. It was a connection Charles could never make with Gideon.

They passed the windows in the foyer and the sunlight glinted off her hair. It was an odd combination of light blonde and deep honey gold strands, as if it couldn't decide what it wanted to be. She had it pulled back rather tightly, exposing her mark for all to see. Another similarity to Gideon. But it looked as if it would be long and thick when it was free. Charles absently ran a hand through his curly blond hair. He'd noticed his forehead getting noticeably larger lately. He smiled ruefully at the thought. As if he was in competition with the lovely Miss Whitley. No matter how Charles felt, Gideon did not think of him that way. It was best he remember that. Best that he think about how good it would be for Gideon to have a wife like her, pretty and strong and seemingly unconcerned with his scars. It was what Charles had been hoping for, after all.

* * * * *

Well, at least he hadn't recoiled in horror. Although truly, that was the best Sarah could say about Mr. North's reaction to her face. She'd thought she could be braver about the whole business, brazen out the fact that they'd withheld something so important from him. She'd known about his scars. The duchess had written to her and her father and described Mr. North's injuries. She had imagined an infirm veteran, grateful that any woman would consider his suit.

Instead she had been met by a man who carried himself as if he commanded the world. He had stood unsteadily behind his desk when they arrived but sat down immediately. From behind his desk he had glowered at them, broad-shouldered and lean. His scars pulled down the corner of his left eye and the corner of his mouth. She had almost convinced herself that was why he appeared so displeased at their arrival. But his eyes, so unusually light blue they seemed to shine from his face like a beacon, were hard and assessing. He had already found her wanting and he hadn't even seen the birthmark yet.

She knew an overwhelming sense of defeat sitting across from him. This man could pick and choose his wife. He need not take a disfigured girl such as her He'd been her last hope for a home and family of her own unless she considered marrying beneath her, which she was reluctant to do. Marriages like that rarely worked in Sarah's experience. She wanted her own life but had no desire to be unhappy in it. When he had insisted she remove her coat and bonnet, Sarah had actually flinched in fear. But she was made of sterner stuff than that. She'd had the mark her whole life, had dealt with a wide range of reactions to it, and she knew in that moment she could deal with Mr. North's as well.

But she had cheated, just a little. She'd turned to that nice Mr. Borden, who had escorted them from Ashton Park, riding beside their carriage on his horse. She had been in the carriage with her father so hadn't spoken to Mr. Borden, but the duchess was quite fond of him and he was so congenial to everyone they met on the road. So she let his reaction be the first she saw. It had not soothed her fears. The shock on his face was like a douse of cold water to her bravado. The pity that followed was no better. But she'd turned to Mr. North and she had been so proud of her calm and steady demeanor.

Mr. North had surprised her by not showing much of a reaction at all. He'd fallen back on tea, which amused Sarah to no end. Tea had certainly solved a great many English dilemmas, had it not? And so here they were, making polite conversation in the drawing room.

She was a little surprised that Mr. Borden was still here. As the estate manager he was a retainer, but he was treated as family. From what little the duchess had told her, he had been with Mr. North since the war. Perhaps that explained his esteemed position in the household.

"You are very quiet, Miss Whitley," Mr. North said suddenly, with the sharpness of impatience. She was surprised and fumbled her teacup, nearly dropping it. She sighed with disgust and forced herself to put the cup down calmly. She accepted the handkerchief Mr. Borden held out to her with a firm "Thank you" and matter-of-factly dabbed the spot of tea on her gown before answering.

"And what would you have me discuss, Mr. North?" she responded with a smile. "I have exhausted tea and the weather."

Mr. North's eyes widened in surprise and then the unscarred side of his mouth quirked with amusement. "Have you? I thought ladies were taught to discuss those topics at length with great animation."

"North," Mr. Borden said with ill-disguised warning.

"Sarah has been raised as a lady, sir," her father said calmly. She was quite proud of how well he was handling himself here. This was the first time he'd had to negotiate a marriage for a daughter, and Mr. North was intimidating.

"I did not doubt it," Mr. North said with a slight inclination of his head to her. "I apologize if I indicated otherwise."

"Accepted," Sarah murmured with a polite nod of her own. She secretly found Mr. North's gruff manner amusing. She was tired of people who tried too hard to say the right thing at all times.

"Well then," Mr. North began, setting his cup down on the table, "let us get to the heart of the matter."

Sarah could hardly wait to hear what he was going to say next. "Oh yes, let us do exactly that," she agreed with conviction. Both Mr. North and Mr. Borden looked at her as if they'd never seen anything like her before. Well, that was certainly not a first for Sarah.

"Tell me why you wish to marry me, Miss Whitley," Mr. North demanded, and Sarah almost clapped in appreciation of his forthrightness.

"Now see here, North," her father protested. "We have not established that Sarah wishes to marry you at all. We are here to determine if an alliance between you is acceptable."

Mr. North nodded. "You are correct, Reverend." He looked at Sarah with those eyes that seemed to see everything. "And is it, Miss Whitley?"

It took Sarah a moment to realize he meant did she wish to marry him. "Yes," she answered, perhaps a little too fervently, at least based on her father's frown.

"Why?" Mr. North sat back in his seat and calmly waited for her answer.

Sarah smoothed her skirts and glanced at Mr. Borden out of the corner of her eye. He seemed quite pleased by the turn in the conversation. She licked her lips and looked back at Mr. North, who was still intently watching her.

"I am the eldest of eleven children, Mr. North." His eyes grew wide with astonishment as he turned his gaze to her plump, balding, mild-mannered father, who calmly sat there drinking his tea. "My mother died in childbirth and I have raised my younger siblings and run my father's house for the last seven years. My father has recently remarried and my stepmother is expecting, and as I am twenty-four years old I felt it was time I married and set up my own home."

Mr. North made no response for a time, as if waiting for her to go on. When she didn't he leaned forward. "That is all very well, Miss Whitley. But why do you wish to marry *me*?"

So, he wanted all of it, did he? Very well. "Because, Mr. North, to be quite frank, you are the only man I've met who might be able to accept me with the mark on my face."

Mr. North smiled, rather gruesomely actually, because of his scars. But Sarah didn't mind. The unscarred half of his face was handsome, and she knew a smile when she saw one.

"And now I must ask you, Mr. North. Why do you wish to marry *me*?"

"Sarah," her father said chidingly.

Mr. North waved him off. "It is only fair," he said. He looked at Sarah, assessing her from head to foot. She felt the heat of a blush spread from her chest to her cheeks, one of the awkward traits that came with pale skin and blonde hair. "Quite frankly, Miss Whitley, you are one of the few women I have met who does not seem to mind my disfigurement."

Sarah smiled grimly. It wasn't much of a compliment, but she was willing to accept it as his reason.

"And," he surprised her by continuing, "you meet almost all of my requirements in a wife."

Sarah blinked, not sure what to make of that. "And those requirements are, sir?"

He waved his scarred hand in the air dismissively. Two of the fingers had been injured so badly he could not straighten them completely. "Immaterial, Miss Whitley. What matters is that I think we shall get along quite well together. If you agree, then we shall sign the papers and our betrothal will be announced at once."

Sarah found herself slightly breathless. This was it. It was up to her. If she said yes, she would marry this hard, scarred man, live here in his house, bear and raise his children. This — he — would be her life. He waited patiently, as if understanding what was going through her mind. She examined him closely. His close-cropped hair showed signs of silver. His eyes were beautiful. Physically he was in his prime. She made herself look at his scars. They were white against his tanned face. But she was already used to them. They didn't detract from his appeal, which lay more in his commanding manner and forthright speech than in his physical attributes. This was a man who would protect and care for her as his wife and who clearly admired her independent streak. Marriages had been built on less.

She nodded slowly. "Yes, Mr. North, I would be honored to be your wife."

He smiled again. "Good. In three weeks time, then."

And just like that, Sarah's life changed forever.

Chapter Three

❧

"Sarah?"

Sarah turned and leaned around the tree at her back. "Here, Papa. I'm over here." She was sitting on a comfortable bench by the fence surrounding the pasture, watching the horses. Did Mr. North sit here, she wondered? It was a beautiful view, enchanting in its quiet simplicity. The pasture lay before her looking bright green in the sunlight, the horses dotting the landscape. She couldn't believe this was to be her home. After today she would be Mrs. Gideon North. She felt a shiver race down her back. It was excitement, anticipation.

Today. Today her life would start. Today was her wedding day. *Please let this be a good day,* she silently asked. When her mother had been dying after Winnie was born, she had lingered for several weeks. Each morning Sarah had asked the same thing. She had asked every day since. She had compromised on what was and was not a good day over the years. She didn't want to compromise anymore.

Her father sat down next to her with a sigh. They had traveled all day yesterday. He had wanted to get here earlier this week, but he'd been needed in the parish. He had been so upset, worried that he'd ruined her wedding. They had arrived at Ashton Park late last night and the duke had sent a message to Blakely House.

The duke. Sarah couldn't believe she knew one, much less had stayed in his home. She had almost convinced herself in the last three weeks that her trip to Ashton on the Green had been a dream, that Mr. North had been a dream. But he'd sent her Papa some money so she could buy new clothes and a wedding dress. Her stepmother had been beside herself trying to get Sarah ready, and jealous that she hadn't gone with them and wouldn't be going this time either. The younger children simply couldn't be left alone with their one servant.

"Are you sure, Sarah?" Her father reached out and touched her hand. Sarah turned in surprise. He was a kind father, but theirs was not an overly demonstrative affection. "You needn't marry him if you don't want to, Sarah girl."

"Why would I not want to?" she asked with very real bewilderment.

Her father cleared his throat. "You don't know him. We know *of* him, of course, and we know his business, but that's not the same." He sighed. "I worry, my dear, that I might not be doing the right thing to let you marry a stranger and go far from us."

"Oh, Papa." Sarah impulsively took his hand and squeezed it, and he squeezed back. "I'm sure, Papa." She looked around at the pasture and back up to the house, content with her decision. "I can be happy here, I know I can."

"I don't want you to feel that you're being forced into this." Her father rubbed his cheek. "I know that your stepmother... Well, she doesn't mean harm."

Sarah felt sorry for him. He was in the middle, wasn't he? It wasn't that Sarah disliked her stepmother, but she disliked being replaced as the woman of the house. Suddenly it wasn't Sarah who was making the household decisions or caring for the children. And her stepmother was uncomfortable around Sarah. She tried to hide it, but Sarah's mark upset her. It was best for everyone that she leave. "I know" was all she said.

She turned on the bench and looked at her father. "I have wanted this all my life, Papa. A place of my own, a family of my own. It is my decision and I think I have chosen wisely."

Her father nodded. "I believe so."

She looked away. "He could have anyone." She was trying so very hard not to let her weak confidence ruin the day.

"Yes, he could." Her father tugged on her hand and Sarah turned back to him. "But he was smart enough to wait for the perfect woman. He has chosen quite wisely as well."

Sarah blushed with pleasure. On impulse she kissed his cheek. "Oh, Papa, I *will* be happy. I will."

He patted her hand and they sat and watched the horses together until it was time to leave for the church.

* * * * *

The wedding ceremony was short and practical. Mr. North, Sarah thought with amusement, would have it no other way. She was almost giddy with relief when she realized the guests were few and seated behind them. She didn't need to face his friends. She was pathetically grateful.

He had given her one more chance to politely bow out of the marriage. He'd asked to speak with her alone right before the ceremony and Mr. Matthews, the vicar, had offered them the small office next to the church.

"Miss Whitley," Mr. North said, "I wanted to assure you that if you have had second thoughts during your absence, I will not hold you to our agreement." For a moment Sarah panicked, thinking he was the one who had changed his mind.

Then he moved, ungainly on his crutches, to stand directly in front of the window, the bright morning sun on his ruined face. Sarah knew it was deliberate. He wanted her to see what she was getting. She looked at him in his somber wedding clothes of black coat and gray trousers, the width of his shoulders stretching the fine material, and the pinned-back trouser leg emphasizing the muscular thigh filling out the other leg. His look was direct, his mouth a harsh slash, the one corner turned down. She knew exactly what she was getting.

She made sure he knew too. Before answering him she removed her bonnet and moved to stand in front of him in the sunlight. She smoothed her hair back and raised her face to his and saw a look in his eyes that could have been fear before he could tame it. When she answered, his face wore its usual mask of bland unconcern, all emotion leashed. But Sarah knew differently. She knew there was more underneath his calm. And she understood it.

"Mr. North," she answered firmly. "I do not wish to release you from our agreement. Indeed, I will not."

He seemed taken aback for a moment and then an amused gleam entered his unusual eyes. It struck her that as composed as he appeared outwardly, his eyes would always give him away. They burned with a spirit that was anything but tame. A spirit that called to her own.

He nodded slowly in acknowledgment. "Very well, Miss Whitley," he said. "Then let us get this business over with." She nodded briskly, the picture of practicality. But when she walked back to the church beside him, slowing her steps to match his unsightly gait, she was rather sure he could hear the wild, nervous beat of her heart.

By the time they signed the register after their brief vows, the other guests had left the church for the wedding breakfast at Ashton Park. Sarah was breathless and excited and trying not to show it. She was a married woman. Married to the taciturn, scarred man who moved by her side. Chained to him for all eternity. Now, why didn't that alarm her more? She grinned foolishly.

"I am glad to see that you are still smiling, Mrs. North," a voice called out to them. Sarah was startled. She'd thought they were the last ones to leave the church. She glanced over and saw Mr. Borden waiting for them beside the carriage that had brought her and her father to the church. He was smiling at them both but his look was guarded.

Mr. North stopped abruptly at the sound of Mr. Borden's voice. He started walking again without acknowledging the other man. Sarah moved with him.

"And why would I not be smiling, Mr. Borden?" she answered, curious at the undercurrents between the two men.

Here was the most unfamiliar ground in her new life. What was their relationship? They were inseparable it seemed, and yet continually at odds.

"Gideon's unsmiling demeanor has been more than enough to wipe the smiles from many faces," was Mr. Borden's wry reply as he turned to open the carriage door.

Mr. North didn't like that one bit, judging by the stiffening of his shoulders. Sarah wasn't sure she did either. "Mine shall not be one of them, Mr. Borden," she responded coolly. "Unlike others who maintain a wary distance, I am close enough to see the smile in his eyes."

Mr. Borden spun back around to face her with an expression of shock on his face. Mr. North stopped again and so did Sarah. He turned his head slowly to gaze at her with narrowed eyes. "My eyes smile?"

Sarah snorted. "You may frighten small children and animals, Mr. North, but you do not frighten me." She raised an eyebrow, hoping she wasn't taking her teasing too far. "Your eyes give you away. If you do not wish me to know how you feel, then I suggest you make every attempt not to look at me."

Mr. North actually chuckled and a real smile crept across his face and then fell away. "Now why would I deny myself the pleasure of looking at you, Mrs. North?" he asked quietly. "I begin to have doubts that I will be able to retain any secrets from you, no matter what precautions I take."

What an odd answer. Sarah felt herself blush at his insincere compliment. Pleasure looking at her, indeed. She humphed impatiently in response, earning another smile from Mr. North. She was learning. He appreciated her rather starchy, practical façade. No weak-kneed, whimpering ninny for Mr. Gideon North. So when she felt that way, she had best conceal it well. "I am not a mind reader, Mr. North," she told him crisply. "I dare say a great many of your secrets are safe from me."

Strangely enough he turned then to glance at Mr. Borden. But when Sarah followed the direction of his gaze, Mr. Borden had turned away. They resumed their uneven pace to the carriage.

"My apologies, madam," Mr. Borden said rather stiffly. He refused to look at them. "I didn't realize you had come to know Mr. North quite so well yet."

Sarah couldn't contain her slight, rather wild laugh at his comment. Mr. Borden looked at her then, unusually enigmatic. "Mr. Borden, I do not know him at all. That is what marriage is for."

He reluctantly smiled. "Ah, now the mystery is explained." His face blanched as he realized how his comment could be taken as an insult. Sarah did not take offense. She knew he hadn't meant it that way, as if Mr. North's reasons for marrying her were a mystery.

"Is it?" she replied, amused at his consternation. "Then you must explain the mystery of marriage to me as well. For I believe I have gotten myself into a situation in which I have no practical experience to fall back on."

They had reached the carriage and Sarah could see Mr. Borden's eyes gleaming with amusement as he grinned widely, and beside her Mr. North tried to cover his laughter with a discreet cough.

"In the case of marriage, Mrs. North," Mr. Borden said, offering his hand to help her into the carriage, "no experience is preferred."

* * * * *

Sarah's nerves were frayed to the breaking point. Mr. North's friends and acquaintances had been extremely pleasant to her, but being the center of attention in a large group was not a comfortable situation for her. She had carried herself well thus far, she thought, but she knew she had to get away if only for a few minutes to gather her composure. She did not wish to embarrass Mr. North by running screaming from their scrutiny, her skirts over her face.

"Would you care to walk through the garden with me?"

Sarah turned to see the Duchess of Ashland standing next to her, smiling in invitation. She nodded eagerly. "Yes, please. That would be lovely." *Reprieved*, she rejoiced inwardly. The duchess locked their arms together and led her off down a well-used path, waving at Mr. Haversham as they went past him. Sarah watched Mr. Haversham as his eyes followed the duchess. She knew he was the duke's closest friend and obviously was close to the duchess as well. The two times Sarah had stayed here Mr. Haversham had been in residence, and from conversation she had overheard, Sarah understood that he lived here at Ashton Park with them.

The sunlight glinted off the duchess's dark, curly hair. Sarah hadn't said anything, but in the three weeks she was away the duchess had grown. She was clearly with child and yet still very attractive. She turned her smiling face and caught Sarah staring. Sarah blushed but the duchess just laughed.

"Yes," she answered the unasked question. "We are expecting a new arrival sometime in October."

"How wonderful," Sarah said sincerely. "I am very happy for you and the duke."

"Hmmm, yes, we are all very happy," the duchess answered, looking away with a wistful smile.

Sarah got the feeling she was missing something, and she felt quite awkward and gauche. The duchess turned back, her ever-present smile in place.

"But today is your day, my dear," she said, squeezing Sarah's arm affectionately. "Are you happy with North?"

Sarah blinked several times, confused by the question. "I have only just married him, Your Grace. I didn't expect happiness quite so soon. He still has time to come up to snuff."

The duchess laughed delightedly. "Oh, you will be good for him."

"I hope so."

The duchess pulled her to a stop in front of some garden chairs tucked away in a small bower protected from the sun by a rose-covered arch. She sat down and gestured Sarah into the other chair. "I find myself tiring rather easily these days."

Sarah sat down. "I'm sorry. I should have taken your condition into consideration. I do appreciate your thoughtfulness, Your Grace." The duchess looked at her inquiringly. Sarah swallowed nervously and continued. "I know you must have seen my discomfort. I do not often mingle among strangers, much less find myself the center of attention. It is...disconcerting."

The duchess reached over and patted her hand. "You must call me Anne. We are neighbors now. We spend most of our time here at Ashton Park. So you see, we shall see a great deal of each other from now on." She settled back in the chair rather inelegantly, her hands unconsciously going to her stomach. "And you mustn't feel nervous about being around us, Sarah. We are very happy for North." She was leisurely looking around the garden but turned then and snared Sarah with a serious expression. "You must give him time, Sarah. North is... Well, he takes getting used to. But he means well. He tries to drive people away, you know. You mustn't let him."

Sarah laughed softly. "How odd. I always thought someone would be having this conversation with my future husband. 'You must forgive Sarah, she simply avoids people. She is different, you know'." The situation was turned backward and Sarah wasn't sure how she felt about that. She still felt different, vulnerable, weak. North was the strong one. She shook her head.

Anne smiled. "You are different. But not in the way you think, Sarah." She ran her finger along the arm of her chair. "You were not the first."

Sarah was confused again. "The first what?"

"The first to answer his advertisement." Anne clasped her hands over her stomach. "The others, however, barely made it past the front door before Mr. Borden was ordered to usher them right out again. You are the only one he gave serious consideration to."

Sarah wasn't sure what to make of that. Because of her birthmark? She focused instead on something else the duchess had said. "What is the relationship between Mr. North and Mr. Borden?"

Instead of answering Anne stood and held out her hand to Sarah, who rose and followed her as they began to walk back to the house. They walked in silence for a time and Sarah thought Anne would not answer her question. She was startled when Anne finally spoke.

"They met in the war." Anne stopped and so did Sarah. They were on the edge of the garden, partially hidden by low-hanging branches and the curve of the path. They could see everyone in the garden, however. As if they sensed her presence, the duke and Mr. Haversham turned and scanned the trees for Anne. When they saw her they smiled and returned to their separate conversations. "Most of the men here met during the war, on the Peninsula."

Anne paused as if waiting for Sarah to say something. "Is that where Mr. North served, on the Peninsula?"

"You didn't know?" Anne seemed surprised, but it was quickly replaced by exasperation. "Of course you don't. North wouldn't offer and you wouldn't ask."

Sarah didn't know how to defend herself against that. Anne was right. She didn't know him well enough to ask such things yet.

"Did you know I was the daughter of a vicar, like you?" The change of subject took Sarah by surprise, but not nearly as much as Anne's startling background.

"You?" Sarah exclaimed. "But you are a duchess."

Anne laughed. "Well, yes, now I am a duchess. But I used to be the only daughter of the local vicar. My father served the parish here before Mr. Matthews." She paused and scanned the crowd again, catching the duke's eye. They smiled at each other. "I was engaged to the duke's older brother, Viscount Talmadge. He died on the Peninsula."

Sarah just nodded. She had the feeling Anne was leading to something as she revealed her past.

"Brett—Mr. Haversham—was my fiancé's dearest friend during the war. He was injured in the same battle where Bertie was killed. When he returned to England, Freddy took care of him." She turned and gave Sarah a meaningful look. "They have been inseparable since then."

Ah. Sarah nodded with a smile. "I see. And you are saying that Mr. North and Mr. Borden are similar?"

Anne chuckled. "I think I can say with certainty they are similar, although not quite the same."

Again Sarah got the impression she was missing something important. Anne sighed. She put her hand on Sarah's shoulder and turned her to face the guests. Sarah had unconsciously taken a sideways stance with her unmarred cheek exposed to that side of the garden. "There," Anne pointed, "did you meet Mr. and Mrs. Westridge? And their friend, Mr. Schillig?"

"Yes, I met them earlier. The baby is beautiful." Sarah had cooed over the gorgeous baby girl with plump cheeks and bright blue eyes, making herself very agreeable to the Westridges. The baby really was adorable, bald as could be but lively and happy.

"Oh, isn't she? I absolutely adore Violet. Leah made me promise not to whisk her off to the nursery and stay there all day." Anne laughed. Sarah liked her laugh. She seemed to do it all the time, laughing at everything and everyone, including herself. Sarah had never met anyone like her. Anne wagged a finger at Sarah. "Now, don't get me started on babies. I am trying to have a serious conversation with you."

"I am sorry," Sarah said a little desperately. "I know you are trying to tell me something, but I simply don't understand. I am very gauche, aren't I?"

Anne impulsively hugged her. Sarah was shocked but pleased and hugged her back awkwardly. She didn't have a great deal of experience with hugs between adults. She'd really only hugged the children when they were small.

"Don't be silly," Anne told her. "You are not gauche. But you are unfamiliar with all this, I understand that." Anne sighed. "Mr. Schillig lives with Mr. and Mrs. Westridge, just as Mr. Haversham lives here with us." She shook her head. "Just remember, Sarah, that the war was a terrible thing, and hardest on Gideon. These men..." She paused again and sniffed and pulled out a handkerchief to dab at her cheeks and Sarah realized she was crying.

"Your Grace," Sarah exclaimed. She reached out to touch Anne on the sleeve but pulled back at the last second. It seemed too familiar a gesture.

From the corner of her eye Sarah saw the duke crossing the garden toward them, but Anne waved him off. She sniffed and tried again. "These men have been through so much, and they need each other. They helped one another through the worst of times, and they can't, won't, give up the closeness they shared during the war." She gave a watery laugh. "I am overly emotional because of the baby." Anne shook her head. "I know you don't understand, not yet. But you will."

Sarah rushed to reassure her. "I have no desire to make Mr. Borden leave, Anne. I was just unsure as to the exact nature of their relationship. They seem inseparable, and yet they are always at odds."

Anne nodded with a laugh. "Yes, yes they are. I think Mr. Borden was the one thing that made North so annoyed he had no choice but to survive and get well, simply so he could give Borden a piece of his mind."

Sarah bit her lip to hide her smile. "I do believe you may be right."

Anne reached out and took Sarah's hand, clasping it gently. "When the time comes and you need someone to talk to, you must come to me."

Sarah was lost in the quagmire of the conversation again. She shook her head in confusion.

"You will know what I am talking about very soon," Anne said, turning back to the garden, where the duke would no longer be held at bay. He was walking toward them purposefully, and as he passed Mr. Haversham he paused and the other man joined him. Anne gave Sarah a secretive little smile. "I wish you joy, Sarah. I think you will find it with Mr. North."

Chapter Four

80

"Jesus bloody wept, Gideon!" Charles exclaimed in frustration. "She's your wife. I won't do it."

They were standing on the veranda that looked out over the gardens of Ashton Park, watching laughing guests attempt to find their way through the maze. Charles had gone through it with Mrs. North and Mrs. Westridge earlier. Gideon wouldn't attempt it because of the uneven ground, so Charles volunteered.

Mrs. North was quiet and so serious with her honey hair and pretty brown eyes that saw too much. She made him nervous and self-conscious, which was quite out of the ordinary for him. He'd let the two women chat as they got to know each other. Watching Leah Westridge dance around her relationship with Valentine and Kurt had been highly amusing. But one thing had become clear—Gideon's new bride was as innocent as a newborn foal.

"It is precisely because she is my wife that you will." Gideon's calm only fueled Charles' ire.

"I will not interfere between you two on your wedding night," he spit out between gritted teeth. "She is so innocent that to do so would surely cause her distress."

"And this won't?" For the first time in the conversation Gideon lost his control, holding his ruined hand up to scars on his face. "If you were a young, innocent bride, would you want this to be what you found in your marriage bed?"

"Yes." Charles answered without thinking it through and then winced. Gideon's face immediately closed down.

"You knew me before Badajoz." Gideon turned away to look out at the garden again.

"Yes, I did," Charles said softly, a wealth of meaning in those three words.

Gideon took a deep breath and Charles saw his nostrils flare in irritation.

"She deserves her first time with someone...perfect."

Gideon's observation was both reluctant and sincere. Charles wasn't sure whether or not to be pleased. "I am not perfect."

Gideon turned a baleful eye on him. "Do not play coy, Charles. Physically you are perfect. You are fit and strong, attractive, a male in his prime."

Charles was amused in spite of his anger. "Shall I let her check my teeth?"

Gideon snorted. "If she wishes to, yes."

"And while the perfectly fit and attractive me is divesting your new wife of her virginity, where will you be?"

"I do not want you to fuck her." Gideon slowly turned to face him. "I am not a complete idiot. She is my wife. And I am able to perform my duties. I simply want you there so that she has something pleasant to occupy her while I am, as you so aptly put it, divesting her of her virginity."

"Bloody hell, Gideon," Charles whispered. He had to turn away. His anger was gone, replaced by despair. "You ask too much of me. You want me to be a...a plaything. Is that my value, then? After all these years? To amuse your wife but not to touch her?"

Gideon moved closer on his crutches. "It is because I value you so much that I ask." He spoke right over Charles' shoulder, so that he felt Gideon's breath against his neck. It made him shiver. "I would ask no other to do this. But you have seen me at my weakest, Charles, and at my best. You know me. You know I cannot do this without you." Gideon gripped his upper arm and it was then Charles realized how stiff his arm was, how tightly he was holding himself in check. He fought his grief over the memories Gideon pulled forth.

"Why is this different than the other times we have done it? It does not have to be different."

Charles spun around to face him. "But it does have to be different, Gideon. It must be different. She is your wife. So much depends on this night." Charles wiped his hand across his mouth and chin. "She is not like the others. She is not a whore. She is an innocent woman who has entrusted you with her future."

"I know that. I know." Gideon sounded as distressed as Charles felt. For the first time in a very long time he did not try to control his emotions. Charles would have rejoiced in any other situation. But not here, not now. "It is different for me. But it need not be different for you. You don't have to care for her. But surely you can see she is beautiful? It would not be a hardship to help me bed her."

"Not care for her? Gideon, have you gone mad?" Charles tried to keep his voice down. "Of course I care for her! She is your wife. As such, I will care for and protect her to my dying breath. And that includes protecting her from you and your idiotic notions." He ran a hand through his hair in frustration. "She does not find you offensive, Gideon. I've seen her watching you. She is fascinated by you. Every word you utter is gospel to her ears. Trust me, bedding you will be no burden for her."

"If you watched her so closely, then you saw her shudder today when I took her hand in mine." He raised his scarred left hand. "In this one."

Charles was taken aback. "No, I did not see that. You are being overly sensitive."

Gideon's laugh was bitter. "You call me insensitive twenty times a day. Now I am overly sensitive." He turned away. "What if I can't do it?" Gideon's whisper was harsh. "It has happened before."

He didn't have to explain. Charles knew how difficult it was for Gideon to talk about that. Gideon hated to show his weaknesses. But he had them. His lack of confidence with women was one of the worst scars he carried from the war. Once again Charles silently cursed the French defenders at the fortress of Badajoz. "That was with a whore. An uneducated, coarse girl who knew nothing. It was my fault, really. I chose unwisely. Neither of us performed that night, and you know it."

Gideon waved away his assurances and moved over to a chair against the wall. He sank into it and then leaned his head against his crutch. He looked so defeated. Charles' hands began to shake.

"Please," was all Gideon said. And Charles knew he was going to say yes.

* * * * *

Sarah was nervous. Not worried, exactly. Surely every woman was nervous on her wedding night. It was expected. And she knew Mr. North would be gentle. He may be gruff and silent most of the time, but she'd seen something in his eyes when he'd offered to release her from her obligation before the wedding. He'd been happy she had declined. He must desire her in some way. Mustn't he?

But he was an experienced man. A soldier. Sarah was not so ignorant she didn't understand what that meant. Loose women followed the drum, and soldiers certainly took advantage of their availability. It was impossible that he should expect Sarah to know what she was about tonight, no matter what he was used to.

She was pacing, and when she realized it she stopped immediately and sat down in an overstuffed chair before the empty fireplace. She'd opened the window earlier and the breeze carried in the scent of newly cropped hay. Sarah tried to relax. She rolled her shoulders and leaned back in the chair, attempting an inelegant, nonchalant sprawl and failing miserably. She simply wasn't the kind to sprawl, unfortunately. She refused to give up and stiffly laid her head along the back of the chair and closed her eyes.

It had been a lovely day. Ashton Park was glorious, and Sarah had floated through the day as if under some enchantment. There was a brief moment of self-consciousness, but her walk with Anne settled her nerves in spite of their odd conversation. Mr. Borden took her through the maze with Mrs. Westridge. Poor Mr. Borden was so nervous he was overly solicitous the whole way. He was so gentle with everyone else and so terse and cross with Mr. North. Sarah hoped she could smooth the way for the two men. They clearly cared for each other. She would figure out why they always seemed at odds. Surely it would be a simple matter to settle.

Sarah pictured her groom. Mr. North had looked austere and quite sophisticated in his somber clothes. He had the most amazing eyes. The more she saw of him the more mesmerizing those eyes became. Anne had described them as sea-glass blue today, and the description fit. They could seem so cold one moment and the next appear as the blue center of the hottest flame. The contradictory combination was fitting for the man.

Sarah compared him to the other men present today, her mind naturally going to Mr. Borden since she had spent so much time in his company. The two men were so different physically. Mr. North was tall, or would be if he did not have to lean on his crutches. He was dark, swarthy almost. His light eyes had bushy, dark brows accentuating them. He was quite handsome in a rather ruthless way. He more than held his own against Mr. Borden.

Although, to be fair, Mr. Borden was quite attractive as well. He was shorter than Mr. North but more muscular, which made sense. He did a great deal of manual labor with the horses. His face was ruddy and tanned from the sun, and his blond hair thin and slightly curly. His brown eyes were the soft brown of a doe. He was quiet and approachable and usually unfailingly polite. And in spite of his cross words she could tell he had a great affection for Mr. North. He was always by his side, watching, waiting, jumping to help if North needed it. Sarah smiled. He was a bit of a mother hen, actually. No wonder North became irritated with him.

Sarah forced herself to stop avoiding her main concern. She had a vague idea of what was to happen tonight, and perhaps if she thought about it dispassionately, it would calm her nerves. She took a deep breath and remembered the times Mr. North had touched her. According to her stepmother, there would be a great deal of touching, and in places no one but Sarah had touched since she was a babe. She could feel her face heating.

This morning Mr. Borden had kissed her hand in greeting. Sarah had been astonished. No one had ever done that before. His hand was callused from work and she liked that about him. Then North had taken her hand from Mr. Borden's with his scarred left hand. She'd been surprised since she had already noticed how he tended to keep that hand out of sight. She'd looked at him then, and he must have realized what he'd done. He slowly pulled his hand from hers, his face devoid of expression. The scars on his hand slid along her palm like a rough caress. It felt different, real, and she liked it. This morning she shivered at the feeling. Sarah shivered again now, thinking of that hand touching her in other places.

There was a knock at the door. A short, sharp rap. Sarah started in the chair, sitting up so quickly her head spun a little. She looked around the room in a panic, not sure what to do.

"Mrs. North?" It was Mr. North's voice. He was here.

Sarah jumped up. She allowed herself one quick wring of her hands before she smoothed the front of her nightclothes and straightened her shoulders and walked to the door. She refused to acknowledge that walking was difficult because her knees felt weak. She opened the door quickly, her knuckles white because she was gripping the handle so tightly. Then she took a surprised step back.

Mr. Borden was with him. Sarah quickly wrapped her arms around her waist. She was dressed as befitted a new bride, in a thin muslin nightgown that clung to her body. The seamstress in her little village had insisted that a bride needed such an ensemble, and the girl who was acting as her ladies maid had insisted just as strenuously that Sarah wear it tonight. She had been slightly uncomfortable in the revealing gown before, but now in the presence of the two men she felt next to naked.

"Yes?" she asked. She hated the tremble in her voice. She cleared her throat. "Is there something wrong?" Clearly there was. Mr. North wouldn't meet her eyes and Mr. Borden's mouth was a thin, angry line.

"May we come in?" Mr. North asked formally.

"Both of you?" Sarah's response came out alarmingly like a squeak.

"Gideon," Mr. Borden growled, but Mr. North ignored him.

"Yes, both of us," he answered as he moved into the room. Sarah stumbled back a few more steps. When North was in he turned his head and looked at Mr. Borden, who remained outside her door. "Charles," he said quietly. Mr. Borden stood there for another moment, angry and defiant. Then he marched in the door and closed it behind him. He didn't move far into the room. He stood there with his back against the door and looked everywhere but at Sarah.

"Mr. Borden will be joining us this evening."

Sarah could only gape at North.

"Bloody hell, Gideon," Mr. Borden ground out between clenched teeth. "This isn't a supper party, you fool. Explain yourself to her."

Mr. North glared at Mr. Borden. "If you would give me a chance, Charles, I had every intention of explaining the situation to Mrs. North."

Mr. Borden gestured wildly in her direction. "Then do it."

Sarah stared at North, waiting. She had no idea what to think, or what to do for that matter. How exactly was she supposed to respond? Was this normal? Surely not.

"I require Mr. Borden's...assistance."

"That's it? That's your explanation?" Mr. Borden burst out a few seconds later when no further explanation was forthcoming. Sarah had been thinking much the same thing.

"What kind of assistance?" Sarah said, although it came out as more of whisper than she had intended. She felt a little clammy as her stomach rolled over nervously, and the breeze suddenly felt too cool. Mr. Borden's gaze swung to her and she watched as his face heated. He was staring at her chest and Sarah looked down to see her nipples raised in stark relief beneath her thin attire. She spun around and walked jerkily over to her chair and sat down, wrapping both arms around herself.

When she looked at North she could tell he was agitated. His frown was more pronounced than usual, and his good hand kept opening and closing reflexively around his crutch handle. His eyes burned bright in the firelight. "Since the war," he began, but then he just stopped.

Oh dear. Sarah hadn't thought that he might be unable to perform in the marriage bed. But his injuries were rather severe. "I see," she said in a small voice. Is this what Anne had meant when she said these men needed each other?

"No, you do not," Mr. Borden said in a tight voice. "Gideon is your husband, and he can and will do all that the title gives him the privilege to do."

Sarah blinked at Mr. Borden in confusion. Did that mean that Mr. North could...copulate? She cringed inwardly at the choice of words, but really, she'd never had to give it a name before. "Then why are you here?" she asked bluntly, tired of all the word games she was woefully inadequate at. First Anne this afternoon, and now these two. Why couldn't they all just say what they meant?

"I will be most happy to consummate our marriage, Mrs. North." Mr. North finally spoke in that stiff, formal tone again. "Mr. Borden is here to make sure that the experience is pleasant for you and that there are no difficulties."

Difficulties? Was Borden here to make sure North didn't injure himself? Was he merely here to help North if need be? Would he watch them? Sarah shivered.

"If you agree to his presence, then we can get started."

"Bloody hell!" Mr. Borden exclaimed again.

North glared at him. "Would you stop saying that in front of my wife?"

"You are handling this like a horse's arse," Mr. Borden told him disdainfully.

"You would know," North said coldly. "Feel free to handle it your way, then."

"Fine," Mr. Borden growled. He jerked away from the door and in two steps was standing in front of Sarah. Without a by your leave he grabbed her arm and yanked her out of the chair. She fell into him with a squeak, a little frightened, but not much. It was Mr. Borden, after all, and North was here. Then he slammed his mouth down on hers and wrapped his arms around her, bending her backward over his arm. She was dizzy and shocked and grabbed his shoulders in an attempt to keep from falling. At the same time she cried out. He thrust his tongue inside her mouth and slanted his lips across hers and Sarah's shock turned to something else. Something that made her feel as if she had a fever, and she began to tremble.

Mr. Borden broke the kiss, if that's what that was, with a curse. "She's never been kissed, Gideon," he rasped.

She was gasping, unable to take in enough air, drowning in the scents of newly cut hay, overheated linen and a musky odor that she couldn't identify, but she associated it with men and what they were doing now. She saw Mr. Borden's flushed face scant inches from her own, his breath warm and sweet against her cheek, his eyes hard and hot, so different from what they had been before. This was what North meant. This was the pleasure Mr. Borden was here to ensure. She turned her face away and met Mr. North's stare. He stood immobile, watching them. She saw the ragged rise and fall of his chest, and the candle flame flickered, making his light eyes shine like gems.

"Then you had better do it again," he told Mr. Borden in a quiet, silky voice, a voice Sarah had not heard before, "but gently this time." When his words registered, Sarah knew a brief moment of nervous terror, and then it was gone, lost in Mr. Borden's kiss.

Chapter Five

80

She tasted so good. That was all Charles could think. He felt a great deal. Felt her heat and the softness of her curves crushed against him. The fine, delicate fabric of her gown. But what he thought was that she tasted wonderful, like wine-dulled mint. He wanted to eat her up in sinfully slow bites, from the tip of her slightly pug nose to the tiny, round toes she had had curled against the carpet as she stood there listening to Gideon's pronouncements with slack-jawed astonishment.

It was that last thought that made Charles break away from Sarah's mouth with a gasping breath. She was Gideon's wife, not his. Gideon, not Charles, should be kissing her. Slowly so as not to frighten her, Charles raised Sarah until she could stand on her own. He took a step back, and she stared at him uncomprehendingly for a moment before she blushed a painful red, almost dark enough to disguise her birthmark, and then she snatched her hands away from his shoulders. Without her heat he felt cold. He licked his lips and cleared his throat.

"I'm sorry."

Sarah wrapped her arms around herself as she'd done when they'd first entered. "No, I..." She shook her head and looked at Gideon. "I don't know what I'm supposed to do."

"Damn." Charles bit back the rest of his curse as Sarah flinched. "I'm sorry."

Sarah laughed. Actually laughed. He was fairly certain there were few women of his acquaintance who would be able to laugh in this situation. "Are we going to be continually saying that this evening? Could we just agree that we are all sorry and then someone could tell me exactly what I'm supposed to do?" she asked in tremulous voice.

"I want you to be comfortable, Mrs. North," Gideon said. "I want you to enjoy this evening." He sounded rough, his voice slightly harsh. Gideon usually sounded like that, whether he meant to or not. Charles watched Sarah's reaction. Many people were put off by Gideon's demeanor.

Sarah looked down at her skirt and picked at the material, making it flutter against her legs. Charles' stomach tightened at the unconsciously alluring display. "Well then, let's start by you calling me Sarah." She peeked up at Gideon around her hair, which had fallen over her shoulder. Charles had been right—it was long and straight and thick when it was loose. It came all the way to her hipbones. "I am not accustomed to being Mrs. North yet."

"You are not Mrs. North yet," Gideon told her gruffly. "That is what this exercise is about."

Charles started to laugh but he stopped himself. He didn't want Sarah to think they were laughing at her. She surprised him again by picking up on Gideon's meaning. She chuckled.

"Exercise, is it? Well, then, Captain, by all means let us begin the drill so I can learn the maneuvers."

Charles didn't stop his laughter this time, and Gideon glared at him. "I did not mean to sound as if…" Gideon seemed at a loss for words.

"You were ordering the troops?" Charles suggested. Gideon glared harder.

Sarah took a tentative step toward Gideon and reached out to touch his arm. He hastily took a step back, and Sarah yanked her hand away. "Who, exactly, am I to be with?"

"Gideon," Charles said.

"Both of us," Gideon replied.

Charles and Gideon answered simultaneously. Sarah looked between them in confusion.

"Is Mr. Borden just going to kiss me, then?" She hesitated on the word kiss, as if she wasn't sure that's what he'd done. Charles closed his eyes. He'd been right. She was so bloody innocent it was a crime, what they were doing. He was about to say so when Gideon spoke up.

"Do you want him to?" Gideon's question froze the words in Charles' throat.

Sarah licked her lips. She stole a glance at him, blushing. Then she looked at Gideon. "Yes?" It was more question than answer.

"Don't look at Gideon, Sarah," Charles told her quietly. "Look at me and tell us truly. Do you want me to stay, or should I go?"

Sarah didn't look away from Gideon. "I want what Mr. North wants."

Gideon's eyes were so bright Charles was surprised they weren't burning a hole through her. "Call me Gideon. And I want him here."

Sarah nodded firmly and finally turned back to Charles. "Then so do I."

Sarah waited for one of them to do something. She was surprisingly more impatient than anything. Both men seemed to be concerned about Sarah's wishes tonight. Well, she wished to know what the great mystery was about. She was a married woman now. And if her husband said he wanted another man there, then all right. But if they didn't do something soon, she was going to scream in frustration and lose what little courage she had mustered. Surely they didn't think she was going to lead the way, did they? Although she supposed they needed to be on the bed. It was referred to as bedding, wasn't it? She cleared her throat nervously.

"Well, then, should I get on the bed?" She couldn't look at either of them. Gideon was so intense he was a little frightening. And Mr. Borden... Well, he made her distinctly uncomfortable. He was so perfect. Handsome and healthy and desirable in a way that she could never be. Did he really want to be here, she wondered, or was it just his affection for Gideon that kept him here?

She heard Gideon move behind her, and then she felt his hand lightly brush her arm. "If you want to."

She shivered at his touch and the roughness in his voice, and he withdrew his hand. Without a word she spun on her heel and walked briskly over to the bed. She climbed up on the bed awkwardly. Her skirts were not made for that sort of thing. They were too narrow. Embarrassment made her avert her eyes as she kneeled on the bed and tried to cover her legs. Her heart was pounding in her chest. What next?

There was a rustle of clothing off to the side, and Sarah wasn't sure whose it was. But it was an act of sheer willpower not to look. She was dying of curiosity. And then panic set in. Did they expect her to disrobe as well? Suddenly a hot, callused hand came down over her hands, which she had been wringing in her lap.

"Sarah." She froze. "Look at me."

It was Mr. Borden. She would have much preferred Gideon. For some reason Gideon soothed her. Mr. Borden threw her into panic and indecision.

"Sarah." His voice was quiet, kind but firm. It told her he would not relent. So she looked. And forgot to breathe.

He had partially disrobed. His upper body was bare and in the candlelight he was a classical sculpture of golden-hued marble, his muscles casting shadows as he moved. He looked rough, wild, beautiful and so strong. His clothes had hidden all that. How could she have thought him gentle? Her skin broke out in goose bumps and she clenched her hands to keep from touching him to see if he was as hard as he looked. She wanted him to be hard, with that glowing, smooth skin beneath her fingertips.

Mr. Borden picked up one of her hands and gently forced her to unclench her fist. She couldn't take her eyes away from his hands on hers. His fingers were blunt, rough, thick. They were the hands of a laborer. She imagined them running up her arms, cupping her cheeks, and with just that touch he had her breathing roughly, shaking with anticipation and dread. Dread that he would find her lacking. Hadn't all men before Gideon found her lacking?

Then he placed her open palm against his chest, holding it right over his pounding heart. She started at the heat of him. His skin was sticky with a fine sheen of sweat, even as the breeze fluttered the curtains. Sarah realized she was sweating too. She felt the damp on her temples, under her arms, between her breasts. She was overheating too. He did that to her. Was she doing it to him?

With his free hand he reached up to cup her cheek. Her marked cheek. In a panic she turned her face away and jerked out of his reach. She frantically looked over at Gideon. "Gideon, please."

Gideon was watching them, leaning on his crutches in the shadows. "What do you want, Sarah?" His voice was as gentle as she had ever heard it.

"I want you here too." He had appreciated her honesty up to this point. She had no intention of prevaricating now. They wanted her to enjoy this bedding. She needed Gideon to truly do that. Mr. Borden was everything desirable, but the way he was making her body react made her feel guilty. Gideon, not Mr. Borden, was her husband. He should be here, shouldn't he?

"Are you sure?" Gideon sounded strangely unsure, not reluctant, but there was a hesitation in him she hadn't encountered before.

"Yes." Her whisper was almost lost in the flap of the curtain as a strong breeze blew in, stuttering the candle's flame.

Mr. Borden started to let go of her hand, but Sarah's fingers flexed, digging into the hard muscles of his chest. She heard him take a sharp breath and then he pressed her hand harder against him. Gideon had begun to walk over to the bed, avoiding the light as best he could. Sarah turned to look at Mr. Borden then and he was watching Gideon too, with a heart-wrenching expression. And Sarah understood at that moment why Mr. Borden was there. Gideon needed him there because Gideon was afraid.

When Gideon reached the bed he set his crutches against the wall and awkwardly settled behind her. She started to turn, but he stopped her by leaning in close and wrapping an arm around her waist. Sarah got a little lightheaded at the feel of his weight supporting her back, his thickly muscled arm pressing against the side of her breast. Under her hand Mr. Borden's heart beat faster.

"Like this?" Gideon asked quietly, his breath warm against the nape of her neck.

Sarah began to nod but then shook her head. "No," she answered honestly, if a little breathlessly. "Like Mr. Borden."

Gideon went still. "What do you mean?"

"I want to feel you." Sarah could feel the blush burning her cheeks at her boldness. When she tried to move her hand on Mr. Borden's chest, he let her go immediately. In an act that took more courage than Sarah had known she possessed, she ran her shaking hand across his chest lightly, through the small patch of blond hair in the middle and then, after a moment's hesitation, over one of his nipples.

"How does he feel?" Gideon's voice was a raspy whisper behind her.

"Mr. Borden—" she began, but he cut her off.

"Call me Charles." His voice was as rough as Gideon's now. Sarah's hand shook harder, but she wasn't afraid anymore. She didn't feel afraid.

"Charles feels hard." Behind her Gideon made a sound that might have been laughter, but it was so quiet and subtle she wasn't sure. "But his skin is soft, smooth, like marble."

"Surely I am warmer than marble," Charles said, sounding amused. "I feel rather warm, truly."

Sarah licked her lips. "You're very warm." She was finding it hard to speak above a whisper. The whole situation was so fantastic, so unbelievable. No man had wanted to bed her in her entire life. And now she was with two very desirable men. Two men who seemed to want her. "You're sweating."

Charles started to pull away. "I'm sorry."

"Don't be silly," Sarah said quickly. "I like it."

"Sarah," Gideon laid his forehead on her shoulder and rolled his head, rubbing his face in her hair.

"Is that wrong?" Sarah asked in sudden concern. "It just... It just makes him so real. It makes me know this isn't a dream. That's why I need to feel you too, Gideon. I need to know my new life is not a dream."

* * * * *

Gideon couldn't deny her. She was so innocent, Charles had been right. But at the same time there was an unconscious sensuality to her that made him hungrier for her than he could ever remember being. Was it because she was his? His wife? His in a way no one had ever been before, not even Charles? And she meant what she said. She wasn't playing at desire or trying to sweeten her pay by loosening his purse strings with empty flattery. She wanted to feel him.

He pulled back slightly, going slowly so as not to overset his balance. Everything he did these days had to be done slowly. He felt a moment's anger as he remembered how he used to be—quick, decisive, strong. He was a shell of that man now. But he could still please his own wife, dammit.

He tugged off his cravat first and let it drop to the floor. Sarah must have seen something in the corner of her eye, because she began to turn around.

"No," he told her. "Charles." He didn't know what to tell the other man, he only knew he wanted Charles to keep her occupied. She could feel him but she couldn't see him, not yet. It was true the scars ended at his collarbone and only began again on his left wrist. But he didn't want her to see him just the same.

Charles knew. Charles always knew. He reached up and cupped Sarah's breasts through her thin nightdress and Sarah gasped. Just knowing that Charles held those soft, full mounds in his hands made Gideon's cock twitch. He'd grown accustomed to that. He'd been disconcerted by it the first few times they'd fucked a woman together, the arousal he felt at watching Charles with someone else. But now he embraced it. It would work out tonight, it would. And Sarah would be more pleasured than any other bride in the country. They'd make sure of it.

Charles climbed up on the bed still holding her breasts in his hands. He was so graceful in everything he did. He was kneeling in front of Sarah now, mirroring her position on the bed.

"Let me kiss you again, Sarah," Charles whispered.

Gideon worked on the buttons of his waistcoat as he watched Charles lean in and take Sarah's mouth. His hands were trembling as he watched them. Would he ever kiss Sarah? There'd been a whore once, but she'd closed her eyes. Charles claimed he was still quite a desirable man. Gideon felt his skin heat and thrust aside old memories that tried to surface. He focused on the present. It was a tactic that had served him well the last few years.

When he had his coat, waistcoat and shirt off he moved in behind Sarah again. Charles gently broke his and Sarah's kiss and pushed her back against Gideon. It was almost instinctive, the way Charles knew what he was doing and reacted to

Gideon's needs without being told. That was why Gideon wanted him here. Gideon was not good with words, and this...this physical closeness with others made him nervous and fumbling. But Charles smoothed the way for him. Charles made it all work.

"Gideon," Sarah sighed, and snuggled back against him. She reached back and dragged his arm around her again.

Gideon was having trouble breathing through the lump in his throat at her obvious enjoyment of him. He leaned over and pressed the unscarred side of his face against the side of her head. He could feel better with that side. Feel the softness of her heavy fall of beautiful hair, the warmth of her. He rubbed his cheek against her, wishing he could carry the sweet smell of her always. Gideon tightened his arm around her and she ran a trembling hand from his wrist to his upper arm, just skimming the surface slowly. He broke out in gooseflesh at the caress.

"You're so warm," Sarah whispered, "and hard too."

Charles laughed lightly and Gideon shivered. "Yes." He didn't know what else to say.

Sarah reached up and wrapped one hand around his biceps, and he couldn't stop the instinctive flexing of his arm. She held on while she slid the other hand along his forearm. Gideon nuzzled her hair out of the way and kissed her neck. Very gently he dragged the tip of his tongue along her pulse and Sarah pulled in a shaky breath. Her head fell back on his shoulder and he let his lips trail along her soft, fragrant skin until he softly kissed her cheek. She began to turn her face to him, and Gideon pulled back.

"Sarah, let me see you." He couldn't believe he'd had the nerve to ask that. It was too soon. He would frighten her with his demands.

She struggled to turn. "I'm trying..."

"No." Gideon stopped her again. "I mean let Charles and me undress you."

She stopped struggling and her heartbeat raced like a small bird trapped beneath his hand.

"Everything?" Her voice was small but steady.

Charles smiled. Gideon could see the gleam of his teeth in the candlelight. "You aren't wearing that much," he said. "But if you don't want to, Sarah, that's all right. Gideon and I don't mind."

"Would you like that?" she asked, the curiosity in her tone making her voice stronger. "The way I like to see you both?"

Both. Gideon closed his eyes. She hadn't seen him yet. But she didn't realize that. She felt him. She liked it too. She hadn't fabricated the pleasure in her caresses. He would keep her that way, enjoying this, enjoying him. He watched as she reached for Charles' chest again. He had sat back on his heels, putting distance between him and Sarah, but as her hand moved he sat up again and met her halfway. Charles put his hand over hers and ran it over his chest, rubbing her palm across his nipples. It was obvious they both enjoyed it. Gideon could see the outline of Charles hard prick through his breeches. He wanted her. He wanted Gideon's wife. Gideon felt a deep, smug satisfaction at the sight.

"Yes." Charles answered for both of them.

Sarah moved then, a little tentatively. She slowly pulled the hem of her nightdress from under her knees so that it pooled on her thighs. Gideon held his breath. Her face was down, hidden by her hair. She clutched the material in her hands, seeming unable to take the next step.

"Let me," Charles said softly. He pushed her hands away and she allowed it. Then he hooked his thumbs in the hem and slid his hands up her thighs, pulling the gown with them. "Raise your arms," he told her in the same soft voice, and Sarah rose high on her knees and raised her arms as he instructed. Gideon caught a side view of her face. Her eyes were closed.

He watched as Charles slowly raised the gown, loosely held with just his thumbs as his hands glided up over her hips and along her sides. Sarah shivered, and Gideon wasn't sure if it was the breeze on her newly bared skin or the feel of Charles' hands on her. A little whimper escaped her but it was not of distress, and Gideon had his answer. It was Charles' hands, then. Gideon understood that.

Gideon pulled back and looked at Sarah's exposed back and buttocks. She was exquisite. Her skin was pale, smooth alabaster, a temptation in itself. But covering such delicious curves. Without thought Gideon let his hands, both hands, reach for her. The dimples in her lower back were pronounced, punctuation marks separating a long, elegant back from a full, round derriere. He set his thumbs in the dimples and wrapped his hands around her generous hips just as Charles pulled the nightdress over her head and let it flutter to the floor beside the bed.

"Jesus bloody wept," Charles whispered worshipfully as he sat back and gazed at Sarah's naked form with awe.

"Charles," Sarah said, and she sounded so prim, so shocked at his language that Gideon laughed.

"Beg your pardon, Sarah," Charles told her with a grin, a blush staining his cheeks. "But you are so bloody gorgeous I forgot myself."

Sarah laughed self-consciously. "Yes, of course I am," she answered wryly. She sighed. "I forget sometimes that you used to be soldiers."

Charles moved in close to her again, crowding her back against Gideon until her hot flesh was pressed against both men, trapping her between them. Sarah was shaking, but she wrapped a hand around Gideon's wrist and one around Charles' upper arm as if steadying herself. She wasn't shying away.

"If we are too rough, you must tell us," Gideon told her, hating the rasp in his voice that made him sound harsh.

Sarah didn't seem to notice it. She shook her head. "No, no, you are not." She sounded breathless and aroused, and Gideon wanted to lay her down and mount her and fuck her until they both cried out. He squeezed his eyes shut. But he couldn't do that. Not to Sarah. And even if Sarah let him, he couldn't do it. He didn't have the balance for it anymore. But there were other things they could do to her.

Gideon slid his hands up her sides and along the underside of her arms, raising them until they were held straight out from her shoulders. He used his good hand to caress her arm and then glided his hand down and under her breast, cupping it. Sarah jumped and a little squeak broke free. Gideon smiled. He rubbed his thumb over her distended nipple. It felt plump and hard, the size of a firm raspberry. Her body was racked by a shudder.

"Wrap your arms back around my neck," he whispered. Sarah complied. The movement thrust her chest out, and Gideon cupped her other breast then and treated her nipples to another caress. Charles leaned down as soon as Gideon's thumb rubbed over and off, and he licked her right nipple slowly with the flat of his tongue.

"Oh," Sarah said hoarsely. Just that one word. But there was shock and surprise and pleasure in it. Gideon squeezed the mounds of her breasts gently and Charles licked her nipple again, this time swirling his tongue around it before sliding over it. Sarah's breathing was ragged. Her hands clutched Gideon's back and her head fell onto his shoulder again.

"Do you like this?" Gideon whispered in her ear.

Sarah nodded and licked her lips. "Yes."

"Good."

Gideon couldn't get enough of her skin. It was so smooth, like the finest silk—perfect. It was a shock, really. She had been so practical, so no-nonsense in their encounters thus far. He hadn't expected this. Hadn't expected her to be this yielding woman melting in his arms, this lush feminine softness under his hands. He caressed every inch of her he could as Charles worshipped her breasts. He had always loved a woman's breasts, Charles had. And Sarah's were full. They had been heavy in his hands when he'd held them.

Gideon's hands were continually in motion, rubbing her stomach, her sides, her arms, then gliding to her hips and even around to cup the plump cheeks of her bottom. After only a few minutes of their caresses, Sarah was relaxed and pliant in Gideon's arms, her body straining for their touch. Experimentally Gideon ran his hands down to Sarah's thighs and dragged his fingers gently along the crease between them. Sarah jumped a little but Gideon maintained the soft caress, up and down that hot crevice, wishing, hoping that she would open them and let him in.

Finally Gideon could wait no more. He pressed on her thighs, seeking entrance. Sarah resisted for only a moment and then, with a little hiccup of a sigh, she spread her legs.

"More," Gideon whispered. Charles had pulled off the breast he'd been kissing and sucking. Gideon could actually see it gleaming in the candlelight, wet from Charles' mouth, and his cock jerked. It felt good. Gideon wanted more. More of all of it, not just Sarah, but Sarah and Charles and him.

Charles moved back, sliding his knees on the bed to give Sarah room to spread her legs. He watched unabashedly, his desire and anticipation filling the air with a heady sense of expectation. He wanted to see her. And Gideon wanted to show him. Gideon slid his palms down the slight break Sarah had made between her legs, pushing them farther apart. She moved as he directed, letting him press her open, letting him show Charles her secrets.

Gideon pressed close against her back, his arm wrapped tightly around her waist. He wanted her to stay like this, where Charles could see. Gideon moved his good hand along her inner thigh and Sarah moaned softly.

"Damn," Charles whispered in wonder. "She's gorgeous, Gideon. All swollen and wet."

At his words Sarah tried to close her legs, but Gideon pressed harder on her thigh. "No," he said firmly, and she stopped. He continued to slide his hand up her thigh until it was cupped over the curls on her mound. They were thick like her hair, and Gideon enjoyed the feel of them on his palm. He circled his hand, rubbing against her, and Sarah squirmed.

"Gideon," she protested, feebly trying to move his hand.

"This is where I need to be, Sarah," he told her softly, continuing his circling motion. "This is where I will take you." He stopped and slid a finger down her crease to her entrance and Sarah cried out.

She was wet. So bloody wet it made Gideon lightheaded. Clearly she had more than liked their intimacies so far. He moved his hand in a slight rocking motion, increasing the motion little by little until the tip of his finger slid inside her. She was so soft, softer here than her outer skin. Soft and swollen and untried. Again Gideon had the urge to mount her, to claim her roughly, and subdued it.

"Gideon," she groaned.

"Bloody, fucking beautiful," Charles said in a whisper.

"Charles," both Gideon and Sarah said chidingly at the same time, and they all three froze for a moment in surprise.

Charles broke the silence with a hoarse groan as he shuffled his knees forward again. He made his way between her thighs, spreading her even wider, and her hips thrust just slightly but enough to force Gideon's finger deeper. She gasped and Gideon was about to remove his hand when she did it again. And again.

Her hands had fallen to her sides and Sarah now gripped his arm around her waist as Charles got close enough for Gideon to feel the heat of his breath. Charles was staring down at Gideon's hand between her legs and Sarah moaned as she thrust down again and again, her rhythm awkward but undeniably sensuous and pleasurable.

Charles looked up at Sarah's face and moved to nuzzle her cheek. Sarah murmured in protest and tried to shy away, but she didn't have enough space between them.

"Sarah, what is it?" Gideon asked, pressing his hand against her sex, pulling her closer.

"Not my cheek," she said in distress. "Don't look."

Gideon didn't know what to do. He'd forgotten about her birthmark. "Does it hurt?"

She shook her head.

Charles hadn't moved. He was still right there, his lips a breath away from her. He moved then and nuzzled her cheek, then kissed it. Sarah was panting, her hips still, her heart pounding. Charles still did not move away. He spent endless moments making love to that cheek. Gideon watched in amazement as Charles kissed it, rubbed his nose against it, licked the soft contour of her cheekbone beneath the strawberry mark and then licked her tears away as they fell silently from her eyes.

"You are beautiful," Charles whispered, and Sarah shuddered in his arms.

Gideon gently pushed Sarah toward Charles, pulling his hand from the warm cavern between her thighs. He needed to kiss Sarah too. But he was too damn afraid to do it like Charles. So he'd do it his way.

Chapter Six

ဇာ

Charles wrapped Sarah in his arms and she clung to him. He looked at Gideon and with a twist of his head Gideon indicated that Charles should lay her down on the bed. Without words, Charles knew exactly what Gideon wanted. He leaned her back over one arm and smoothed her hair off her cheek.

"Sarah," he whispered. He kissed her, softly at first and then passionately. He felt no remorse for being here in their marriage bed. It felt right, so incredibly right. He wanted to watch them together. He wanted to watch Sarah and Gideon come together for the first time. He wanted to give Gideon to Sarah. Wanted her to know the pleasure of being fucked by Gideon. She was beautiful. That moment, when she shied away from his kiss, was the first time he'd seen her so unsure since that first day in Gideon's office. Surely she must know the birthmark did not detract from her beauty in any way? If she didn't, they would show her.

He laid her down across the bed so that her legs were by Gideon's hip, and then he followed her down. He lay down on his stomach next to her, holding himself up on one forearm, wrapping the other around her and pulling her close to his side. His erection was pressed almost painfully into the bed. He liked the feel of it. He liked to be this excited by a woman.

He closed his eyes and shivered a little as the bed moved while Gideon re-situated himself between her legs. Anticipation fired his blood. He wanted to watch Gideon eat her. Maybe that wasn't the gentlemanly term for it, but that's what it was. He wasn't born a gentleman. He was a common man and he liked common things, like the taste of a woman's cunt or watching and feeling her squirm while another man's mouth ate at her. Gideon, actually. He liked to watch Gideon eat them.

"What?" Sarah was confused, her eyes slightly unfocused. They'd done that to her with their hands and mouths. He looked down at her succulent breasts. They were full and heavy, her nipples dark red and swollen still from his mouth. He wanted to suck them some more. Suck them hard so that her hips thrust up and pressed her sex against Gideon's mouth. Sarah's eyes flew wide and she gasped then cried out. He'd started. Gideon was on her.

"Shhhh," he whispered against her temple. "We like this. We like to taste you, Sarah. A woman's passion tastes so sweet." He breathed in her smell. She smelled like lavender and some other flower. And sex. He could smell her wet cunt. One of his favorite things in the world. He took several more deep breaths while Sarah squirmed beneath him.

Sarah moaned and he had to look. He couldn't resist anymore. It had been a pleasant torture not to allow himself to look at Gideon. But he had to look. He kissed Sarah's temple and then turned and looked down her body. He didn't know what to focus on first. She was a feast, not just for Gideon but also for Charles. Her beautiful breasts gave way to the swell of her womanly belly, so soft and warm. He reached down and ran his fingers across it, dipping one finger into her little bellybutton. He smiled when she laughed and squirmed a little and Gideon looked up at him from between her legs. Christ, he was so amazingly gorgeous down there. His eyes shone like exotic sapphires over her dark blonde curls. Gideon began to pull away, and Sarah delighted both men when she blindly reached down and pressed his mouth back to her with a hand against the back of his head.

She sounded...juicy, like an overripe peach. Charles mouth watered. He could hear Gideon lapping up her cream, watched as Gideon's eyes closed in rapture at her taste. Gideon reached down with both hands and pressed behind her knees. Sarah allowed him to raise her legs, bending her knees obediently, letting Gideon spread her wide as he devoured her. Her head thrashed on the bed and her hand fisted in a puddle of her thick hair near her shoulder.

Charles leaned down and took her breast in his mouth again, sucking her nipple roughly, and Sarah cried out, thrusting up into Gideon's mouth as Charles wanted. He hummed appreciatively around her and Sarah thrust up again, moaning. God, she was incredible. There was no shyness in her now. She was wanton, desperate for it. He wanted to watch her climax for them. Then he would help Gideon fuck her. He had never seen a woman who needed to be fucked so badly.

"Oh, oh," Sarah stuttered, her hips moving without finesse. But she was getting the job done. If Charles didn't miss his guess, she was about to come. He pulled off her breast with a final, deep tug and Sarah arched her back in pleasure. Charles was smug and satisfied. He knew what she liked now. She didn't know how to ask for it, but Charles knew. He always knew, didn't he? Sarah's pretty mouth was open as she panted in her excitement and Charles had to have that again too. He moved to kiss her and a stunning thought hit him. He was still the only man to kiss her. Gideon wouldn't. He'd been rejected rather badly in the past. Now he wouldn't risk it. But somehow Charles knew that Sarah would kiss Gideon. She'd kiss Gideon with the same abandon he'd found in her mouth. When he finally pressed his open mouth to hers, it was with the understanding that he was teaching her how to kiss Gideon when the time came.

Gideon was groaning at her cunt now. Christ, she must taste good. Charles wondered if he would ever find out. He wanted to, more than he ought to, probably. The right thing to do was to make this the last time for the three of them. But he'd never been very good at doing the right thing, had he? If they asked, he'd be here again. And again. Because he knew this was where he wanted to be. With Gideon and Sarah.

Sarah was wild beneath him, biting his lip and sucking it desperately as her hips tried to fly out of Gideon's hands. Gideon was trying to hold her down for his mouth. Charles moved his hand from her stomach to her slit and rubbed the hard little knot of pleasure there. He'd never known a woman who wouldn't come from that.

Sarah's breath stuttered in his mouth. Christ, that was arousing. He rubbed harder and she fell away from his lips as a keening cry broke free and she stiffened on the bed, her hips arched into Gideon's mouth. Gideon moved his hand between her legs as Charles pinched her little knot and she convulsed with a sob. Charles watched her face as she came. She was gorgeous, dammit. She came apart, coming and crying and shaking.

"Yes, Sarah," Gideon rasped from between her legs, and Charles looked down and watched as Gideon licked his fingers around Sarah's knot. Her hips jerked up at the same time Charles pressed his hard cock into the bed at the feel of Gideon's tongue on him.

When it was over Sarah went limp, breathing as if they'd put her through her paces too hard. She moaned and then covered her eyes with her arm. Charles turned and saw Gideon kissing and licking her thigh softly.

"Was that it?" Sarah asked breathlessly. "Am I Mrs. North now?"

Gideon chuckled as he awkwardly moved from between her legs. "In one sense, yes. But truthfully, no."

"Dear Lord," Sarah whispered, "there's more?"

* * * * *

Sarah looked away as both men took off their trousers. Gideon had told her they needed to be unclothed for the actual act. She desperately hoped it felt like what Gideon had just done. His mouth on her sex had been wondrous. She truly hadn't known. Had not known this was what it was like between a man and wife. She blushed as she remembered that Charles was not her husband. The secret of adultery was now unlocked to her as well. She looked at Charles out of the corner of her eye and then slammed her eyes shut. Even his backside was muscular. How was that possible?

She felt self-conscious lying there naked. The breeze was still blowing through the curtains, and she could hear night creatures calling to one another outside. She was chilled. There had been so much heat between the three of them, and now she was alone and cold, the sweat and...other things cooling on her skin and her sex. She rolled to her side and reached for the blanket.

"Stay like that." Gideon's voice made her freeze, lying there on her side with her arm stretched out. She shivered at his gruff, commanding tone. How could anyone not respond to that voice? Sarah certainly did, to an embarrassing extent.

She felt him stand beside the bed and then heard him awkwardly hop around. The blankets were pulled up behind her and the bed dipped as he got back in. Sarah's heartbeat accelerated. Suddenly he touched her arm and she forced herself not to jerk in surprise. He didn't like that. Every time she'd done it before, he'd retreated. Her senses were fine-tuned to his movements, to his breathing. Should she turn now?

Charles stepped in front of her beside the bed. Sarah caught her breath. She had never seen a man's member before. The boys' when they were children, but never a man's. It was smaller than she'd imagined. The way some village women talked about it under their breath, Sarah had expected it to be shaped like a huge mace with a barbed end. She was quite relieved to discover it looked nothing like the specter of her imagination but exactly like the attributes she'd seen on farm animals. Not as small as a dog's, but thankfully not as large as a bull or stallion. Relief coursed through her and she started to smile. But then she wondered, *are all men the same?* Would

Gideon's be different? Because Gideon was the one she was going to be with.

Just then Gideon rolled over and pressed against her bottom. She did jerk in shock but then quickly pressed back against him before he could pull away. What she felt seemed to mirror what she saw between Charles' legs. She closed her eyes and took a calming breath. Good. That was good.

"Sarah, say something," Gideon said quietly. He smoothed a hand over her bare hip and she pressed back harder. He seemed to like that, snuggling closer to her and kissing her shoulder. She couldn't feel his legs. Just blankets. But she could feel the hot flesh of his member, obviously left exposed.

"I am greatly relieved to find the stories about a man's...parts to be vastly exaggerated," Sarah said weakly.

Charles burst into laughter beside the bed while Gideon chuckled behind her. "I think we'll do all right with what we've got," Charles told her with a grin. He climbed on the bed and offered Sarah a hand. When she took it he pulled her up gently to kneel in front of him, and his smile dimmed a little. "Or Gideon will. Sarah, you must know that I won't...that is to say, you are Gideon's wife and I respect that. I'm honored that you let me be here tonight, that I was allowed to help Gideon...anyway, Sarah..." he trailed off again.

"I understand," she told him quietly, squeezing his hand. "Thank you."

Gideon moved behind her and she turned to see him lying on his back. He didn't force her to turn away. He let her look at him. His shoulders and chest were even thicker than Charles'. It had appeared that way in his clothes. His upper arms were heavy with muscle. She'd felt them when he had wrapped his arm around her. She liked it, liked the way it felt when he had flexed those muscles for her. His chest had more hair than Charles' and it was dark and curly. The hair on his head was so short it was hard to tell if it was curly. Did a man's chest hair mirror that on his head? Charles' hair was very curly and so was his chest hair, the little he had. She could just see Gideon's nipples peeking out among the hair. They seemed pale pink like hers. Charles' were browner. Sarah was a little surprised at how much she had noticed about Charles without realizing it. She couldn't help but make comparisons. These were the only two naked men she'd ever seen, after all.

She told herself not to be a ninny and finally looked down between his legs. His member was quite similar to Charles', perhaps a bit longer maybe, and paler, but hardly frightening. It looked peculiar. They both did. It was just odd to see that pole sticking out from between a man's legs.

"Why are you smiling?" Gideon asked coolly.

Oh dear. She'd upset him. She stopped smiling and cleared her throat. "It's just odd, that's all. I've never seen a…a man's member, and it looks peculiar sticking out like that."

Charles laughed and she turned to him with a frown. He smoothed a finger between her brows.

"Don't frown, pretty Sarah," he whispered, and kissed the end of her nose. "It's just that you are not much of a flatterer."

Sarah blushed. "I wasn't aware I was supposed to flatter a man in bed. Do you really like that?" She tried to imagine insincerely praising the length or girth of a man's parts and truly didn't think she could muster the necessary dramatic skills.

"No," Gideon said roughly in that way of his. "I don't like it. I'd rather be vastly exaggerated and peculiar. Come here."

Charles smiled at her and grabbed her under her arms lifting her up. She clutched his shoulders for support and bit back a cry of surprise as he lifted her and then set her down so she straddled Gideon's lap with her back to him, looking at Charles.

This wasn't right. She should be facing Gideon. She shook her head at Charles, just looking at him. She wasn't sure what he saw in her face, but he smiled kindly. "No?" he asked so softly she wasn't sure Gideon heard.

"No," Sarah whispered. She lifted her right leg and Charles again held her hand to support her as she awkwardly turned around.

"No," Gideon bit out. Sarah and Charles ignored him. He sat up, leaning on his hands and frowning. When Sarah finally faced him full-on, he quickly turned his head to the side, showing her the unmarked side of his face. Sarah cupped his chin in her hand and caressed that cheek with her thumb.

"Oh no," she said softly, "if I can't, you can't." She applied gentle pressure until he gave in and jerked his head aside, dislodging her hand. The look he gave her was more ferocious than ever. Suddenly she felt Charles at her back, his hands on her hips, and he moved in close enough to rest his chin on her shoulder.

"She's got you there, Gideon," he said with amusement. "And I think it will be easier for her this first time if she faces you." The last was said quite seriously, and Gideon's expression changed. He looked chagrined.

"You're right, of course," he agreed. "I hadn't thought of that." He shook his head. "I'm sorry, Sarah."

"I thought we agreed not to say that anymore tonight." Her voice was shaky again. She could feel his stiff member rubbing on her inner thigh. The skin there was shockingly soft and hot. And damp. Was he sweating? There?

Charles reached around to cup her breasts and massage them. She loved that. It felt delicious. She'd had no idea. She forever banished the wish to be rid of them. Many times she'd wished them gone when they got in the way or her clothing grew too small when she was younger, making an almost vulgar display. But now...now she knew what they were capable of and she would never underestimate her breasts again. Charles seemed fascinated by them. It thrilled her. She tentatively thrust her chest out slightly, into his hands, and his laugh was low, enticing, temptation itself.

"Like that, do you?" he murmured. "Good."

Gideon was watching Charles' hands on her breasts and she felt his erection move against her thigh. Unbelievably, she actually felt her sex quiver. What else was her body capable of? What other surprises were in store for her? Gideon slowly lay down again, watching, always watching. Sarah loved that too. She understood now, understood that Gideon needed Charles to help him overcome the fear, but he also wanted Charles here. He wanted to watch Charles touch her, kiss her. And Sarah didn't mind that. They had both been so wonderful to her tonight, all day today, really. Sarah closed her eyes, trying not to cry. She was so emotional, too emotional. Gideon liked her practical. She placed her hands over Charles' on her breasts. "Yes, I like that." Her voice was low, forced out from the very depths of her as she bared her desire before them.

Charles' chest rose and fell in a deep, rhythmic pattern behind her. He seemed so solid there, much as Gideon had earlier. Had Charles really made her nervous before? She couldn't imagine that now.

"What do I do?" She needed to know. She wanted to do whatever it was right now. She suddenly had a burning need to make Gideon hers. And in so doing, she knew Charles would be satisfied as well.

Gideon touched her leg and Sarah glanced down to see him grasp his member in his fist while he held her thigh in his other hand. Charles wrapped an arm around her waist and pressed her down until the tip of Gideon's erection tapped her entrance.

"Here." Gideon's voice was so low and rough Sarah almost didn't hear him. He was as overcome as she was. It drove her desperation higher, and she pressed down. Gideon arched his neck back with a hoarse cry as the tip penetrated her, much as his finger had earlier. Sarah gasped. It felt marvelous. She started to drive herself down on him, but Charles stopped her with his firm grasp on her waist.

"Sarah, wait," he said quickly. "Not too fast, my sweet, or too rough. Not this first time."

"You must tell me, then," Sarah said, panting suddenly, lightheaded as if she was running a race. "Show me, tell me, do something!"

* * * * *

Gideon was drowning in Sarah's desire. She wanted him. She was looking right at him, watching him, desperate to fuck herself down on him. No one had ever been that desperate for him. The desperation was always his alone. But not tonight. He let instinct take over. He grabbed her hips and pulled her down at the same time he thrust his hips up. He couldn't get a great deal of leverage, but it was enough. He felt the slight resistance only because he was looking for it. It didn't impede his possession of Sarah at all. But it seemed as if he'd broken through a barrier of immense proportions. She was his in every way now.

Just as the thought went through his head, Gideon's gaze met Charles' over Sarah's shoulder. Theirs. In an irrevocable way, theirs. And that was how Gideon wanted it. He wanted this with Charles, had always wanted it. But it wasn't fair to either one. Gideon had forced this on them both, and for him they had agreed. He didn't fool himself. They had enjoyed each other. But the experience was one that neither had sought. And one that Gideon knew should never be repeated, no matter what he desired. He had Sarah now and so must let Charles go.

"Gideon!" Sarah cried out, her back arched against Charles.

Charles turned his face into her hair and shushed her. "It will be all right, Sarah sweet," Charles murmured. "Does it hurt? Tell us if it hurts. We can make it better, Sarah, I swear."

Gideon couldn't find his voice. It should be him soothing Sarah's fears right now, but as usual the words escaped him. Instead he ran his hands over her hips and down her thighs. They were trembling, both he and Sarah.

She nodded and turned her face to rest her cheek on Charles' chest. "It stings a little." She was so quiet and subdued. Had he been too rough? Had he hurt her? Gideon began to panic.

Charles gave him a look that told Gideon to stay still. He didn't need to be told. "Should I pull out?"

"Is that it?" Sarah asked incredulously. "There's no more?"

Charles laughed. He was very free with his laughter tonight. For the last year there had been little of it between them.

"Oh Sarah, there's more. If you think you can take it." Charles kissed the side of her head and then nuzzled her ear, biting the lobe softly, and Sarah gasped. She nodded rapidly.

"Yes, yes, I can take it."

Gideon's nerves were strung tight as a bow. He was straining with the effort not to move. Her declaration nearly did him in.

"Is Gideon all right?" Sarah asked. She sounded as panicked as he felt. "He looks as if he's in pain. Did it hurt him too?"

There it was again, Charles' laughter. Charles' leg moved and touched Gideon's and he felt the laughter down his thigh. He could almost feel it in his toes. Those damn phantom toes he didn't have anymore on that leg.

"I'm fine, Sarah." He hadn't meant to bite that out so sharply. Sarah's gaze clashed with his and he was glad to see she didn't appear to be offended. "I am just...not moving. Which carries its own sort of pain. Which is pleasure."

Sarah just looked confused. "If it is painful for you, then why are we doing it?"

Charles smiled seductively at him over Sarah's shoulder. Gideon shivered. He both loved and hated that look. "Because it feels so good to suffer, Sarah," he told her with another kiss, this one on her neck. Sarah tipped her head to the side to give him better access to her neck, the move unconscious and sensual. Charles licked a path from the curve of her shoulder to that soft spot behind her ear and Sarah moaned. Gideon very nearly embarrassed himself by doing the same.

"Gideon," Sarah said. She pressed on his hands gripping her hips. Gripping them too tightly, he realized. He started to apologize, but Sarah cut him off. "Don't say it." There was laughter in her voice. He was sure at some point she would stop continually amazing him, but now was not that time. He tried to remove his hands, but she wouldn't let him. "Hold me. Just not so tightly." It was then he realized that her hand was covering his. Touching his scarred hand. Then she did the most extraordinary thing. She rubbed his scarred hand on her hip and wiggled against the caress. "I like the way that feels." She was nearly purring like a cat. "So rough."

Gideon had no response. He was stunned and let her continue to caress herself with his hand. Charles was looking at him with a smug smile that said more clearly than words, *I told you so.* Gideon both loved and hated that look too. Sarah wiggled against his hand again, rising slightly and then coming down on his cock again, and she caught her breath.

"Like that too, now, do you?" Charles asked with a chuckle. "That's more."

"More," Sarah said with wonder. "I had almost forgotten that you were inside me, Gideon. I couldn't really feel you until now."

Charles raised his eyebrows at Gideon with a grin. "Her flattery just gets better and better."

Gideon was disgruntled. "I am only peculiar. You were vastly exaggerated."

Sarah lifted herself up and slid down again. "Oh, Gideon."

Oh, indeed. She was so incredibly tight and hot. Gideon had never fucked a woman who felt like Sarah. Smooth as silk inside, smothering his cock. He couldn't think as she tightened her passage around him. He could only feel.

"Like this, Sarah," Charles murmured, and suddenly she was moving in a slow, steady rhythm, her movements shallow, a torturous drag on the sensitive tip of Gideon's cock. "Sarah," he ground out between clenched teeth, his back bowing off the bed.

"Yes," Charles whispered. It was decadent, hearing his voice like that at this moment. When he was buried in his tight virgin bride, and she was riding him so sweetly. And then Charles, like the very devil, whispering encouragement in her ear and teaching her how to fuck Gideon so rightly. Gideon bucked into Sarah's downward glide, ramming his cock deeper into her, and Sarah cried out.

Gideon shook his head against the pillow. "I am too rough but I cannot help myself," he said, then bit his lip to prevent further confessions.

"Is that what you would like, Gideon?" Sarah asked breathlessly. "It was not too rough." And she moved on him like that, deeper and harder. Gideon's vision dimmed.

Through a haze of lust he watched Charles direct Sarah up and down on his cock, moving with her. It looked as if they were both fucking themselves on him. Gideon had to close his eyes. *Don't think about that,* he told himself. *Don't.* Sarah cried out again, and Gideon's eyes flew open. Charles' hand was between her legs. He was rubbing the little knot of sensation there in her slit. The same one he'd played with when Gideon was eating her. He loved that crass expression. Charles had taught him that. Charles had taught him a great deal. And now he was teaching Sarah. Sarah's legs slid open more, and Gideon's cock pierced her deeper. Her hands came to rest on his stomach as her head fell back on Charles' chest in rapture.

Gideon had never thought to see a woman look like that again when he was fucking her. But Sarah, God, she was every man's dream as she rode him.

"Mmm, Sarah, darling, just like that," Charles murmured, his hand still between her legs. "Are you going to come again, Sarah?"

"W-what?" she stammered. She licked her lips, panting through another retreat and downward thrust onto him. Gideon met her thrust and pressed deep, holding himself there.

"The way you felt when my mouth was on you, Sarah," he rasped. "That feeling at the end, the bliss. Is it close? Are you close?"

Sarah ground against him. Christ, it was true. Mating was instinctive. The rut was on them and, innocent as she was, Sarah's body took over, taking what it needed.

"Again?" she asked in breathless wonder. "That will happen this way too?"

Gideon laughed desperately. "Yes, Sarah, yes. But for God's sake, hurry."

"Gideon," she chided breathlessly.

"Hurry, Sarah," he begged. "I cannot hold out much longer."

"I don't understand what you're saying." But she moved faster, harder, her body taking over.

"He's going to come, Sarah," Charles whispered in her ear. "He's going to feel like you did earlier, and he's going to fill you with his seed."

"His…?" Sarah could hardly speak now. The sound of her desire was fuel on the fire of Gideon's lust. He thrust wildly into her and she took it, grinding down on him with a moan. Suddenly Gideon felt the tips of Charles fingers on his cock, sliding along Sarah's folds around him.

"Charles," he ground out. He meant it to be a warning. It came out a plea.

"Oh, oh," Sarah cried out. Then she was driving herself down on him, holding him deep, and he felt the pulsing of her walls squeezing him tight.

"Sarah," he answered her in a hoarse shout, and then he was coming, filling her, making her his. And all the while Charles' voice encouraged and soothed them both.

When it was over Sarah collapsed on Gideon's chest while Charles rubbed her back. "I am going to like this business of being Mrs. North," Sarah murmured sleepily.

And holding his wife spent and satiated in his arms, all Gideon could think as he looked at Charles, still fully aroused, was that Charles should have taken her too. But he was too much of a coward to voice the thought.

Chapter Seven

&

Where the hell was Gideon?

Charles ran past the troops crouching behind cover in the dark, waiting for the order to storm the breaches. Christ, they weren't even supposed to be here. What the hell was Gideon thinking? They didn't have enough battles of their own, they had to borrow someone else's?

The French fired down on them, safe behind the fortress walls of Badajoz. A bullet slammed into the dirt just to Charles' left and he dodged right instinctively, even while thinking that it was foolish. The next one might very well come down to his right. If there was one thing he knew after all this time, it was that there was no rhyme or reason to a bullet. Once it left the gun it made its own decisions.

"Have you seen Captain North?" he hissed to a sergeant who was motioning his troops down behind him.

"Captain who?" the sergeant asked. "What regiment?"

"He's with the 14th Light Dragoons."

The sergeant gave him an odd look. "Didn't even think they were here."

"We're not," Charles answered grimly.

The sergeant smiled widely at what he thought was a jest. "That's right. You're just dreamin', lad. Ain't this what we all dream of?" The soldiers around them laughed quietly in genuine amusement.

"We were on our way to meet up with the 14th when we got wind of this. Captain North came to see the commander of the 4th."

"Well, he's getting quite a show, then, ain't he?" The sergeant turned back to business, dismissing Charles. Charles couldn't blame him. He had more pressing matters to worry about than a stupid missing cavalry captain.

"*I say, are you looking for Captain North?*" *a voice whispered to his left. Charles turned and saw a young lieutenant crouching there, sword drawn as he waited for orders. At Charles' nod, he pointed toward the fortress.* "*He's there with the 4th, with the Forlorn Hope.*"

Charles' heart stuttered to a stop in his chest. "*What?*" *he croaked in disbelief. Surely Gideon wouldn't do something so foolish. Volunteering for the force that led the attack was a suicide mission. Very few survived. This wasn't their fight. Surely he wouldn't. He couldn't.*

The lieutenant nodded enthusiastically. "*Oh yes. 'Pon my word, he's a brave fellow. Heard he arrived just today and begged the commander to be allowed to lead the Forlorn. Commander refused, he'd already picked his man. But North attached himself unofficially to the force. He's got experience, by God. He may not be on a horse but he'll beat the odds. Mark my words!*"

Before Charles could answer, the shout came. "*Now, lads! Forward!*" *All around him men surged to their feet screaming and began running toward the trenches. Charles was unable to move for a moment. Then he leapt to his feet and ran as if the hounds of hell were after him. He carried neither gun nor sword, just ran toward the breach, desperate.*

"*Gideon!*" *His cry was lost in the screams of the men around him.*

The black smoke from the guns and the men falling around him impeded his frantic search. He coughed and then sucked in a lungful of thick, acrid smoke and coughed more. Twice he tripped over dead men, falling to his knees. He grabbed a sword lying there, its dead owner no longer needing it, and he raced on.

He had almost reached the trench when the French blew the mines. The concussion rocked the ground under him and threw him back several feet. He faltered a moment but sprang up and raced into the carnage.

When he reached the trench he slid down the slope, falling on top of a pile of dead bodies. He refused to believe Gideon was among them. Gideon would have reached the top of the breach. Even as he thought it more bodies fell, and Charles slogged over the pile of bloody, mangled flesh. Where was he? He couldn't be too late, he couldn't! What had Gideon been thinking? It was a fuck, for Christ's sake! Nothing, a moment, a mistake, a desperate thing that happened between desperate men who had just done violent unspeakable things in battle and lived.

Charles fell again and came face-to-face with a dead infantryman. Half his head was missing. The bone shone whitely through the red and gray gore, and Charles gagged, crawling backward. He realized the light was brighter than it ought to be and glanced up to see half the trench was burning out of control. The mines had set the debris lining the bottom of the trench on fire.

He pushed away from the dead man and scrambled up the other side of the ditch only to be met by chevaux-de-frise, wooden timbers in which the French had driven sword blades. Men lay bleeding, impaled on the blades, crying out for help. Charles closed his mind to their pleas and climbed over them, using them as a gruesome bridge across the treacherous beams.

"Gideon North!" he screamed over and over.

Suddenly a hand grabbed his ankle and Charles fell forward, barely missing a blade. He kicked, trying to shake off the hand.

"Charles." The voice was so rough it was almost unrecognizable. Almost. Charles reached down and grabbed on to the hand desperately, following it to wrist and to arm, and then there he was. Gideon.

He lay beside a beam. Not impaled, thank God. But Charles' relief turned to horror when he saw what was left of him. His coat sleeve was still burning. Charles tore his neckcloth from around his neck, wrapped his hand in it and grabbed at the smoldering material, ripping the sleeve off and throwing it away. His face... Gideon's face. One side was a mass of black, burned skin.

"Cut it off," Gideon rasped.

"What?" Charles coughed, choking on bile.

"The...leg," Gideon whispered harshly. Charles looked down and what he saw made him fall to his hands and knees and retch violently. Gideon's leg was broken, mangled and nearly torn off. It *was bent at an impossible angle, the bloody, shattered, exposed bone gleaming in the firelight.*

"Cut it off," Gideon said again.

Charles recoiled in horror, incapable of speech, unable to move. Why couldn't he move? He had to help Gideon. He had to save Gideon. Why couldn't he move?

Charles woke, gasping for air, the urge to retch overwhelming. He tumbled off the bed and grabbed the basin, emptying his stomach, his hands trembling and his gut cramping.

The dream had been more accurate today than the last time he'd had it. His mind changed the details routinely. One night he'd be too late and it was Gideon's sightless eyes accusing him, another night it would be Charles lying broken and bleeding. But he hadn't had the dream in a very long time. Why last night? Why after leaving Gideon and Sarah...

Of course. He'd forgotten. It had been so long, he'd forgotten that sharing a woman with Gideon as they had Sarah always brought the dream. Because it was the one time he and Gideon had been intimate that had driven Gideon to such a foolhardy act. It was Charles' fault for always wanting more than Gideon was willing or able to give. Gideon was right to blame him. Both for driving Gideon to such extremes and then for saving his life when all Gideon had wanted was to die.

Charles shook off his melodramatic and damned depressing mood. So he'd had the dream. He'd had it for the last six years, hadn't he? One more time was not alarming. It wasn't even unusual. Going to his pitcher of water, he poured some on a cloth and wiped his face clean. A good cleaning with the basin was out now. He sighed. It would be all over the house by breakfast that Mr. Borden had his dreams again. Damn. The maids were up already. There'd be no sneaking out and dumping the evidence quietly. He smiled grimly. One of the inconveniences of living in each other's pockets here in the country. The only thing for it was to go on as if everything was normal.

Halfway between the dressing stand and his armoire, Charles lost his resolve and sank down onto the end of the bed. He rubbed his face roughly with both hands and then jammed them into his hair. Dammit, why now? He was trying so hard. He really was. Last night had been... There were no words to describe it. It had been unlike any other bed sport Charles had experienced, with or without Gideon. But definitely different than the other times he'd shared with Gideon. In the short time she'd known him, Sarah was already breaking down barriers that Gideon had kept locked tightly in place for the last six years. Last night with Sarah, Gideon had been more tender, more responsive, more himself than Charles had ever seen him be with a woman. It was the marriage. In Gideon's mind it made all the difference. She couldn't reject him now, could she?

Charles finally stopped denying the truth. The dream had come and had been so vivid and so accurate because it was happening again. Charles was on the verge of losing Gideon again. And this time he should let it happen. This time he should walk away. Because Sarah was clearly what Gideon needed and what he wanted. But the way she'd accepted Charles too... He couldn't stop thinking about it. About the way she'd made him feel, about the way he and Gideon had worked together to make the experience pleasurable for her. The way she'd responded to them had been thrilling.

Charles let his hands fall to his lap and stared at them as they lay there. They were covered with calluses and tiny scars, the hands of a laborer, a farmer. Not the hands of a gentleman. He didn't belong with them. He slowly closed his hands into tight fists. But he had always fought for Gideon, hadn't he? Fought by his side in the war, fought for scraps of his affection, fought for his life and his forgiveness. He was a stubborn fool. Because he couldn't seem to accept that the fight was over. But his fight was different now. Now he fought to keep a place in Gideon's life and to make one for himself in Sarah's.

* * * * *

"Good morning, Charles."

He paused in the doorway, keeping his face blank as he met Gideon's stare. Charles blinked first and Gideon smiled triumphantly. Well, that morning ritual was apparently unchanged today. He peered around the room. Sarah was nowhere in sight.

"My wife has not risen yet." Gideon seemed to almost preen as he said the words, and Charles hid a smile. Charles was sure Gideon would not be amused were he to comment on his smug attitude.

"No? She struck me as an early riser." Charles walked over to the sidebar and accepted a plate from Anders. He began to fill it with the hearty breakfast fare laid out for them. He wasn't hungry, which wasn't all that odd. Normally after the dream he skipped breakfast and went straight to the barn to work off his agitation. But he'd felt that an appearance at breakfast was required of him this morning.

"I'm sure we will learn her habits in due time," Gideon said nonchalantly. Charles was delighted at his casual inclusion in Gideon's observation, although he did not show it.

"Yes, quite," was all he said.

They ate their breakfast in a silence that was typical of them. A few years at war made a man appreciate a hot, hearty breakfast and the silence to eat it. There was no awkwardness, just a mutual enjoyment of the quiet and the fare.

Suddenly Sarah appeared in the doorway. Charles hadn't even heard her footsteps on the stairs. Either he was preoccupied or she was stealthier than she looked. Both he and Gideon rose from their chairs as she entered, Gideon reaching for his crutches.

"Good morning, Mr. North, Mr. Borden," she said crisply. She waved them back down. "Please do not interrupt your meal on my account." She walked over to Anders and accepted a plate with a smile and a murmured thank-you.

"Good morning, Sarah," Gideon said, his voice rather formal though the greeting was not. Sarah glanced over her shoulder at him in surprise and then with a blush her gaze cut to Anders, who was busy removing the covers so Sarah could see what was available.

"Good morning, Mrs. North," Charles offered jovially, and he could see her shoulders relax, as if she'd been waiting for an inappropriately intimate greeting from him. She merely nodded at him politely.

When she had all she wanted, Sarah turned to the table and stopped, indecision written on her face. The table was set with far too many places. Charles had wondered at it, but he now realized the staff wasn't sure where she would choose to sit and so had made up all the settings. He stood and walked over to pull out the chair to Gideon's left. "Join us, please," he asked politely.

"Yes, thank you," she replied. When she was seated Charles walked back over to his own place at Gideon's right, directly across from Sarah.

It was painful. What had been a relaxed and quiet breakfast was suddenly fraught with silent tension. Sarah ate quietly, looking at neither Charles nor Gideon. Gideon's jaw was tense, and he set his fork down beside his half-full plate with a precision usually reserved for holy objects and explosive devices. Several times he looked at Sarah as if he would say something but then thought better of it. He finished his tea with a loud swallow and was startled when Anders immediately appeared to refill his cup. The butler looked as tense as the three of them.

Charles was at a loss. Normally he would have interjected some light conversation to ease the tension, but he found himself tongue-tied. Was Sarah's nervousness his fault?

Should he leave? If he left he would be setting a precedent. He would be shutting himself out of their morning routine, and that was not the way to get what he wanted. Gideon caught his eye, and though his expression was fierce his eyes were pleading.

Then Sarah set her fork down on the table with a thump. "I am not sure what is required of me."

Gideon's gaze snapped to Sarah and Charles' followed. She stared down at her lap. "Today." She blew out a breath and her eyes darted up to flash a look between them. There was an edge of panic in it. "And tomorrow. What I mean is, do you wish me to take over the house and accounts or leave things as they are? I have been trained to run a household, as you know, but you have been satisfied with the current arrangement and I do not wish to interfere."

"Sar—" Gideon began, but her eyes grew wide and she glanced at Anders again. "Mrs. North," Gideon said slowly, and Sarah breathed a relieved sigh. "I wish you to do whatever it is that you wish to do. As my wife you have every right to run the household as you see fit. Any action you take will in no way be seen as interference."

Sarah nearly slumped in her seat as the tension in her shoulders disappeared. "Thank you, Mr. North," she said with sincere gratitude, reaching out and lightly touching the back of Gideon's hand. "I am not sure what I would do with myself if you had answered differently." Gideon's hand curled into a fist beneath her touch, his two damaged fingers refusing to hide themselves.

She licked her lips nervously, and though it was completely inappropriate to the situation, Charles felt his cock swell. Damn, she was pretty.

"I was wondering, is there anything that you wish changed? Or anything that you prefer remains exactly the same? Here in the house or around the farm?" Sarah's questions were a bit tentative, but it was clear she was determined to establish the boundaries of her new duties. She moved away from Gideon's hand and nodded her thanks to Anders as he set a fresh cup of tea in front of her.

Gideon's confusion was evident, which was astounding in itself. Sarah seemed to disconcert him routinely, when as long as Charles had known him he had been as stoic as a Spartan. Well, with everyone except Charles. Whether this was good or bad, Charles hadn't yet decided. Gideon's emotional recalcitrance may drive him mad, but it was the way they were used to operating. Charles wasn't sure he wanted to deal with an overly emotional Gideon. God save us. But then Gideon had never had to deal with a wife before. He'd adjust, hopefully.

"I'm agreeable to any changes you should like to make," Gideon said after clearing his throat. He picked up his fork and began eating his now cold breakfast without so much as a grimace.

Charles sat back in his chair and continued to openly observe the conversation. Neither Gideon nor Sarah seemed to be concerned about his presence. He was undecided as to whether that was good or bad too.

"If I may," Sarah said, and Charles could tell she was forcibly interjecting some firmness into her tone. Good for her. *Show him your backbone, my girl,* Charles thought with an inner grin. "I thought I might like to change a few things around the house. It is rather masculine for my tastes. But if that is what you prefer, by all means I shall leave it as it is."

Hardly a firm demand, but a stand all the same. Charles turned to watch Gideon's response.

Gideon was looking at Sarah as if she had two heads. "My dear Mrs. North, I care not one whit what you do with the house. As long as I have a bed and desk on the premises, I shall be content." He looked at Charles in complete bewilderment. "Charles?"

Charles let his smile show this time. "We did not change anything about the house when we took possession, Mrs.

North. None of the decorating is ours. The blame lies solely with the previous owner." He leaned forward and winked at Sarah, which caused another blush. "And I am very curious to see what you can do with the place. Change Blakely House any way you like. You have my blessing also."

"Ah," Gideon said with finality, "and there you have it. Charles approves." Charles glanced over at him with a frown. Gideon did not disappoint. "As in all things that go on at Blakely House, if Charles approves, then it must be done." His tone was dry.

"Of course," Charles responded with a polite nod for Gideon's sally. "One of us has to do more than growl at everyone before anything gets done properly. It's a wonder you haven't driven all the servants off."

"I haven't managed to drive you off. If growling will work that magic, please let me know."

"I am not a servant." Charles was strangely hurt by this morning's back-and-forth, although they had had almost the same exchange every morning for the last six years.

"No, you most certainly are not." Sarah's scandalized tone cut through the room and everyone, including Anders at the sideboard, froze. "Mr. North, I believe that was uncalled for."

Gideon blushed. Charles wasn't sure he'd ever seen that happen before.

"You are correct, Mrs. North," Gideon said coolly. He nodded at Charles. "My apologies, Borden. I did not mean to intimate that you were a servant. Merely that I wish I had driven you off."

Charles burst out laughing. "For a moment I actually thought you were going to apologize and I would need the smelling salts."

"If you faint," Gideon warned, "I shall have you bundled off on the next coach. That really would be the last straw, I'm afraid."

"Duly noted." Charles' sarcasm was ignored.

"Mr. North," Sarah said quietly. She reached out and touched his hand again. "Surely you don't mean it. Mr. Borden is invaluable here at Blakely House."

She frowned and her gaze shifted from Gideon to the window. The frown turned to a delighted smile and she unconsciously began rubbing her fingertip along the top of Gideon's hand. Gideon sat frozen, staring at her hand on his.

Charles turned in his seat to see what had caught her eye. There were several horses close to the fence, frolicking. They were butting each other with their heads and spinning around, and then one rose on his back legs before crashing down and sprinting off. Spring hijinks in the meadow.

"Why is it called Blakely House?" Sarah asked curiously without taking her eyes off the horses. She watched them hungrily. Why? What about them did she hunger for?

"No idea," Gideon answered, back to his gruff ways. "That was what they called it when we bought it. I suppose someone named Blakely owned it once or built it or some such thing."

"Yes, but why House?" Sarah pressed. She looked at Gideon and then Charles. "It is so much more than that now, isn't it?" She pushed her chair back and Anders rushed over to assist her. Charles and Gideon made as if to stand and Sarah waved them back into place. "Oh stop," she said absentmindedly. She wandered over to the window and put her hand on the sill. "I suppose if we called it Blakely Home, people would try to ensconce their invalids here."

She choked and spun to stare wide-eyed at Gideon. "I...I didn't mean... That is, I was making a jest. A very poor one, I think."

Gideon merely raised an eyebrow, his blue eyes piercing her mercilessly. "I am hardly an invalid."

Sarah shook her head and suddenly her eyes were as bright as Gideon's, full of what had happened between them all last night. "No sir. No, you are not," she agreed quietly. The room was suffused with a different kind of tension now.

Gideon stood up abruptly and Anders was there with his crutches. He moved out from the table but didn't leave. "If Blakely House displeases you, then you may choose a different name. Although I do agree that Blakely Home smacks of the infirmary."

Sarah blushed a painful red and Charles took pity on her. "I fear we would begin to receive inquiries as to available space for mental incompetents." Both Sarah and Gideon turned to stare at him and he smiled wickedly. "And we've only room for Gideon."

Gideon smiled back with ill humor. "You become less amusing as the day wears on."

"To you, perhaps. But the rest of the world dotes on me."

"And there you have it again," Gideon rejoined flatly. "We shall name it Borden Home."

Charles laughed and looked at Sarah, who seemed uncomfortable with their banter. "What do you wish to call it, Mrs. North?"

She licked her lips and again Charles had thoughts inappropriate for the breakfast room. "I was thinking perhaps Blakely Farm?" she ventured timidly.

"Blakely Farm," Charles mused. "Yes, I like it. Gideon?"

"If the two of you are satisfied, then I am more than content." The look Gideon gave them both was inscrutable. Charles wished he knew exactly how Gideon meant his comment. But the hard truths of their past convinced him to take it at face value to the conversation.

Charles looked back at Sarah. "Welcome to Blakely Farm, Mrs. North," he said gently. Sarah clasped her hands together and gifted him and Gideon with a smile brimming with possibilities.

Chapter Eight

ℰ

As Sarah inventoried the linen she thought about the conversation she'd had with Gideon and Charles at breakfast the other morning. The morning after her wedding night. Sarah had to stop and put her hands to her burning cheeks as she looked up and down the hallway to make sure no one saw her blushing for no apparent reason.

Refusing to let her mind get sidetracked yet again as it had numerous times in the last few days with thoughts of *that* night, Sarah cleared her throat and took another pile of linen off the shelf. Goodness, they had an awful lot of linen. Someone had clearly been saving for a rainy, cold day. She counted the pillow covers. Twenty-seven. Not only was it an odd number, but she was relatively sure that they did not have that many pillows in the house. They hadn't enough beds to hold them. Thoughts of beds naturally led her to thoughts of that night.

She gave in and closed her eyes, smoothing her fingers over the soft linen beneath her hand. She wished it was a firm, hairy chest instead. She nearly moaned aloud as she remembered the feel of Charles' burly chest against her fingertips, Gideon pressed to her back. And then Charles was against her back as she sat astride Gideon's lap, wanton and full and desperate to feel that pleasure again, the pleasure she'd learned under Gideon's mouth. She felt a pulse in her sex and she grew warm in the closed-off hallway. Her eyes flew open and she frantically looked around. She mustn't let the servants see her daydreaming like this.

Sarah worried her lip as she placed the pillow covers back on the shelf. Gideon had not knocked on her door for the last three nights, not since their wedding night. Neither had

Charles, which was appropriate, after all. He was not her husband. He had only been there at Gideon's request. Her breasts grew heavy and her nipples ached as she remembered Charles touching and sucking them.

In frustration she fell back against the wall beside the linen closet with a loud thump. Why had they not come back? She was a complete wreck, watching and waiting and wondering. It was driving her mad. Had she done something wrong? There had been no indication either way, really. After it was over Sarah had been so tired she could hardly keep her eyes open. First Charles and then Gideon had risen from her bed, dressed and left to go to their own rooms. She hadn't liked that at all. At home Papa and her stepmother slept in the same room. Both men had offered her sincere thanks, which embarrassed her mightily, and then made quiet departures. But they had not uttered one word about whether or not she had performed satisfactorily. Then again, they had let her rename the farm. That made it as much hers now as theirs, didn't it? They wouldn't have done that if they weren't happy with her.

Sarah turned and yanked yet another stack of linen off the shelf. It wasn't as if she could ask them, was it? Conversations had been limited to meals, and those were stilted recitations of her day. She would dearly love to see Gideon's reaction were she to broach the subject at luncheon in front of an astounded Anders. Sarah laughed mirthlessly. She wanted the physical intimacy of marriage. It was part of why she had sought a husband. She sighed and buried her face in the pile of sheets.

She was lonely. A bride should not be lonely mere days after her wedding. The house was so quiet. What were they doing right now? Was Gideon in his office? Was Charles down in the paddock with the horses? She was too afraid to ask. Too afraid of looking like a fool.

"What are you doing?"

The question was asked in a mildly curious tone, but having thought she was alone, Sarah jerked upright and couldn't stop a short shriek of surprise from escaping before she clapped her hand over her mouth.

Charles fell back a step or two, his eyes wide. "Good Lord, I didn't mean to startle you. Are you all right?"

Sarah pulled her hand away. "I'm fine," she squeaked. She cleared her throat. "You just...yes, startled me." She turned back and busied herself with the linen. "I'm taking inventory of the linen."

"By smelling it?"

Charles sounded amused, which made Sarah more than a bit angry. Here she was lonely beyond words and longing for a touch, and he found her desperation amusing?

"It smells a little musty," Sarah snapped without looking at him.

"Oh, Mrs. North! I am so sorry." Sarah's head jerked up and she saw Mrs. Brown standing behind Charles. The housekeeper seemed quite upset at Sarah's comment and she could have kicked herself. In her selfishness she'd lashed out without thought.

"Oh, it's nothing Mrs. Brown," Sarah said quickly. "Simply disuse. A little lavender water sprinkled on the sheets will take care of it, I'm sure."

Mrs. Brown paled. "Lavender water? Well, you see Mrs. North, we haven't much of that. Mr. North and Mr. Borden..." she trailed off.

"Are not prone to smelling like lavender," Charles finished with a grin. "The horses take exception to it. But now that there is a woman in the house they will just have to get used to it."

"You can get some in the village, Mrs. Brown," Sarah told her with a smile. "And while you are there perhaps you could stop at the apothecary? I noticed yesterday we are in need of some items for the medicine chest."

Mrs. Brown wrung her hands. "I cannot go today, Mrs. North," she apologized. "We are short two maids, as I mentioned earlier, and it is baking day. I am needed here."

Sarah waved her off. "That's fine, Mrs. Brown. It isn't urgent. You can get them later in the week. That will be soon enough."

"Have you been to the village, Sarah?" Charles asked with a frown. "Since the wedding?"

It was Sarah's turn to blanche. "No, I…I have not needed to. It has only been a few days, after all." And would be many, many more before she went if she had her way. At least until Sunday. And if handled properly even church need not require a great deal of socializing.

"Let's go." Charles grabbed her arm without waiting for an answer and began to drag her down the hallway.

"What?" Sarah was incredulous. He couldn't just drag her off to the village, could he? She clung tightly to the small pile of sheets she still held and tried to plant her feet, but his pull was inexorable. Mrs. Brown rushed to catch up and they engaged in a brief tug-of-war over the sheets. Mrs. Brown won.

"Now don't worry, Mrs. North, I'll take care of these. You go on to the village with Mr. Borden. I'm sure it will be nice to get away for a little while."

Sarah could only stare wide-eyed with incredulity at Mrs. Brown over her shoulder as Charles dragged her away. Was the woman daft? Did she honestly think Sarah would find it "nice" to be stared at like an oddity from a traveling circus?

Before she knew it she was standing in the hall while Anders shoved her coat over her arms. Charles was adjusting his hat as he watched with approval.

"Blue is quite becoming on you, Mrs. North." His comment was made politely, but Sarah caught a gleam in his eyes that had nothing to do with politeness. Her heart soared and then she blushed and glanced nervously at Anders. He was busy fetching her bonnet and paying them no mind. To him Charles' comment must seem nothing more than the polite flattery practiced by so many gentlemen. Perhaps that's all it was, truly. Sarah mustn't read too much into it.

Suddenly Charles winked from under his rakishly perched hat and Sarah caught her breath.

The study door opened and Gideon appeared on his crutches. He stopped as he saw them all in the hall. "Where are you going?" His question was curious, nothing more. He held a sheaf of papers in his hand.

"To the village," Charles replied. "Mrs. North needs a few things."

Gideon nodded absently. "Good, good." His gaze grew sharp as he watched Sarah put her bonnet on. "When you return I need to speak to you about these." He raised the papers. "But there is no hurry." He turned back to the study and as the door was closing behind him, called out, "Get her a new hat, would you Charles?" Sarah's mouth dropped open and she was about to tell him her hat was none of his business when his sparkling blue eyes met hers briefly over his shoulder. He caught the door with his elbow and held it open. "Make sure that one meets an untimely and violent demise." Then the door swung shut in her astonished face.

"Well!" she said. What else could she say to the closed door? Truthfully she didn't like the bonnet either. That didn't mean she was giving it up without an argument, however. She wore it for a reason. It hid her birthmark beautifully.

She saw a small gig waiting for them in the drive as she and Charles went down the front steps. When had Charles asked for that? It was almost as if the entire house was attuned to Charles' needs at all times. This wasn't the first time that whatever he needed magically appeared without a word being spoken. The servants adored him. He was always unfailingly polite and gracious with them. In the short time she'd been here Sarah had determined that Charles was not a distant estate manager but instead a man who worked right alongside the staff, listened to their problems and helped when he could. Yet they treated him like a gentleman, not an equal. Sarah had the impression that Charles had earned the deference of the servants through his kindness and industry. She hoped to do the same. She didn't want the staff to obey her simply because she was Mrs. North, although they would. But it would be so much better, and easier, if they respected her as a person and not just her station.

"Sarah?" Charles was standing next to the gig, holding out his hand, his head cocked to the side as he waited patiently. She blinked, suddenly aware she had been standing like a dolt staring at him.

"I'm sorry," she apologized. "I was thinking about what I needed in the village." She didn't like to lie and could feel her cheeks heat with shame.

"Were you?" Charles murmured as she took his hand and stepped up into the small carriage. She refused to look at him.

Halfway to the village Charles asked Sarah where they were going. She had been desperately trying not to let his proximity encourage thoughts of the wedding night, concentrating on his driving and the horses and the passing scenery, anything but their past intimacies. She was concentrating so hard it took her several heartbeats to realize he meant what shops she needed to visit. "The apothecary and the general store, please."

"And the milliner," Charles added.

She couldn't see his face around the brim of her hat, but Sarah put a protective hand on it just in case. "What is wrong with my hat?"

Charles cleared his throat and Sarah scooted over to the side in order to turn her head and look at him. He stared straight ahead for a moment, a muscle working in his jaw. When he finally glanced at her, his expression was far too innocent. "Why, there is nothing wrong with your hat. Gideon simply wants to buy you new things. He is newly married, after all. It's only natural he should want to buy you pretty things."

Sarah let her skepticism show. "Is it? Since his money paid for this one, he has already bought me enough hats." She turned to the front again and moved back to a comfortable place on the seat. "I am fond of this hat. I very much like the style of it. Perhaps I should get one just like it."

Next to her Charles choked out a cough and Sarah smiled triumphantly behind the huge brim of her bonnet.

But Charles was not ready to concede defeat. "You are quite right, of course. It is very fetching. May I see it? I've often wondered how they make those bonnets for ladies. Are they similar to a gentleman's hat? Inside?" She saw his hand waving about in front of him, apparently to indicate flipping a hat upside down. At least she assumed it was his hand since she couldn't see where it attached to his body. She almost giggled at the thought.

"I am sure I have no idea," Sarah said primly. "I have not examined gentlemen's clothing to any great extent."

"Pity, that," Charles murmured. He sounded closer than before, although his legs had not moved, and neither had his shoulder against hers. The heat from that contact had been warming her most of the carriage ride. Was he leaning toward her? The skin on her arms got goose bumps and she shivered. "I cannot tell from here," he muttered. "Take it off and show me the inside."

Sarah was suspicious, but he hadn't asked to have the hat so she saw no harm in holding it up for his inspection. The road was empty in front and in back of them, so she needn't fear running into a neighbor without her bonnet. She quickly untied the ribbon at her jaw and took the bonnet off, careful not to disturb her hair arrangement. Lil, Mrs. Brown's young niece and Sarah's new maid, had put it up in the latest fashion today, or so she said. All day it had felt to Sarah as if it were going to fall around her shoulders any minute. She didn't have a headache for a change, but she missed her old, tight fashion.

"I've been meaning to tell you how attractive your hair looks today. I like the way it..."Charles swooped his hand down along his face. "Sort of falls like that."

Sarah blushed and covered her embarrassment by holding the hat out for his inspection. "I'm not sure whether it's supposed to be falling or not." Her confession was made in a crisply wry tone that made Charles laugh.

"I'm not either, but it still looks pretty," he assured her. Then without a by-your-leave he grabbed her bonnet and tossed it in the road under the horses, grabbed Sarah's arm and flicked the reins. The horses broke into a trot and stomped her poor bonnet to shreds.

Sarah spun about in the seat and stared in shock at her crushed bonnet lying broken in the road behind them. Charles slowed the horses with a tug on the reins and Sarah nearly fell off the seat, but Charles put out his arm and stopped her fall.

"My bonnet!" Sarah cried in anger. She turned around and glared at Charles. "You did that on purpose!"

Charles glanced at her and she did not like his smug grin at all. "Yes, I did."

Well, that took the wind out of her sails. She couldn't believe she was almost charmed by his unrepentant response. She frowned harder. "You are no gentleman."

Charles' lips became a thin slash and he trained his gaze on the road before them. "No, I am not."

What? It did not sound as if he meant that the same way she did. How she wished she were more adept at understanding men. But she'd known so few intimately. "I'm sorry," she ventured.

Charles smiled coolly but still would not look at her. "Why? It's the truth. I was not born a gentleman."

"Charles, a gentleman is more than his birth. A gentleman is judged on his behavior, his speech, his noble actions. No one can pass judgment on you in those areas."

He spared her only a glance before he turned away. If she didn't know better, she'd have said he looked both tender and guilty. Her emotions seemed just as tangled today.

"That is the first time since…in the last few days that you have called me Charles."

Sarah was surprised by the unexpected remark. She appreciated his discretion. She was embarrassed enough by the reminder of the things he had done to her that night without him expressly addressing it. She would have to be careful. His name had slipped out unbidden, a visceral reaction to his anger and defensiveness. What if there had been servants about?

"I…" She did not know what to say. She didn't think telling him she had not meant to do it was the right thing at this time. Nor was telling him it felt natural to do so and she had to fight the urge every minute she was with him. How could she long for intimacies with him again and at the same time be afraid to call him by his Christian name? It was all so confusing.

"I understand," he said quietly, and she truly believed he did. He continued, saving her yet again from having to respond. "As for what makes a gentleman," here his glance was chastising, "you are far too naive if you believe all gentlemen are noble creatures. I shall have to keep my eye on you lest some gentleman lead you astray."

"I am not so naive as to believe that," Sarah scoffed. "I said they are judged that way. As for being led astray…" She let the thought trail off, both amazed and horrified at her boldness.

Charles' laugh was genuine. "You should see how you are blushing right now," he teased. He shook his head. "You continue to amaze me, Sarah. You really do." He clicked his tongue and turned the horses at a crossroads and Sarah could see houses up ahead.

"Charles—" she began fearfully, her hand going to her cheek and then traveling up and smoothing her hair as if that was what she'd meant to do.

"I shall have to tell Gideon when we get home that you are learning to be a proper wife," Charles said teasingly, sliding his leg along the bench and nudging Sarah with his knee. At her shocked gasp he chuckled. "You are becoming a very good scold."

For some reason that little touch and his teasing calmed her. She put both hands in her lap over her reticule and sat up straighter on the seat. "Am I? Then I shall continue to scold you both over my poor, wretched bonnet left ignominiously in the lane. What will people think, Mr. North's new wife arriving in the village in such a sorry state as no bonnet?"

Charles placed his hand over his heart and sighed dramatically, earning a whinny from one of the horses. "I will take the blame, dear lady. I am racked with guilt over knocking your pretty bonnet off into the lane. Our first stop— the milliner's." He turned and smiled wickedly at her with a twinkle in his eye. "Where you can replace the one I ruined."

"Destroyed is more like it," Sarah muttered, smoothing her skirts. She pretended to ponder for a moment. "Perhaps Mr. North would not be too devastated if I did not purchase an exact replacement. After all, the milliner here may not have one as fine as my old one. I may have to settle for a different style." Even as she said it, Sarah felt her hands grow cold with dread. She wasn't sure she could come out of hiding so easily.

"We shall see," Charles said noncommittally. "Perhaps Mrs. Duncan will have one that is finer."

Sarah could not answer him through a throat choked with emotion. His comment showed his sensitivity to her plight. If she were not very careful her affection for Charles could grow to something so much more.

"You are a gentleman, Charles," she finally whispered as they entered the village and several people stopped to look at them.

"Don't be fooled for one minute, Mrs. North," Charles told her as he nodded at the villagers. "I am as far from that creature as it is possible to be."

After the nerve-racking experience of driving into the village with Charles, exposed in the carriage with no bonnet or cover of any kind, actually visiting the shops was far less dramatic than Sarah had expected. Mrs. Duncan, the milliner, positively beamed when Charles walked in.

"Mr. Borden!" she cried, coming around the counter with her hand out.

Charles bowed low over her hand. "How do you do, Mrs. Duncan?" he said with a smile in his voice. Sarah had never understood that expression until she met Charles. He turned to Sarah who was hanging back by the door. "This is Mrs. North. I'm afraid I knocked her bonnet off on the way to the village today and the horses crushed it. She is in desperate need of a new hat."

Mrs. Duncan put her hands together under her chin and turned to Sarah with a wide smile, as if she was the cat who got the cream. She was a plump woman in her thirties, a very attractive brunette with big blue eyes. "Mrs. North!" Sarah hid her amusement at the effusive greeting.

"How do you do, Mrs. Duncan?" Sarah asked politely.

"Oh, how good it is to meet you," Mrs. Duncan said, sliding her arm through Sarah's and pulling her farther into the shop. "I would be thrilled to help you find a new bonnet today." She let Sarah go at the counter and walked around behind it. "The whole village has talked of nothing else but your wedding this past week. How romantic."

Sarah wasn't quite sure what the other woman meant. A wedding was romantic? Marrying a man you barely knew was romantic? Gideon was the tragic romantic hero? Sarah decided not to ask, merely sneaked a look at Charles out of the corner of her eye. He was grinning.

"Yes, quite romantic," he agreed with Mrs. Duncan enthusiastically.

Sarah felt a little lost. "Thank you?" she tried.

Mrs. Duncan seemed satisfied and beamed again. "We've all been hoping that Mr. North would find a wife."

Ah, it was Gideon as tragic hero, then, Sarah thought. How he would hate that.

Mrs. Duncan looked slyly at Charles. "And now it is Mr. Borden's turn, is it not?"

Charles looked more than a little alarmed. "I don't believe it is contagious," he answered. "Marriage only affects willing victims."

Mrs. Duncan laughed and Sarah hid a smile. "Now, what kind of hat were you looking for?" Mrs. Duncan asked, all business.

Sarah looked around at the various styles on the shelves behind the counter. She saw Charles sidle over and stand very straight and tall in front of a small section, hiding what was behind him. Sarah pointed directly at him. "I believe I saw a poke bonnet on the shelf there?"

Charles grimaced with a sigh and moved off to the side. Mrs. Duncan looked alarmed. "Are you sure that's the style you want, my dear?" she asked gently. At her question Sarah turned her attention away from Charles but was still able to see him shake his head vigorously at Mrs. Duncan, who seemed to understand immediately. "You see, that bonnet is Mrs. Reed's. She is to pick it up tomorrow. But if you'd like, I can make another one for you. It will take some time…" She let the sentence trail off as she turned to peruse the shelves herself. She picked up a pretty little bonnet with a very small brim and some pink trim. "How about this one?" she asked with a smile as she turned around.

"Oh no," Sarah said, aghast. That little bonnet? Why it wouldn't hide a thing.

"Why not?" Charles asked. He stepped up and took the hat from Mrs. Duncan. "I like it. It's pretty."

"Then you wear it," Sarah said drily. Charles and Mrs. Duncan laughed as if it was a great joke. It wasn't.

"Oh, Mrs. North," Mrs. Duncan giggled. "You and your husband have the same sense of humor. How marvelous."

"Yes, isn't it?" Sarah murmured.

Charles was watching her with a challenging gleam in his eye. "Try it on."

Sarah sighed like a martyr. She'd perfected that with her younger siblings. It had no effect on Charles. He continued to hold the hat out, nearly in front of her face. She snatched the bonnet from him. "Fine." She walked over to a mirror on the counter and set the bonnet on her head.

"Oh," was all she could say. It was beautiful. Sarah had never worn something so frivolous in her life. She turned her head to the right, so only her unmarred cheek was reflected in the mirror. She actually looked pretty. Then she faced the mirror square-on. Well, the hat was pretty. She was passable at best, and not too ridiculous.

"Tie the ribbon, dear," Mrs. Duncan said. But even as she said it Mrs. Duncan pulled Sarah about and began to tie the ribbon herself. "Oh, this looks even better than I'd hoped! See how attractive she is, Mr. Borden! The pink ribbon makes her eyes glow."

Sarah turned back to the mirror and was caught by Charles' gaze as he looked over her shoulder into the reflection. "Her eyes rival the stars, Mrs. Duncan," Charles said somberly. "We will take the hat."

"Oh, I'm so glad!" Mrs. Duncan gushed. She left Sarah staring at Charles in the mirror and bustled over to the counter, pulling out a hatbox.

Sarah broke the spell and turned away from the mirror. "Yes, I will take it," she said firmly, arching her brow at Charles, who just grinned. "It is a little too fine for everyday wear, however." She walked over to Mrs. Duncan. "Have you something else that would work around Blakely Farm?"

"Blakely Farm?" Mrs. Duncan asked curiously.

"Mrs. North has renamed it," Charles told her. "She said it was far more than a house now."

"Oh, that is splendid," Mrs. Duncan said in her friendly, enthusiastic manner. Normally Sarah would have found that grating, but Mrs. Duncan was hard not to like. "And how are things on the farm, Mr. Borden? Have you made your horse yet? And Mr. North? I hope he is doing well?"

Mrs. Duncan's questions were directed at Charles, though Sarah stood right in front of her. Sarah would have said something but Charles answered too quickly.

"No, we have not made our horse yet," he responded with a laugh. "But we are getting closer. And Mr. North is his usual self."

"Good, good," Mrs. Duncan said absently as she looked over the shelves again. She turned to Sarah with a sigh. "I know just the thing, dear, something similar to what you're wearing now, but in a lighter shade with a wider ribbon. Blue to match your pretty pelisse?" She frowned, and though Sarah did not know her well, she could tell it was an unnatural expression for her. "But I don't have it right now. I can have it by next week. Would that be all right?" She pulled down a military-style hat and held it next to Sarah's face. It was peacock blue. "This would look very smart as well. The color is perfect for you." She pointed here and there on the hat. "With a feather here, and perhaps some braid. Also next week?" She looked at Charles.

Sarah cleared her throat before Charles could answer. "I will take your advice, Mrs. Duncan," she answered politely, "and order both." Sarah looked down at what she was wearing and remembered Charles telling her how becoming blue was on her. She tried not to blush. But perhaps Gideon would like the blue too? "But could you make the adornment on this little hat blue to match my coat as well?"

Mrs. Duncan smiled. "What a clever idea! Of course. I shall use a different ribbon on each hat, but they will both complement your coat, ma'am. And your pretty eyes."

Sarah's smile was a little hesitant at Mrs. Duncan's flattery. "It is more practical that they match my coat, I think."

Charles huffed next to her. "You are far too practical, Mrs. North," he muttered.

Sarah walked to the door, her smile hidden from Charles as he paid Mrs. Duncan. "Someone has to be," she replied. "And I am very good at it."

Two hours later they were in the carriage on the way back to Blakely Farm. Sarah thought about her new hats. Charles was incredibly persuasive when he wanted to be. And charming, she mustn't forget charming. He charmed everyone in the village. And not one person acted rudely toward Sarah. No one pointed, no one turned away as if she carried some contagion. Granted, they did not walk the entire village and only spoke with a handful of people, but it was a start. Sarah felt inordinately proud of herself.

A young man named Garret, from the general store, was following them in a wagon loaded down with supplies for the horses. Charles had needed some things in the village as well, although Sarah wondered if he really had been coming all along as he'd claimed.

"What did Mr. Howard mean when he asked how the experiment was going?" Sarah asked. She'd been burning with curiosity ever since she'd overheard the remark.

"We're trying to create a new breed of horse," Charles answered as if it were common to do such a thing.

"A new breed? Why that's amazing! But why? Can it be done?" Sarah's head was spinning. She'd had no idea they were doing that sort of thing. It sounded complicated and time-consuming.

"Yes, it can be done," Charles answered. He sounded amused but not condescending. "Gideon thinks that carriage travel on the new roads requires a new breed of horse, and I think he's right. He wants to breed one of the faster horses with a heavier, stronger breed. The combination of speed, strength, endurance and intelligence should make an excellent carriage horse."

"I had no idea." Sarah felt utterly foolish. She had not asked them about the horses. She hadn't made the effort to find out what her new husband's interests were, what his goals for the farm were. She'd seen the horses and thought they were beautiful and she hadn't thought beyond that. Even Mrs. Duncan had known. She'd asked whether he had "made his horse".

"I'm sorry," she blurted out. "I'm sorry I didn't ask about the horses and the farm. I should have. No wonder..." She broke off before she revealed her fears over the two men not returning to her bed.

"No wonder what?" Charles pounced on her hesitation.

Sarah just shook her head. "Nothing."

"Don't worry, Sarah. You'll learn all about the farm as you go along. It's too soon to castigate yourself for not knowing everything." Sarah smiled at him, letting him believe he'd placated her. Charles let it drop after one more searching look at her.

A few minutes later she broke the silence again. "What exactly is your work, Charles? Are you in charge of the breeding?"

Charles started to shake his head but stopped. "Yes and no. I'm in charge of the day-to-day care of the horses and the management of the farm. But Gideon is the mind behind the breeding program. He is in communication with breeders around the world, decides which horses to buy, which horses to breed with each other. The horses are Gideon's dream."

"Which you are helping him to realize." Sarah spoke without thinking. Charles glanced at her nervously and she could see he was blushing.

"Anyone would need help. What we do is too much for one man to undertake." He tried to minimize his role on the farm, but it was too late. Sarah knew all that he did, and now she knew what his goal was—their goal, really. To create something lasting, something unique and wonderful. Something they could only do together.

Sarah had wondered today if she was underestimating Charles' role on the farm. She understood that Charles was more than just the estate manager. He was Gideon's dearest friend, even if they did exchange cross words frequently. Gideon trusted Charles more than he trusted anyone else, including her. But they were almost strangers still, it seemed, she and Gideon. Most of the villagers had directed their questions about Gideon and the farm to Charles today, not to her. Charles may deny being a gentleman, but he was treated like one in the village. A gentleman of property, as if the farm were as much his as Gideon's. If she had underestimated his role on the farm, perhaps she was underestimating his role in Gideon's life as well. Perhaps that was the real reason they had not been back to see her.

Chapter Nine

ℭ

He was leaning on the rail of the gazebo, one hand resting on the whitewashed wood, a crutch clutched in the other hand. Sarah walked slowly toward the small, delicate building on the lawn facing the fenced horse paddocks. He looked upset. Well, as upset as Gideon got. His face appeared closed off, forced into blankness, which she was learning meant inside he was wrestling strong emotions. As she got closer she could see his knuckles were white, he was clutching the rail so tightly. His jaw was tense, his permanent frown even more pronounced. It was astounding the little building could contain him, he seemed so much larger than life there, a dark, angry beast among the flowers.

And yet she dared approach him. Gideon's gruff fierceness hid many things, but not cruelty. He was never hurtful or callous to her. He was kindness itself, solicitous of her welfare at every turn. But it was the dark beast that drew her today. The fiercer he became the more she wanted to be with him. Who was this man she had married? What did he want from her?

She'd observed him and Charles for the last several days, ever since her visit to the village. Still they did not come to her. It had been a week now. The wedding night had faded to a dream. She saw them rarely, spoke to them sparingly. Yet they were never to be found far from each other. She could see that even now he was watching Charles with the horses. Was it the horses that held his attention, or the man?

"Are you going to stand there peeking around the bushes all day, or do you wish to speak to me?" Gideon turned his head sharply and speared Sarah with his bright gaze.

Sarah hid a flash of trepidation, standing straighter and squaring her shoulders as she walked sedately up the steps to the interior of the gazebo. "I was not peeking. I was merely standing, on the path mind you, observing. If you can stand here and spy on Charles, why can I not stand openly on the path and observe you?"

Gideon raised his eyebrow. "I thought you would be more biddable."

Sarah raised a brow as well. "Did you? Pity, that." Gideon laughed outright at her imitation of Charles' favorite phrase.

"I am not spying," he said. "I am watching him train a horse." He turned and hopped over to a chair, settling his weight on it with a sigh. He laid the crutch on the floor beside his chair and waved Sarah into the seat next to him.

"Did you teach him how to train the horses?" Gideon appeared surprised by Sarah's question. "He told me that you are the thinking half of this partnership." Sarah chose her words deliberately.

"Did he?" Gideon said. He sounded more intrigued than anything else. "What else did he say?"

"He said that the two of you are trying to create a new breed of carriage horse. That you are in charge of the correspondence and research and breeding decisions, and he is in charge of the day-to-day affairs on the farm."

"He said rather a lot, then, didn't he?" Gideon said pensively. "I assume this was on your trip to the village?"

Sarah nodded. "We did not discuss the breeding in detail."

Gideon's lip quirked. She was used to his smiles now, few and far between as they were. "No, I don't suppose you did." Sarah blushed at his double meaning and looked away. "What would you like to know?" he asked pleasantly. "I may not be in charge, but I do know something of the day-to-day."

His answer confirmed what Charles had told her, and convinced her that Gideon harbored no resentment over the situation. He had not corrected her when she had called their relationship a partnership. It was apparent that was how he saw it too.

"Is the horse there with Mr. Borden one of your new breed?" Sarah asked.

Gideon shook his head. "No. That's a Cleveland Bay. It's a carriage horse already. Or will be after Charles is done with it. We are trying to create a new breed, but we also raise and train breeds that are in demand right now, such as the Bay." Gideon pointed to the field beside the paddock. "Do you see the smaller, black horse there? That is a Dartmoor. I'm hoping that cross-breeding with the Bay will create a strong, intelligent, tractable horse." He turned to Sarah and grinned like a schoolboy. "And then I shall introduce the Arabian." He rubbed his hands together. "With the thoroughbred's speed and high spirits tempered by the Bay and Dartmoor's sweet temper and strength, I think we shall have an excellent, heavy-carriage horse."

His enthusiasm was a delight to watch. Sarah had never seen him so animated. "Why carriage horses? Why not thoroughbreds, racehorses?"

Gideon shook his head dismissively. "Because it's not about what they do in one moment, it's about what they are capable of day in and day out. A carriage horse is an investment in time, an integral part of a gentlemen's life. A racehorse is merely an investment to be disposed of if it does not deliver."

He pointed at various horses in the paddocks and the field. "We also have some trotters, Yorkshire and Norfolk both. I'm planning to crossbreed them as well. The result should be a lighter, elegant horse with good stamina." He took a breath as if to say more, but then grimaced and looked at Sarah. "I'm sorry. I get carried away."

Sarah shook her head. "No, it's fascinating, truly." She wrinkled her nose. "I must confess that I've never thought much about the breeding of horses for specific tasks. A horse is a horse to me."

Gideon frowned in mock ferocity. "You blaspheme, my dear."

Sarah laughed. "Gideon," she chided halfheartedly. She turned to watch Charles with the horse. "I shall learn as I go, as Charles told me the other day."

"Yes," Gideon said quietly, "you will. Particularly if Charles has decreed it."

Sarah turned to him, but she could detect no malice in his remark, just amusement. "I will learn because I choose to, not because Charles has decreed it."

"Bravo, my dear Mrs. North," Gideon said with a wry bow of his head. "I am put in my place."

Sarah sighed. "I do not wish to place you anywhere you do not wish to go," she said in exasperation. "I am trying to learn, Gideon. I am trying to learn about you."

She couldn't have surprised him more if she'd stripped naked and danced on the lawn. "Why?" The question burst out unbidden, but he did not want to take it back.

Sarah sighed again and shook her head as she smoothed her skirts. He'd noticed she did that when she was nervous or thinking. She was always thinking. Gideon could almost hear the wheels turning in her head sometimes. But he never knew what she was thinking. She was quiet as a mouse, watching. If she'd only say something, anything to let him know how she felt about this marriage of theirs. About what they'd done on the wedding night. He closed his eyes and turned away, as if cutting off the sight of the sun glinting off her shining hair would stop the memories of how that hair felt against his face, how it smelled, how it shimmered in the candlelight around her shoulders and hips like a cape of honey as she rode him. He opened his eyes and saw Charles watching them. And he remembered how Charles had watched them then too.

"How can I be your wife if I don't know you, Gideon?" Sarah asked quietly beside him. He had almost forgotten his question.

Gideon took a deep breath. Her answer did not reassure him. "You are my wife now," he drawled, "whether you know me or not."

Sarah made a noise that may have been frustration, but when Gideon looked at her she was serenely watching Charles in the paddock. She spent as much time watching Charles as she did watching Gideon, though she tried to be surreptitious about it. Gideon supposed that was natural. She had shared her body with Charles as much as she had with Gideon, intercourse be damned. His one regret was that he had not let Charles have her. But he had not spoken of it. Neither had Charles, nor had Sarah. Blakely Farm had become a house of unspoken thoughts in the last week.

"If you were to know me better, madam, you might find that you do not wish to be my wife."

Sarah scoffed. She must think he was joking. But he wasn't. Surely she knew what kind of man he was by now. The kind of man who could not bed his wife alone. The kind of man who would share a beautiful, innocent girl with another man. The kind of man who enjoyed it, had enjoyed watching his friend touch her, kiss her, fondle her. The kind of man who wanted to do it again.

"Gideon, you say the most outrageous things. You do not know me either. Perhaps you are finding that the more you know the more you regret the poor choice you made for a wife?"

Gideon glared at her. "Do not ever say that again, Sarah. You are the one who must now have regrets. I am sure I am not what you hoped for."

He couldn't decipher her look. Why must his wife be so enigmatic? He was not adept in these emotional minefields. What had he been thinking to believe he could handle a wife?

"Why were you here watching Charles?" she asked quietly. He could tell that the question had an underlying meaning, but he had no idea what it was. Another attempt to "know" him?

"I like to watch him train the horses. To see the fruition of my work. I also keep an eye on how he trains them."

"Did you teach him?" She had asked him that when she first entered.

He shook his head. "No. Charles' father was a well-to-do farmer. I understand breeding and lineage, he knows training. But I have learned from him."

"He said he was not a gentleman."

Gideon felt the familiar irritation whenever he heard Charles say the same thing to him. "That's rubbish. He is as much a gentleman as I."

"I do not know your background, Gideon." Sarah sounded surprised. "I should have asked before now. You said you had no family and I did not pursue it. I assumed because you were an officer you were well connected."

Gideon waved it off. "Well, of course I had a family. But they are dead now. My father was a merchant in Bath. I was the youngest of three children. He bought me a commission, and while I was away he lost his business and all but my oldest brother died of a fever. He died several years ago. I am not a gentleman by birth either." He stared off in the distance. "But I earned that commission and my pension in the war." He raised his left hand and looked at it, flexing his fingers as best as he could. "This made me a gentleman farmer, my dear."

"Are you telling Mrs. North I am too rough with the horses, Gideon?" Charles called from the path outside the gazebo. Gideon refocused on the paddock and saw a groom leading the Bay to the barn. He hadn't noticed Charles leaving. He turned and saw Charles just rounding the bend in the path, and then he was there, jumping over the steps, too impatient to take the time to climb them.

"He does not take the lead well," Gideon replied smoothly. "You bully him when you should praise."

Sarah seemed to melt into her chair at Charles' arrival. It wasn't that she shrank, but rather that she went very still and quiet, the better to observe them, he supposed. Charles bowed briefly and Sarah nodded. So stiff and formal today, yet they had been bosom beaux on their trip to the village, apparently. Gideon took a deep breath again. He couldn't decide which annoyed him more. Yes, he could. He did not like to see them this way. He wanted to be privy to the two when they were sharing their secrets with each other. His jealousy had less to do with their growing friendship and more to do with being left out of it.

"If you want to train the horses, then get off your arse and get down there and do it."

That certainly got Sarah to sit up. "Mr. Borden," she gasped.

Gideon smiled sarcastically. "Yes, that would be amusing. Dragging me around the paddock by the lead should help train them to pull dead weight in no time."

"You could ride a horse to train. You know you can take the lead from atop a horse. And they need to be trained to work with other horses eventually. You could do that."

"I do not ride." Gideon's jaw tensed as he clenched his teeth. They had had this argument innumerable times. He did not wish to have it again in front of Sarah.

"You could ride," Charles said, anger coloring his voice. "We have the saddle for you. I've seen you use it. You choose not to ride."

"It is uncomfortable and awkward," Gideon ground out, "as I have told you before."

"Then get a prosthesis." Charles was relentless. "You have the name of a maker in London. With the proper prosthesis you could work in the paddock."

"Enough." Gideon grabbed his crutches from the floor and stood up. "Simply because you cannot train a horse properly does not excuse your boorish behavior in front of my wife."

Charles looked at Sarah and his mouth thinned to a razor sharp line. "My apologies, madam." He turned back to Gideon. "But do not hide behind her skirts, Gideon. You are afraid to ride, afraid the cavalry officer cannot ride as well as he used to."

Gideon's anger exploded. "You know nothing about why I do or do not choose to ride, Charles, so kindly do not presume that you do. I am well aware that cavalry officer no longer exists. I will not pretend otherwise by getting up on a horse again. Now act the gentleman if you can and give Sarah a proper apology, and then go and wash the dirt off. You should have cleaned up before coming here."

"You will not pretend to be something you are not, but I am supposed to? I am no gentleman, Gideon, just as you are no officer." On those words Charles turned and jumped down the stairs as easily as he had jumped up a few minutes before. He angrily stalked toward the house.

Gideon stomped over to the rail and grabbed it with one hand. Only Charles could make him so angry. But then again, only Charles had the nerve to confront him like that. Damn him. Why now, in front of Sarah?

"Gideon." Sarah said his name quietly and he flinched, anticipating her questions. She rose from her chair and walked over to stand next to him. He could feel her skirt brush his leg, smell the subtle flowery scent she wore. "This is probably not the right time to say this. No, actually, I know this is not the right time."

She placed her hand over his on the rail and Gideon felt her touch everywhere. It was a small, tentative touch, and yet more powerful than a kiss. She had not touched him since the morning after the wedding.

"I want my marital rights."

Gideon shook his head, sure he had heard her incorrectly. He turned to her and saw her cheeks were so bright he could hardly discern her birthmark. She refused to look at him. "Excuse me?" he asked inanely.

Sarah licked her lips and he noticed she was breathing rather erratically. "I wish to enjoy the physical intimacies of marriage again." Her hand tightened on his. "With you." She suddenly whirled away and began to pace the gazebo, her arms wrapped around her waist. "I have been…distraught this past week that you have not come to my room. I was worried that I did something wrong."

Gideon turned to face her so he could lean against the rail, dumbfounded at her confession. "You did nothing wrong. Nothing at all. It was…an enjoyable experience." He nearly groaned aloud at how awkward he sounded. Where had Charles gone? How dare he let an old argument drive him off?

Sarah spared him a tight smile. "Yes, it was." She took a deep breath. "I need you to know that I will not ask you to give up Charles. I understand how…close you are. If you wish to have both of us, then I will not complain. But I desire that aspect of our marriage. It was one of the reasons I sought a husband, to enjoy…well…" She trailed off and then blurted out, "And I want children."

Gideon was so astonished it was hard to form a reply. "Give up Charles? If you do not want him in our bed again, then I will concede to your wishes. I do not need him there." Which was not entirely true. "I, too, desire the physical intimacies of marriage. I wanted to give you time to adjust to your new life here."

Sarah was facing him now, clearly nervous but determined. "Good. And you may go to Charles as well. I will not say a thing about it."

Gideon had to force his features to stay blank. "Go to Charles? Madam, I assure you, Charles and I are not intimate in the way you imply."

Sarah gaped. "But...but, I mean, the way you two act, the lovers' quarrels..."

"My astonishment knows no bounds at this moment," Gideon said grimly. "Lovers' quarrels indeed. Madam, I will blame your erroneous assumption on your lack of experience. We may quarrel but we are not lovers."

"Then I want him back in my bed. With you."

Gideon had to sit down. He turned back to the chair and fell into it. "What?" He was having a very hard time grasping the fact that what Sarah had apparently been thinking about all week was exactly what Gideon had been thinking about.

Sarah covered the painful blush on her cheeks with her hands. "I am trying to figure out how you feel about that, Gideon," she said tremulously. "It is quite possibly the hardest thing I have ever had to say. But you showed me something the other night, you and Charles, and I want it back. I want that in my life. My new life here with you."

"And Charles," Gideon murmured.

"You are my husband," Sarah said firmly. "You brought him to my bed. Do you not want him there now? I am more confused than you can know, Gideon, about what is right or wrong in this situation. Help me, please."

It was her heartfelt plea that did it. How could he deny her when he wanted the same thing? Right or wrong, those were not concerns to him. Fair or unfair, that was the question. Was it fair to Charles to drag him into his life even deeper? To rely on him more, to make Sarah dependent on him as well? It would become harder and harder for Charles to leave, to have his own life and his own family, if they invited him to their bed again. Gideon knew it because he knew Charles. But if Sarah wanted Charles, well, Gideon was learning that he could refuse her nothing.

"We will ask Charles tonight." Gideon's voice was a rough whisper.

Sarah nodded. "Tonight." She turned to flee but stopped on the top step, her back to him. "Thank you," she whispered, and then she hurried down the steps only to slow her walk to a sedate pace on the path to the house. He watched her until she was out of sight.

Chapter Ten

ဢ

"That will be all, Anders. Thank you."

Charles was as surprised as Anders at Gideon's dismissal. They'd only just finished dinner and Anders had set the port and whiskey on the table, with a cup of tea for Sarah. They had fallen into a routine this past week. He and Gideon talked about what they planned for the next day while Sarah listened and then they all said a polite good night and went to bed.

Was this because of their fight this afternoon?

Charles had regretted his words as soon as he stormed off. When would he learn not to push Gideon so much? He just got so frustrated with the damn fool. And he was brimming with frustration of another kind, as well. The only real contact he'd had with Sarah in the past week had been their trip to town. Other than that he had seen her only briefly in passing and suffered through stilted conversations over meals. Yet he was constantly aware of her. Her scent permeated the house, and he found himself trying to sniff her out like a dog on the hunt. And Gideon was so painfully uncomfortable and irritable that Charles dared not confront him about Sarah. Had Gideon been to her since they'd shared her on the wedding night? The possibility tormented him.

When Charles had seen them together in the gazebo, watching him and talking like a...well, like a married couple, he had been so jealous he shocked himself. He was being shut out. Gideon had Sarah now, and Sarah had Gideon, and they didn't need him. And didn't he just sound like a pathetic old woman?

Christ, he needed a drink. Thank God for Anders and whiskey.

"We would like you to join us again this evening, Charles," Gideon calmly said a few minutes later after Anders' footsteps had faded down the hallway.

Charles had just taken a drink and choked on it.

"Oh dear," Sarah said. She jumped up and rushed around the table to pound him on the back. "Are you all right?"

Charles pushed her away and shoved his chair back from the table, bending over coughing.

"No more whiskey," Gideon drawled beside him. "We'd prefer you still breathing if possible."

"Gideon," Sarah chided, and Charles couldn't help it—he began to laugh, which caused more coughing.

"Good...scold," he gasped when he was able to get his breath back.

"Between the two of you I shall have peace no more," Gideon lamented drily. He stood up and made his way slowly to the door of the dining room. "Come on."

Charles looked around and found Sarah standing in the shadows of the corner near the door. "Wait." His voice was still a little raspy, but it was strong enough to stop Gideon before he opened the door. He turned back to Charles with an inquiring look. "Who? You or Sarah?"

"I beg your pardon?" Gideon asked coolly.

"Me." Sarah's reply was firm, though she still hid in the shadows. Then she stepped forward, just far enough for the flickering candlelight to barely illuminate her. "I asked Gideon for my marital rights. And I told him I wanted you to join us."

"Clearly I left too soon," Charles commented in astonishment. Sarah wanted him. Not Gideon this time. But Gideon had agreed. Why?

He walked over to Sarah. He could see her eyes widen as he approached, and she clasped her hands together before smoothing them down her skirt. Without warning he put his hands on her waist and picked her up, turning around and setting her on the edge of the table. Sarah gasped, her hands going to his shoulders, but she didn't push him away or protest.

"Charles..." Gideon said in a low, warning voice.

Charles could see him over Sarah's shoulder. In spite of his warning he just stood there, leaning on his crutches, watching them. Very slowly Charles reached down and wrapped his hands around Sarah's ankles. Then he slid them up, pushing her skirt before them. He didn't stop until his hands were on her hips. He stepped between her fully exposed legs, nestling right into her woman's heat. Then he nuzzled her shoulder, his eyes on Gideon the entire time. "Want me, do you?" he murmured.

Gideon was transfixed. His cheeks were flushed, his breathing ragged, his fist clenched so tight around his crutch Charles was surprised it didn't break. This was why Gideon had agreed. Because he wanted to watch them, Charles and Sarah. He liked to watch them. Charles felt a victorious thrill shoot down his spine, a thrill that turned to maddening need when Sarah tentatively ran her fingers from his shoulder to his nape, her touch light and so achingly hesitant.

"Yes," she whispered. Charles looked into her face and she bit her lip then glanced nervously back at Gideon. What she saw relaxed her and she became slightly more pliant in his arms. She knew too. She knew how much Gideon liked this. Was that why she had asked for him? To please Gideon? Charles wasn't sure how he felt about that. But he knew he was going to say yes. He would say yes to almost anything they wanted of him. Charles gently kissed her cheek. "Well, come on, then," he said quietly, and he stepped back, helped Sarah off the table, and they followed Gideon through the door.

"Gideon," Sarah cried out. Her voice was ragged but his name from her sounded better to him than the sweetest music. He didn't stop nibbling the peak of her breast. It had clearly been a cry of pleasure and not pain. Her hands tightened on his head, pulling his hair and he grinned, not that she could see it. She was straddling his lap, wild in their arms.

He still wasn't sure how they'd gotten to this point. Somehow, as soon as they'd entered her bedroom, Charles had orchestrated the removal of their clothing. Sarah's had disappeared first. How Gideon loved that—watching her standing there naked, ready for them, flushed with shy anticipation. Gideon had pulled the pins from her hair one at a time while she stood before him, her bare skin rosy, the heat of her beating at him, her scent surrounding him. Her hair fell in a waterfall of shimmering gold down her back to cover her plump bottom and Gideon lost his breath.

Then Sarah was taking his jacket off and Charles had moved behind him to support him while he'd pulled the jacket down Gideon's arms and off. Gideon had ended up on the bed as they pulled his boots and trousers off, and then Sarah was sprawled next to him and he had been unable to resist the allure of her beautiful body and sweet-smelling skin. He had pulled her to him, pressed her against him, and it wasn't until he was kissing his way to her breasts that he'd realized he'd forgotten to cover his bare leg. And Sarah had not said a word. She had not pulled away or averted her face from the unsightly stump. Instead she had wrapped herself around him like a living blanket and held his mouth to her breast as her soft, warm thigh slid over his, clasping him closer.

Then she had moaned Charles' name. Yet Gideon had not flinched. This was what they all wanted. There were no fences here, no boundaries to be left uncrossed. He raised his head from her breast and rasped, "Join us." And a moment later Charles had done just that, adding his heat and bare skin to theirs.

Sarah was sweating. They all were. But the salty taste of her on his lips was intoxicating. He could smell their sweat, her arousal and perfume, even the lavender on the sheets and it all went to his head until he was dizzy with need. He felt the bed move and suddenly Charles was straddling his lap behind Sarah. Gideon didn't pause, but kept laving Sarah's rough, pebbled nipple. Then Charles sank down so that his backside rested partially on Gideon's legs. Gideon pulled sharply away from Sarah and swallowed a cry of surprised arousal at the touch.

"Yes, Sarah," Charles murmured, and Gideon looked down to see Charles' fingers appear between Sarah's legs, caressing her mound, lingering at the top of her slit, rubbing the button there. Sarah moaned and thrust against his hand. Gideon looked at her face then. Her eyes were closed, her lashes feathered along flushed cheeks. Her mouth was open as she panted. She was gorgeous.

Gideon slid his left hand up her side and Sarah shuddered. How she loved the rough texture of his scars on her smooth skin. He let his hand travel all the way to her breast and cupped it, bringing it back to his mouth.

"Gideon." It was Charles.

"Hmm?" Gideon murmured, loath to leave Sarah's breast for something as mundane as talking. She was so delicious and so responsive to him. Even before the war, no woman had been like this with him.

"I've got to have this." Now that Gideon thought about it, Charles sounded rather desperate.

"What?" Gideon forced himself to pay attention.

Sarah's breath was coming in short, sharp bursts now, a little hiccuping cry at the end of each one. Gideon buried his face between her breasts as he slid his hands up her back. He rubbed his entire face against her, the mounds of her breasts pressed to his cheeks as he kissed her feverish skin. Sarah cried out and clutched him as Charles rubbed his bottom against his leg, and Gideon had a profound moment of absolute rightness.

Then Charles was prying his hands off Sarah. "Please," Charles growled. "I must have it." Charles carefully climbed off Gideon and then rolled Sarah over onto her back next to him. Charles wasted no time scooting down the bed, spreading her legs and burying his face in her sex. Sarah cried out in a strangled voice and then grabbed Charles' head and wrapped her legs around his shoulders.

"Oh, that," Gideon drawled. They were on his right. He lay down on his side, his weight supported on his forearm to watch them. He was too unbalanced and had to rest the ragged edge of his mangled leg on the bed next to Sarah's hip, careful not to touch her with it. Then he realized she wouldn't notice if he did. She was completely taken by the pleasure of Charles' mouth. Her back was arched off the bed, both hands grasping fistfuls of Charles' curly hair, her heels planted on his back. She rode his face with abandon as Charles hummed his appreciation, his hands on her bottom holding her to him, and Gideon had to look away or he was going to spend right then and there.

He focused on her breasts and stomach. The colors of her skin in the candlelight were mesmerizing. She shimmered gold and pink and the shadows painted across her body flickered with the flame. Gideon reached out and traced the shadows, and then he felt the pulse in her neck where he could see it pounding. He followed it down to her heart and pressed his palm there.

"Gideon," she whispered. She arched deliberately, pressing her breast to his hand. His left hand. Of course. She wanted to feel the roughness of that palm on her breast again. Gideon cupped and then squeezed the pale mound, rubbing his thumb over the peak, and Sarah moaned. It was still unbelievable to him, how much she loved to be touched by that hand.

He let go and she said "No" in a husky voice and tried to grab his hand. Gideon laughed and held it out of reach. She gasped and Gideon looked down to see Charles nipping her inner thigh.

"Behave," Charles said, then kissed the spot he'd bitten. She nodded and Charles rewarded her by returning his attention to her sex with another hum that made Gideon smile.

Gideon idly ran his finger along her shoulder and down her arm. He came to her hand holding Charles' head and he traced the bones in the back of that hand, feeling the silky brush of his hair on his fingertip. What would they both do if Gideon traced the whorls in Charles' ear as his finger was itching to do? He stopped himself. That wasn't where this should go. Sarah was here now. If he and Charles were together, it would only be with Sarah now.

He didn't begrudge Charles this time between Sarah's thighs. If the truth were known, he loved it. He loved to watch them together. It was unexpected, the intense enjoyment he received from watching Charles with his wife. He'd never felt that way with the whores. He'd watched Charles fuck them but hadn't really cared one way or the other. He considered it the whore's reward for putting up with him.

Perhaps it was because they made Gideon part of what they were doing in a way the whores never had. He didn't doubt for one moment that if he were not there, Sarah would not be with Charles this way. But she enjoyed what Charles did to her, and Gideon wanted to give that to her. And he wanted to give her to Charles as well. She was delectable, everything a man could want in bed.

Gently Gideon cupped his hand over Sarah's. He wasn't touching Charles, not really, but he held Sarah's hand against him, held Charles to her.

"Gideon," Sarah groaned, and then she pulled her hips off the bed, straining, and cried out. "Yes," she sobbed quietly. Gideon felt the tension in her hand as she gripped Charles tightly while she came. He leaned down and pressed his cheek to her chest, listened to her thundering heartbeat and watched Charles sucking her lightly, his eyes closed.

When she was shuddering in the aftermath and her legs slid off his shoulders, Charles finally broke away. Gideon could see his face gleaming with her essence in the candlelight. He wanted to lick it off but instead he looked away, hiding his reaction.

"Your turn," Charles said, his voice rough.

Gideon shook his head. "No, I want to be inside her." He started to roll onto his back, but Charles stopped him with a hand on his arm. The contact caused awareness to streak between them, and Charles looked shocked for a moment.

"Atop her," Charles ordered. "She can't always ride you. Show her something else."

His words unconsciously mirrored Sarah's, when she'd pleaded with him in the gazebo. She deserved more, but Gideon couldn't. He wasn't physically able. He shook his head again. "You know I can't." He waved at his absent leg. "I can't. You do it."

Charles stared at him for a moment and then firmly shook his head. "No. I'm not her husband."

"I—"

Charles interrupted him before he could say it again. "Yes, you can," Charles insisted. "Come here." Charles moved out of the way.

Gideon was about to refuse when Sarah's hand cupped his cheek. "Please, Gideon. Show me."

Reluctantly he rolled over on top of Sarah. He held himself up with his hands, trying not to crush her, and came up on one knee.

"Kneel," Charles ordered him.

"I am," Gideon barked in frustration.

"No you're not. Not with both legs."

Suddenly Charles was there behind him, wrapping his arm around Gideon's middle, pulling him up and shoving his left knee behind Gideon's, forcing him onto the stump, pressing it against Sarah's lush bottom.

Gideon could feel every inch of Charles pressed against him. The fierceness of his response caused him to overreact and he jerked in Charles' embrace, fighting to get free.

"Easy," Charles whispered in his ear. "Let me help, Gideon. It's why I'm here, isn't it? To help you fuck Sarah. You can do it."

Gideon froze. There were so many things careening through his mind. The feel of Charles against him, the sight of Sarah beneath him, the sounds of his breath sawing the air and Charles panting in his ear, Sarah murmuring his name. Then her hand slid along his thigh and he shuddered at the sensation.

"I want to watch, Gideon," Charles whispered roughly. "Let me watch you and Sarah."

That was a desire Gideon understood perfectly.

Sarah held her breath for fear of drawing their attention. This was something, oddly enough, that seemed to be between Gideon and Charles, although it obviously involved her as well. Sarah simply enjoyed watching them. She had never seen two men in such an intimate embrace. It was arousing seeing Charles' arm heavy with muscles wrapped around Gideon's leaner frame, Charles whispering in Gideon's ear. Sarah could imagine the things he was telling Gideon. She shivered, but not in trepidation.

Whatever Charles said convinced Gideon. He nodded and Charles pushed him down over Sarah again. "Leave your thigh there, Gideon. Spread her legs with yours."

Gideon hesitated, actually pulling his injured leg back slightly from her, and Sarah suddenly understood that he was afraid to touch her with it, afraid she would be repulsed. She was not. That leg was a part of Gideon, a warm, rough, naked part of Gideon touching her intimately. She wanted more of it, not less. Sarah followed that leg, scooted down and pressed herself wide on it. Gideon was startled and jerked it back.

Sarah simply followed it again. "I'll follow it down until I fall off the bed," she told him with determination. To make her point she rubbed her thigh along the side of his. Over his shoulder she saw Charles smile approvingly.

"Sarah..." Gideon seemed to change his mind and let whatever he was going to say trail off. "All right." Sarah tried not to gloat. Gideon raised his brow. "Victory is yours," he murmured, almost as if he could read her mind.

He moved closer and her legs were forced wider apart, his hips snuggly secure between them.

"That's right," Charles whispered. "Keep your left leg up like that. You'll have to use it for leverage, Gideon. You'll have to dig in with your leg, just as if it were your foot."

"You've got it all figured out, have you?" Gideon asked tartly. But he followed Charles' instruction.

"Of course," Charles said with that smile in his voice. "I have thought a great deal about how to fuck Sarah."

That caused a delicious shiver down her back. She liked the idea of that very much.

"Haven't you?" Charles continued, curiosity in his voice.

"Not like this," Gideon replied stiffly. "I try not to think about things I cannot do."

Sarah's heart broke. Charles stopped what he was doing behind Gideon. Then he just ran his hand down Gideon's back in a gentle caress and Sarah watched Gideon close his eyes as the muscles in his shoulders and arms quivered. But before she could say anything, Gideon was pressing inside her and she could hardly catch her breath.

When he was deeply inside her, he slowly lowered his chest until it pressed against her breasts. "I will try, Sarah," he whispered to her, his light eyes gleaming in the weak light.

Sarah reached for him, wrapping her arms around his neck and her legs around his waist. "Oh, Gideon," she said with a ragged sigh. "Yes." She tried to kiss him, but he turned away and buried his face in her shoulder, kissing her there.

His hands pushed under her until he gripped her shoulders from behind, and then he began to move. He was tentative at first, but it felt so marvelous Sarah couldn't contain a moan of sheer pleasure.

Charles moved to the bed beside them, and his pose perfectly mirrored Gideon's earlier. "Can you feel him now, Sarah?" he asked. It took her a second to remember the first time they'd all been together and she blushed. Gideon pressed deeper inside on a hard stroke, and Sarah cried out.

"Gideon," she pleaded, her mouth seeking his. How she wanted to taste him, to kiss him and share his breath as he shared her body right now. She was desperate for his kiss.

He did not understand what she wanted. He kept turning away, kept his face hidden in her hair as he moved in and out of her. She could hear it, hear the movements of his body in hers as she grew wetter with her arousal, and it embarrassed her.

"Sarah," Charles whispered, and then he had his hand in her hair and was turning her face to his. His mouth claimed hers, mated with hers, and Sarah moaned against his lips, his tongue. Charles had known what she needed. It was decadent to be kissing Charles with abandon while Gideon...fucked her. She moaned again as she thought the word, feeling a blush stain her cheeks. To even think something like that was so new and exciting.

"Yes, Sarah, yes," Gideon whispered harshly in her ear. His back was slick with sweat, the hair on his chest rubbing her sensitive breasts, his voice hot in her ear, and then he bit her earlobe. He moved faster, harder, and Sarah found herself panting, unable to catch her breath as pleasure spiraled low in her belly. It was as if a knot grew tighter and tighter there, and she sought the relief she knew climax would bring her. Gideon lost the rhythm of his strokes as he readjusted his legs, and when he pushed inside of her again he did something that made Sarah cry out and arch in ecstasy against him. She sank her nails into his back, wanting the almost painful pleasure to stop but at the same time hoping it would never end. Gideon hissed and moved harder inside her.

Charles broke the kiss and moaned, jerking on the bed beside them. His head hung right next to their shoulders, and his hair tickled Sarah's skin.

"Touch him, Sarah," Gideon rasped out in a breathless, rough voice. "He needs it. Wrap your hand around his cock. Do it."

All three of them froze. Charles raised his head slowly and met Sarah's eyes, and above her Gideon turned his head to look at Charles. Charles pulled his hips back, and Sarah couldn't keep from looking down. His member was long and hard, raised high against his stomach, the end shiny with moisture.

Gideon pulled his arm from under her, took her hand in his and guided it to Charles' cock. The word fit. It looked hard and fierce and proud. Gideon wrapped her hand around it and then left her to stay or go. Charles shuddered at her touch. She stayed. Gideon pressed deep within her as Charles showed her how to move her hand on him. He sucked in a breath as she caught the same rhythm Gideon was using in her.

Soon they were all moving. There were no more words, as if the spiraling tension was choking off all but their breath. The sounds of their mating were earthy and harsh and Sarah tried to catch them, to remember them. She loved the crass sounds, the exquisitely wanton things she was doing. Gideon found that spot inside her again, and Sarah knew she couldn't last, she was going to come and she wanted them with her. She wrapped her legs tighter around Gideon, moved her hand faster along the silky smooth rod of Charles' cock, loving the heat and hardness of it in her hand.

Her thoughts were base, her focus on Gideon's cock tunneling into her, Charles' breath against her shoulder, his hips moving his cock in her fist. And then it was there, stealing her breath, her voice, her very thoughts. She let out a low keening cry and thrust her hips up, pressing Gideon so wonderfully deep as she felt her sheath grip him and tremble with pleasure. Charles cried out then and Sarah felt a wash of hot, sticky moisture coat her hand and her side and then Gideon gasped and his release inside her triggered another ripple of pleasure in her core, this one slow and long and deep, and Sarah actually laughed weakly at how wonderful it was.

"Where are you going?" Sarah spoke quietly, still lying there under the bedcover. She'd been dozing lightly and wasn't sure what time it was, although she knew it was not morning yet.

Both men paused as they were rising from the bed. "We were going to let you sleep," Gideon answered politely. How she hated that polite voice. "We do not wish to disturb you."

Sarah tossed aside her pride yet again. She sat up, clutching the blanket to her chest. "Don't leave me."

Gideon looked surprised. She held out her hand to him. Hesitatingly he took it and slid in next to her, lying on his back stiffly. On the other side of the bed Charles slid back under the cover with her. "Sarah," he said, and kissed her shoulder.

Sarah snuggled down under the covers and put her head on Gideon's shoulder. "Gideon." He didn't look at her, just made an inquiring noise. She became more insistent. She put her hand on his cheek and turned his face to her. She was on his left side. She could see that it took every nerve he possessed not to turn away from her. "Thank you." She raised her face to his for a kiss and he did pull against her hand then, but she held him tightly. "Please," she whispered.

Gideon stilled and let her place her lips on his, but he remained passive. She didn't give up. She employed all the lessons Charles had taught her. She rubbed her lips along his, licked the seam of his lips, nibbled his lower lip. Finally he relented and his lips softened. After a moment he took over the kiss, turning them so Sarah lay on her back. He devoured her, kissed her like a starving man, and she fed him all the passion she had for him. His hands trembled as he held her and Sarah moaned at his taste and the rasp of his beard against her. The hunger of his kiss overwhelmed her. But she understood what it meant, the warm touch of another after a lifetime of that kind of unsatisfied hunger.

The bed moved and creaked and Gideon broke the kiss. Breathing hard, he looked over at Charles. "Stay." It wasn't a request. Before Charles could protest, Sarah tempered Gideon's order by reaching over and touching Charles' hip with one hand, pulling him to her. He came with a gentle smile, pressed against her side and slid his leg over hers. She caressed his bottom and leg and he made a noise that sounded like a satisfied purr as he nuzzled her neck. Gideon turned her head with the backs of his fingers pressed to her cheek and came close to kiss her again.

"I don't want to sleep," Sarah whispered against his lips, and behind her Charles chuckled while Gideon smiled slightly before his lips met hers again.

Chapter Eleven

ᏚᎧ

Sarah stared out her bedroom window at the early morning sun shining over the meadow. The grooms were bringing the horses from the barn. Those lucky enough to be released in the meadow were frolicking in the high grass. Is that what one called it? Did horses frolic? It certainly seemed so to her. She couldn't blame them for their high spirits. It was a glorious morning.

Sarah set her open palm against the window, feeling the heat of the sun warming her. *Let this be a good day,* she silently asked. But inside she knew it would be. She felt the smile curving her lips with smug satisfaction. She'd done it. She'd asked Gideon to come back to her bed, and he had come. And he had brought Charles. She was almost afraid of how perfectly happy she'd been this morning when she woke with the two men still beside her. They had both been asleep and she'd simply lain there listening to their deep breathing, feeling their big, warm, hair-rough bodies against hers. It had felt divine, as if the hand of a benevolent God had answered her morning prayers.

Sarah laughed. The situation could hardly be classified as divine. After all, she'd woken up with two men, one of who was most definitely not her husband. As far as Sarah knew, there was no church that condoned such behavior, not even the papists.

She turned from the window and was confronted by the rumpled linen of her bed. She could smell the lingering scent of last night's exertions. She bit her nail in indecision. Should she strip the bed? The maid would certainly find that odd. She shook her head. No, she would merely ask for new linen. Lord knew they had enough of it. And even if the staff knew what had gone on here last night, they would not know with whom. They would assume it had been Gideon, and of course it had. But they would not know that Charles had lain here with them.

Sarah's cheeks heated with her blush and she huffed in exasperation. For heaven's sake, there was no else in the room! And she'd only thought it, not even said it out loud. Why on earth was she blushing? Why couldn't she control her embarrassment? It was extremely vexing to know that every illicit thought was reflected in cheeks as red as cherries.

Sarah stumbled. She hadn't thought about her birthmark once last night. Nor this morning as she had kissed Gideon and Charles goodbye at her door before the sun rose. She could not remember a time when the mark was not on her mind in some way. But last night there had been so much more going on here than Sarah's petty fears about her physical inadequacies. Gideon had needed them last night. His fears had taken precedence. And they had given him back something of himself last night that the war took away. Something Charles alone had been unable to give him, though he had tried in different ways. But Sarah had done it with Charles' help. Sarah had shown Gideon in the most basic of ways that he was still a man—her man.

Sarah fell back against her bedroom door with a huge grin on her face. She clasped her hands together and brought them to her chin, hardly able to contain her happiness. This is what she had dreamed of for them. A marriage of equals, a marriage where Sarah was able to give as much as she received. Gideon needed her. He needed *her*. She was not a substitute, as she'd been for her younger siblings, filling in the void left by their mother's passing. She was the woman Gideon wanted, the woman who finally gave him back a vital part of himself. His wife.

Sarah's smile faded as she remembered there were more than just the two of them involved. What about Charles? What was he to her and she to him? She cared for him a great deal, she knew that much. He was a rock, and more and more she found herself wanting to lean on him for advice and support. He made her feel stronger, as if she could handle anything this new life threw at her. But he had refused to consummate their relationship last night on the grounds that he was not her husband. Sarah felt no shame in admitting she would have welcomed him into her body. Was the lack of vows between them insurmountable to Charles? Was he only in her bed for Gideon?

Which made her wonder yet again, what were Charles and Gideon to each other? They were friends but not lovers. She believed Gideon. After watching them last night, even in the most intimate of embraces, they had not spoken, touched or looked at each other as lovers. And yet Sarah believed there was love there. But there was enmity too. Why? What had happened between them? She was sure it led all the way back to the war and to Gideon's injuries. They were bound together by that experience. Perhaps it was time she found out exactly what had happened to the two of them on the Peninsula.

Sarah nervously sipped her tea and watched Gideon and Charles eating silently as they sat at the breakfast table. The two men were very much alike in their morning routine. They liked to eat heartily, and they liked to do it silently. It was a trial. Sarah was usually brimming with ideas and plans for her day and felt constrained to sit quietly contemplating her china. She summoned up some courage from her rapidly dwindling supply and cleared her throat.

"Ah, Anders, I believe that I would like to talk with…with Mr. North, if that is all right? We are fine? Aren't we?" she asked Gideon and Charles a little helplessly. She was not good at dismissing the servants. She really needed to work on being more authoritative. But Anders was quite, quite nice and very proficient at his duties. She didn't want to offend.

Gideon put down his fork and looked at her. Then he waved his hand negligently over his shoulder. "Leave us."

"Very good, sir," Anders replied politely. He didn't seem offended at Gideon's high-handed manner at all, but quickly gathered up the tea tray, handed it to the footman and closed the door as they left.

"Gideon, really," Sarah reprimanded him gently. "You must be more polite to the servants."

"Why?" He seemed genuinely perplexed. "I pay them handsomely. I don't feel the need to compound their income with unnecessary pleasantries." He surprised her by taking her hand and kissing it gallantly. "Those I shall reserve for you."

Sarah couldn't resist teasing him. "I shall only get the unnecessary pleasantries? I consider myself duly warned."

Across the table Charles laughed and winked at Sarah.

Gideon had the last word. "My dear, to me all pleasantries are unnecessary."

Charles laughed even louder at Gideon's remark. "I can attest to the truth of that," he agreed. "Gideon is tightfisted with his pleasantries."

Sarah pondered that a moment with a puzzled look on her face. "Wouldn't that be tightlipped?" she asked innocently.

Gideon grinned at her. "Touché, my dear." After their laughter subsided, Gideon took her hand in his. His touch was still tentative, as if he was unsure whether she would welcome it. Foolish man. She clasped his hand tightly in hers. "Is there something amiss, Sarah?" he asked gently. "Are you all right?"

This time she was perplexed. "Yes, of course. Why do you ask?"

Charles leaned back in his chair and crossed his arms over his chest. "You did ask to speak with Gideon privately, Sarah," he reminded her. "Would you like me to leave?"

Outrage and disbelief coursed through her at his question. "How can you ask me that? You know I do not. But I cannot ask to speak privately with you, Charles. Not even here in our home." She pulled her hand from Gideon's and crossed her arms. "I'm sorry that you think I would do so." She shook her head. "I cannot." The last was said in a whisper as the enormity of their situation hit Sarah. How hurtful it must be for Charles to be treated that way.

It was Charles who reached out first. He sat forward and stretched his hands across the table, palms up. She uncrossed her arms and placed her hands in his. "I'm sorry, Sarah," he whispered. "I know. I understand." And the awful thing was he meant it. His understanding and forbearance humbled her. With a squeeze of her hands he let go and sat back. "Is this about last night?"

Sarah blushed and looked down at her lap, smoothing her skirts. "No, no it isn't. Last night was..." She paused and raised her head. How to describe such a wonderful thing as last night? She shrugged helplessly.

"Yes, it was," Charles agreed with a grin. She looked at Gideon and he was smiling too.

"Yes, well," she cleared her throat. "I was wondering, Gideon, if I might ask how you were injured. In the war."

Gideon looked surprised. "Have I not told you? I thought you knew."

Sarah shook her head. She glanced at Charles and was shocked to see him pale and shaken. When he realized she was watching him he stood abruptly and paced over to the window, turning his back to them.

"It was at the fortress of Badajoz, at the second siege there. I was part of the Forlorn Hope." Gideon spoke dispassionately, going as far as to pick up his fork to begin eating again.

Sarah gasped in horror. "The Forlorn Hope! Gideon, why? Why would you do such a thing?" Sarah had heard of the Forlorn Hope, the men who volunteered to be the first to storm the battlements. But they were men with nothing to lose, men who hoped to gain rank or influence if they survived. But very few survived. It was sanctioned suicide. She had not imagined Gideon among that group. Even hearing it from him she could scarce believe it.

Gideon merely shrugged. "For the same reason everyone does, I suppose. I hoped to gain rank and a fat pension from it." He smiled mirthlessly. "The rank became a moot point, but the pension has been very useful."

Sarah watched Charles grip the window frame tightly. There was more. What wasn't Gideon telling her?

"You were a captain, were you not? In war, is there not ample opportunity for the advancement of a good officer?" Sarah could scarce wrap her head around the idea of Gideon being so foolhardy.

Gideon's laugh was short and sharp. "If he has the funds or influence to purchase it, certainly. But for those of us who did not, then we had to earn it the hard way. We had to survive trial by fire to gain what others were given." He was becoming agitated. His voice was as sharp as his laugh. He tossed his fork down and it clattered against his plate. "I had plans, Sarah. Plans for the future that could not be realized on a captain's pay. I did not plan to waste my life in the army. It was merely the first step."

Sarah gripped his sleeve tightly. "And the Forlorn Hope? Was that part of your plan from the beginning?"

He placed his hand over hers, his anger visibly dissipating. He sighed. "No. But I reached a point..." He looked over at Charles by the window. "I realized that if I hoped to achieve the life I wanted, I had to take more risks. And I believed it was worth it."

"The horses, the farm... This is what you dreamed of, isn't it?" Sarah asked gently.

Gideon patted her hand. "Yes, yes it is."

"Was it worth it?" She had to know.

Before Gideon could answer, Charles spun around to face them. "Are you mad? Could anything be worth the price he has paid?" he asked harshly. He began to pace along the wall.

Gideon was noticeably taken aback at Charles' vehemence. "I believe it was worth it, yes," Gideon finally answered quietly. He was answering Sarah's question, but it was directed at Charles.

Charles laughed wildly. "Worth it? You *are* mad. All that you endured? For a horse? A farm? A patch of land?" He shook his head bitterly. "I do not understand how you can say that."

"I had nothing. No prospects, no income, no future. Look at me, Charles." Gideon waited but Charles turned his face away. "Look at me." Gideon's tone was harsh and Charles finally obeyed. "I have all that I dreamed of then. This place," he looked at Sarah and took her hand, "a wife," he looked back at Charles, "a future. And most of that I owe to you."

Charles nodded grimly. "Yes, yes you do. This place," he indicated all around them, his arms open wide, and then he pointed directly at Gideon, "and your condition. I am responsible for that as well."

Sarah closed her eyes. And that was it, wasn't it? That was what drove Charles.

"What?" Gideon's shock was evident. "What are you talking about?"

"I know that I drove you to Badajoz, to the Forlorn Hope. I know, Gideon." Charles' tone was accusatory. "I know that...what happened between us drove you to do such a stupid, suicidal thing."

"What happened between us?" Gideon's face was flushed, either with embarrassment or guilt, Sarah wasn't sure. But she knew that she should not ask, not now. Was it one of their fights that tormented Charles? "That had nothing to do with my decision," Gideon continued stiffly.

Charles scoffed. "No? I think you lie, Gideon. Not only to me but to yourself."

"Fine." Gideon's voice was cold. "It influenced the timing, but that is all. I had already been thinking about it, about after the war. I needed to make plans, and…what happened between us merely underscored the importance and necessity of doing so."

The tension in the room was nearly choking Sarah. She should not have brought this up. It was a festering wound between them. Last night they had all crossed a line. This morning she had redrawn that line firmly separating them again.

"What did you mean, Gideon, when you said you owed it all to Charles?" she asked, trying to make them both remember what they meant to each other.

"He saved my life that day."

"That's a lie," Charles retorted immediately. "I stole it that day. I took the life you knew and the life you dreamed of and killed them."

"What are you talking about?" Gideon demanded angrily.

"Tell me, Charles," Sarah urged him quietly. "Tell me how you saved Gideon's life."

Charles went back to the window and stared out. "I found him. He'd been burned badly and his leg was broken. Shattered, really, barely still attached. He was dying there among the *chevaux-de-frise*."

"The what? I'm sorry, I don't know what that is," Sarah said.

Charles put his hands on his hips and shook his head. "Bloody awful things those goddamned French bastards came up with," he answered. He slammed his fist into the palm of his other hand. "They rammed sword blades into wooden beams and lined the trenches with them. Getting across was almost impossible. The only thing that worked was to wait until enough dead bodies piled up on them to climb across."

He said it so matter-of-factly it took Sarah a moment to understand what he was describing. When the full horror hit her, she covered her mouth to keep from screaming or vomiting. She felt like doing both. Gideon had been trapped in that hell. She reached blindly for him, and he grasped her hand.

Charles continued without turning around. "He didn't tell me what he was going to do, you know. I found out too late, the Forlorn had already left. And I couldn't very well go yelling into the night after them and alert the French, could I? I had to let him go. When the charge rang out I ran as fast as I could."

"It was not your decision whether to let me go or not," Gideon told him frankly. "I knew you would make a fuss, and so I didn't tell you. I would have gone anyway."

Charles shook his head. "No, I would have stopped you, if it meant knocking you senseless and carrying you away."

"How—" Sarah had to stop and clear her throat, her voice was rough from holding back her reactions. "How did you save him?"

Charles finally turned and leaned tiredly against the wall beside the window. "When I found him he was bleeding out, barely conscious, burned, his clothes were still on fire. He'd been caught in the explosion from the mines, you see. He was thrown into the blades. God knows how he managed to avoid being impaled on them, but he must have hit one, or one of the timbers more likely, and it snapped his leg nearly clean off." Charles stopped and licked his lips. He was still pale, and his hands were shaking. "He begged me to cut if off. His leg. I'd picked up some officer's fallen sword along the way, and I..." He paused and rubbed his hands against his pant legs. "I cut it off. I picked him up and climbed over all those dead bodies. I don't really remember much of that."

"I don't remember any of it, thank God," Gideon said. "The last thing I remember is running into the trench, the lads' battle cries behind me. Then I woke up screaming a week later, with half my leg and face gone."

"You were able to get him to a doctor before he bled to death?" Sarah asked incredulously. "But how? That must have been a monumental feat."

Charles was shaking his head before she finished. "No. I couldn't. He was bleeding too much." He smiled grimly. "But fate sent me a doctor. Doctor Thomas Peters to be precise. He was there on the battlefield, trying to save the wounded." Charles ran his shaking hand through his hair. "He wasn't like the others. Most of the surgeons waited in their bloody, reeking tents for poor bastards who were already more dead than alive. But Peters, he went out and brought them back. Or did what he had to. There on the battlefield."

Sarah didn't want to know what he meant by "did what he had to". "He saved Gideon there?"

"Yes. I made him. I dragged him away from some poor blighter and I put a knife to his throat and I told him I didn't care how he did it, but he had better save him or else."

"What?" Gideon was aghast. "You could have been court-martialed!"

"I never told you that, eh?" Charles asked with a genuine chuckle. "Luckily Peters didn't hold a grudge. Saw him last time I was in London. He's a very forgiving fellow."

"What did he do?" Sarah asked, breathless with awe. What Charles had done for Gideon was amazing. He talked of what Gideon had endured, but certainly he had endured as much that night.

"We did the only thing we could think of. We burned it closed. Peters poured some gunpowder on his leg and we lit it on fire."

"My God," Sarah whispered. She was numb. It was horrendous what they had been through. Her hand tightened in Gideon's.

Charles looked at Gideon then. "You may not remember it, but I do. You woke up screaming. It was the second time you'd been on fire in as many hours. I'll never forget your screams. Or the smell of it."

Charles rubbed his face with his hands and blew out a breath. "He was delirious for over a week, begging to be allowed to die. He nearly did, several times. But I bullied him and berated him, so damn angry at him I wanted him to live just so I could kill him." Beside her Gideon snorted. "A little Spanish whore helped me to tend him. She belonged to a couple of officers in the Dragoons. She was a sweet girl. Died not too long after that, I think."

"Yes, she did," Gideon confirmed quietly.

Charles slowly straightened from the wall and walked to the door. "I don't blame you, you know," he told Gideon. "For holding me responsible. I am. I forced you into that position and then I saved your life and refused to let you die. And I know you regret it all. Everything."

"Charles," Gideon said, clearly exasperated. But Charles was already gone.

Chapter Twelve

ॐ

"You wanted to see me?" Charles' voice was as cool as his demeanor when he walked into Gideon's study later that morning. It only added fuel to Gideon's simmering anger.

"Yes." He didn't dare say anything else just yet. He'd thought he had his temper under control, but Charles' arrival proved him wrong.

Charles stood just inside the door and raised his brow with wry humor. "Down to one word, are we? That's never good."

"Close the door."

"Is three words an improvement? We shall see." Charles' amusement did nothing to douse Gideon's anger.

When the door was closed Gideon indicated the chair across from his desk.

"The inquisition, then?" Charles said sarcastically. "Bring on your torture devices." He threw himself into the chair and sprawled there negligently, but Gideon could see the tension around his eyes and in the hand he wrapped into a tight fist against his thigh.

"You should leave." Gideon hadn't meant to blurt it out like that, but he was so angry.

Charles looked confused. "I thought you wanted to see me?"

Gideon took a deep breath, trying to gather his thoughts. Finding out that Charles had stayed all these years out of guilt was a shock that he had not yet recovered from. He looked out the window at the horses in the meadow. He'd thought this place meant as much to Charles as it did to him. But he'd been wrong. He'd been wrong about a lot of things.

"I meant you should leave Blakely Farm."

His statement hung in the silence between them like a tangible thing. Finally Charles answered.

"That's it? After all the times you've thrown me out with anger and sarcasm, that's the best you could to today?"

Charles sounded angry, and that made Gideon angrier. What right did Charles have to his anger? Gideon was the one who'd been wronged. Gideon had been deceived about why Charles was here, why he had stayed through all the hardships they'd endured. Gideon had thought... Well, it didn't matter what he'd thought, did it? He'd been wrong.

"Your guilt is misplaced. If it has kept you here, then you should go." Gideon could hear how clipped his words were, how icy his tone. He was furious and unable to hide it.

"My guilt is misplaced?" Charles rose from his chair to stand behind it gripping the back. "My guilt has been placed precisely where it ought to be — behind your actions."

"You are not, nor were you ever, in charge of my life or my actions." Gideon tried to rise from his chair but sat down abruptly when he lost his balance. He glared at Charles from where he was sitting.

Charles had gone pale. He pointed at Gideon with a shaking hand. "That — that is what I'm responsible for. I pursued you, Gideon. You know I did. I forced you —" He turned away.

"You did no such thing. What happened between us was by mutual consent." Gideon did not want to talk about it. He thought about it nearly every damn day and had for six years. But he did not want to talk about it.

"What happened between us?" Charles gave a snort of disgust. "I'll tell you what happened. We *fucked*, Gideon," he hissed quietly. "I chased and I chased and finally I caught you in a weak moment and I begged you to take me. And you did.

139

And then you hated yourself and me for it. Hated yourself enough to go on a suicide mission. I might as well have just killed you when it was done."

Gideon couldn't have been more stunned if Charles had picked up his chair and hit him over the head with it. "Is that what you think? That I hated it? That I hated you?"

"Please," Charles said angrily, "don't try to deny it. You have not spoken of it, ever. It is as if once it was over it never happened. Don't try to tell me it meant something. I'm not a woman, to believe that lie."

"No," Gideon said calmly, "but you are more a fool than I ever thought you could be."

Charles stared at him incredulously. "What?"

"I will say this once and never again. I liked it. I wanted it, and when you offered that day I finally let myself give in. I thought I'd lost you. I watched you fall and thought a bullet had taken you and all I could think was that I hadn't had you. So as soon as I could I dragged you off to the woods and I fucked you. There, now you know." Charles was gaping at him. Gideon nodded. "Oh yes. You thought all this time you were the great seducer. Well, I was willing. Willing and able and eager." He was spitting his words out now.

He couldn't sit still anymore. He rose from his chair carefully and grabbed his crutches and walked over to the other side of the room. "I liked it too much. I knew that if I didn't keep my distance we'd be found out, because I had a damn hard time hiding how much I wanted you. And that is what drove me to Badajoz. I knew that if I wanted you again it had to be somewhere of our own, somewhere no one could gainsay us. And I didn't have the wherewithal to make that kind of place for us. But with the pension from the Forlorn Hope I could. And I was willing to die trying."

"Gideon—" Charles was dumbfounded, his voice disbelieving.

Gideon cut him off. "After this—" He waved a hand at his missing leg, at his face. "After I was ruined and turned into this, that couldn't happen. I understood that. You became nursemaid to me more than anything else. How I hated that." For the first time Gideon let it show. His disgust and frustration at what he had become, what he had lost. "My dreams changed then, and I assumed yours did as well. Because if I have not spoken of it, Charles, neither have you. And no matter what lies you tell yourself, the reason is obvious. And I have never, never blamed you for that. Not for the fuck, not for what happened to me and not for changing toward me."

Gideon breathed deeply. It was a method that had worked for him since the war. It helped him to stifle his anger and frustration. Charles started to say something, but Gideon held up his hand to stop the flow of words. He was not ready to hear what Charles had to say.

"Sarah has changed everything." Gideon moved back to his desk and Charles warily sat back down in his chair. "It is all for her now. All this—" He waved his hand outside to indicate the horses and the farm. "Everything I do, I do for her and our future." Charles was pale again. "You can leave with the assurance that whatever debt you feel you owe me has been repaid." He softened his tone. "You deserve more, Charles. You deserve your own life, a normal life." He cleared his throat and spoke briskly. "So we shall find someone to take your place and I can give you an allowance of some sort until you settle somewhere."

"Will he take my place in your bed, as well?" Charles question was filled with so much venom Gideon jerked back in his chair. Charles stood before his desk now, his fists planted on the sturdy wood, leaning toward Gideon aggressively. "Is that all I've been these many years? An employee who can be replaced? A whore to help you fuck someone else? Your 'boy' to be shoved off with an allowance until I disappear?"

"No." Gideon kept his response simple because his anger was back again.

"No? No? That's all you have to say? You bastard." Charles voice was rising with every word. "I have worried myself to death over you. I have sacrificed, bullied, begged and pleaded, dragging you into this life of ours with all I have. Do you think guilt made me do it? You call me foolish. Look in the glass, Gideon. You are the greatest fool I know."

Gideon grabbed his edge of the desk and leaned forward until their faces were mere inches apart. "That is exactly what I am talking about," he ground out. "You have wasted enough of your life playing nursemaid. Your responsibility here, whatever kind you thought you had, is over. Yes, I owe you. I owe you this farm, this dream, Sarah, my life. Is that what you want to hear? Will that make you stop feeling sorry for yourself and get on with your life? Or are you too afraid to do it? I begin to think that this guilt of yours is an excuse to avoid your own problems."

"My greatest problem is you." Charles' words were laced with disgust. "It always has been and always will be. You refuse to see what is right in front of your face. You claim you wanted all this for us, and yet now you tell me it is all for Sarah. Make up your mind, Gideon. I may chase and chase, but you tease. You let me almost catch you, and then you pull away. Now Sarah is here. Now you have given me Sarah." He pointed a rigid finger at Gideon. "She is more than you deserve. God knows she's more than I deserve. But I will not let you ruin her happiness. She is content. She is stronger than she was when we first met her. I'm not going anywhere. I didn't build you both up just to walk away before I could enjoy the fruits of my labor. Oh no. If you want me gone you'll have to do better than that."

"Build us up? As if we were castles of sand? Clay to be molded by your almighty hands?" Gideon had had enough. "It wasn't you who had to learn to live with this body, Charles. You witnessed my struggles, you did not make them for me. It is not you who faces your fears of going out in public, it is Sarah. Yes, you bully. You bully us both until we do your bidding just to shut you up. But what we are, what we have become, is due to our own strength and our own desires, not yours. If you stay you will be sorely disillusioned. We will not bow and scrape to you for what we have. You may enjoy us all you like, but you may not take credit for us."

Charles looked as if he'd taken a blow. "Perhaps I do bully you. But you are both so...so...stupid," Charles finished vehemently. "That you think what you are outside matters to me or to anyone worth your time. You are both so much more than what people see on the outside. You are beautiful to me. But it's like banging my head against the barn door."

Beautiful? "Sarah is and always was beautiful. I agree." Gideon made himself speak ruthlessly. "But if you feel as if being with us is banging your head against a barn door, then leave. I have asked you to do so. I have begged you to do so. I implore you now to do so."

Charles went on as if Gideon hadn't spoken. "And the way you see me? The way you treat me? Sometimes I wonder if you see past what is outside." Gideon narrowed his eyes, ready to deny it. "I see it, Gideon. I see the way you watch me. You talk of my perfection, my physical attributes as if I am a horse for sale. You wanted me for Sarah as a pretty toy. Do you even know or care what I feel? What I think? I may not be a gentleman or well educated, but I have ideas, Gideon. I have feelings. You trample on both with impunity."

"If you feel so ill-used, then go," Gideon barked. He was incredulous that Charles would accuse him of such shallowness. Of course he saw him. He saw everything. He saw how hard Charles worked, how much the success of the farm meant to him. He could see past his earlier anger to the truth of that. Gideon knew that without Charles there would be no success, no farm, no Gideon. If Charles left...Gideon saw himself standing on the edge of an abyss with no lifeline to keep him safe. He thrust the thought aside. "You tell me I am nothing without you, and then you tell me that I do not see you for who you are, that I do not appreciate your feelings or ideas. How can both of these be true? If there is one of us confused here, it is you, Charles. You do not know what you want."

"I have known what I wanted from the first moment I followed you into battle," Charles yelled. "Yet you still treat me as that green recruit. Have I not proven my loyalty to you? Have I not proven my abilities? My determination? You make me prove them every day. Every damn day, Gideon. You are so hard to love. Why do you make it so bloody hard?"

"Then go," Gideon yelled back. He was not the man Charles was describing. He was not. Charles did not have to prove a thing to him. It was Gideon who had to prove every day that he was still a man. That he was still that man that Charles had followed into battle, the man worthy of such trust and devotion. And he knew he failed. Every day he failed. Because he was not that man anymore.

"Stop!" Sarah's voice cut through the tension in the room and both men looked at the door in surprise. Gideon had not heard her come in. She closed the door behind her. "The whole house can hear you. What is going on?"

"I'm leaving, apparently," Charles said. He stalked past Sarah but stopped and turned back to her to kiss her hand. "Goodbye." He straightened and looked directly at Gideon for a moment and then he spun on his heel and left the room. The door slammed behind him.

"Gideon?" Sarah sounded upset. He had not meant to upset her. Not this way. He'd known she would be upset when Charles left. And that was his fault. Charles was right about that, at least. Gideon had given her to Charles, and he had given Charles to her. Did he have the right to take that away now? When he didn't answer her Sarah walked around the desk and touched his shoulder. "Are you all right?"

Gideon grabbed her and pulled her onto his lap before he buried his face in her shoulder. She smelled so damn good. She felt perfect, so soft and yielding. He would do anything for her. She wrapped her arms around him and ran a hand through his hair. "You must stop fighting with Charles, Gideon. He cares for you, you know. And I know you care for him."

Gideon's breath caught. Did she know? Did she truly know what Charles meant to him? He wasn't sure himself anymore.

Gideon buried his hand in Sarah's hair and raised his mouth to hers, holding her tightly just out of reach. "He means nothing to me," he whispered harshly. He pulled her to him then and kissed her savagely. He felt savage, wild and out of control, as if his tether had snapped and he had nothing to hold him back. After a brief moment of surprised hesitation, Sarah dug her fingers into his scalp and held him tightly to her, kissing him as roughly as he was her. Their teeth scraped and Gideon wasn't sure if it was a moan or a growl that worked its way up from his throat. But it pulled him back to himself and he tore his mouth from Sarah's.

They were both breathing hard and stared in shock at each other. Her eyes were wide and bright, their soft brown turned sharp with emotion. "That's a lie," she told him vehemently. "Charles means everything to you. Nothing you can say or do will change that."

"You're wrong," Gideon replied as he wrapped his arm around her waist and pulled her torso tight against him, her breasts pressing against his coat. "He does not mean everything to me. There is more now. There is you."

Sarah's hand caressed his cheek. "Oh, Gideon. I know that. But I cannot take Charles' place. I do not wish to. I can only make a place for myself. Do you understand?"

Gideon shook his head. He didn't understand anything these days. His life was changing too quickly, leaving him confused. Part of him wanted to barricade himself inside his old life, protecting his isolation. Another part, a part he hadn't been familiar with a few short weeks ago, wanted to embrace the changes. He was fighting a losing battle against himself, and though logically he knew it was foolish and futile, emotionally he was not prepared to concede.

"There will always be a place for you," he told her honestly. It was the one thing he could guarantee with any certainty.

"But it has to be my place," Sarah whispered, "and not an empty place left by someone else."

"Am I too hard, Sarah?" he found himself asking. He wanted to kick himself after the plaintive question escaped.

"Of course you are," she answered with a small smile. "I wouldn't want anything that wasn't. The effort is minimal but so are the rewards. To make the victory sweeter, it has to be difficult to attain."

Gideon managed a weak smile. "I want to be worth it, but honestly, Sarah, I tire of difficult."

She stroked his cheek and then playfully flicked his good ear. "Poor Gideon. To be difficult or not to be difficult, that is the dilemma."

This was new, this playful side of Sarah. It was entirely new territory for Gideon. With chagrin he realized that he'd spent the last few years either fighting or brooding. He nipped at her bottom lip. "There is no question of hard, then," he murmured, maneuvering Sarah on his lap so she couldn't help but feel his growing arousal.

Sarah laughed throatily. The sound shot straight down to Gideon's cock. "No, no question about that. You are extremely hard."

Gideon looked at her askance. Yes, she was blushing. But she had managed the risqué banter without hesitation. Charles was right. She was gaining confidence with them. Gideon frowned. Would that confidence desert her if Charles left?

As if conjured by his thoughts the door opened and Charles barged in. "I'm sorry, I shouldn't have left that way." He ran a hand through his hair, leaving the curls shooting off in every direction. "I—" He stopped abruptly when he saw Gideon and Sarah. His back stiffened and his face lost all expression. "I'm sorry again. I'm intruding." He turned to leave.

"No," Sarah called out. She peered through the door in a panic. "Don't leave," she whispered just loud enough for Charles to hear her. "Close the door."

Charles looked at Gideon. Gideon nodded. "Close the door."

Very slowly Charles walked back and quietly shut the door. He turned and leaned against it. "Back to that, are we? Isn't this where we began not too long ago?"

Sarah pinched Gideon. "Apologize," she whispered in his ear. He shook his head slightly. He would not. Charles had as much to be sorry for. And Charles had apologized, hadn't he? Gideon nearly groaned aloud. He leaned his forehead on Sarah's shoulder in misery. He was going to have to do it. Sarah pinched him again, harder, and he raised his head to glare at her. She jerked her head in Charles' direction with wide, determined eyes.

"I'm sorry," he bit out, refusing to look at Charles.

"You're...what?" Charles asked with exaggerated confusion. Gideon turned and glared at him. Charles leaned forward as if he couldn't hear.

"I said I'm sorry." Gideon enunciated each word carefully but kept his tone distant.

Charles shook his head in wonder. "I do believe that is the first time you have ever uttered those words to me with at least a modicum of sincerity."

"Charles, behave," Sarah chided. "You know that was not easy for Gideon." She gave Gideon a private smile. "He can be so hard, you know."

Behind her back Charles started at her comment, so similar to his just a few moments ago. "Yes, I do know," Charles told her. "I just didn't realize you knew it."

Sarah gave that throaty laugh again. "I'm learning rather quickly."

"I'm right here," Gideon said sarcastically. "In case you'd forgotten."

"How could I?" Sarah teased as she wiggled in his lap. Gideon hissed in a breath and clamped his arm around her.

"Should I stay?" Charles asked, his voice low and turning rough. "Or should I go?"

Gideon closed his eyes and breathed in Sarah's scent with the sound of Charles' breath in the background, the rustle of his clothing. The knowledge that he was there with them coursed through Gideon in a rush he knew only with these two. "Stay," he whispered.

Charles walked over and bent his knees to squat before Gideon's chair, his face level with Sarah's. Sarah leaned forward and kissed him lightly. "You won't leave, will you, Charles?" she asked. She sounded so hopeful, so beseeching. Gideon met Charles' stare over Sarah's head.

"No, Sarah darling, I won't leave," Charles whispered, and then he leaned his hand on Gideon's thigh as he gave Sarah a more thorough kiss.

Gideon slid his hand over Charles' on his thigh and squeezed it tight.

Chapter Thirteen

ℬ

Sarah couldn't resist the beauty of the morning. So she sneaked out of bed and now she sat on the bench beside the pasture, watching the sunrise. She was in her nightclothes, but no one would see her. No one else was awake yet, although they would be soon. She sat with her feet pulled up on the bench, her arms wrapped around her legs. A decidedly inelegant pose but, again, who would see her?

It was a little chilly in the pale early morning light. She didn't care. She had never been able to do this at her father's house. She had too many responsibilities. She'd forgotten that she could enjoy something so simple. Was that the problem? Was that why she had prayed for good days? Because she could no longer see the good in each day? Gideon and Charles had given that back to her. It was a wondrous gift.

She rested her head on her upraised knee. Gideon and Charles. It was hard to think of one without the other. They were so different and yet so alike. How she wished they would not fight. It had been weeks since that awful fight in Gideon's study. But they bickered constantly, finding fault with each other. Perhaps they had the same problem as Sarah. Perhaps they longed so much for what they did not have, they could not enjoy what they did have. And they had so much in each other. Where one ended, the other began.

She was in love with them. She had never been in love before, but she knew what this feeling was. Gideon needed her so much. He was wounded, not just on the outside but inside, and he tried to hide it behind his gruff exterior. But she felt his pain and was determined to end it. In so many ways, no matter how gruff he became, he showed her how tender and compassionate he could be. And Charles, he had been harder to figure out. But once she realized that he was in love with Gideon, she understood him and loved him too. He was so strong, so steady and so desperate for every crumb of Gideon's affection. And he'd transferred all that to Sarah. She could see it in his face when he looked at her. When he bullied her and forced her to face her unspoken fears, she knew he did it because he cared deeply for her. And when he was in bed with her and Gideon, he showed her. Every touch that was meant to inflame revealed his passion and tender feelings for her.

She longed to consummate her union with Charles. But he refused. At first Sarah had been hurt and miserable. She'd thought he refused because he didn't want her. But after so many weeks together she knew differently. He wanted her desperately. He struggled not to take what she offered. Why? He claimed it was because he was not her husband and that only Gideon had the right to take her that way.

She blushed as she remembered all the things she'd done with both men. They had taught her how to please them in many ways and taught her how to take her own pleasure. She'd taken them in her mouth. It was wicked and wonderful. And they loved it. They loved to watch her do it. That was one of the ways they were so much alike. They loved to watch each other pleasure Sarah, and she them. Sarah could feel the smug satisfaction in her private little grin. Sarah liked that very much too. To be watched by both of them.

There was a reason Charles wouldn't take the final intimate step with her. And she was quite sure it had something to do with Gideon. Was he afraid that Gideon would object? Sarah was quite sure he wouldn't. He had said as much many times. Was he afraid it would change their relationship? She didn't see how. They were already as close as man and wife. He knew her as well as Gideon did, better than anyone had ever known her before. She shared almost every aspect of herself with both men.

But there were some things she kept to herself. Such as her fear that this perfect time would not last. Her fear that they would realize what a fraud she was, pretending to be strong and brave and resourceful, when each day, each step filled her with apprehension. Perhaps Charles knew that—he seemed to know everything without being told. Perhaps that was why he denied her. Because she was weak and he knew it.

She stared out over the green grass of the pasture glistening with dew. The morning held its breath, waiting for the sun to rise. Sarah wondered what she was waiting for. Charles to relent? Explain? She sighed. She was doing it again. She was so busy worrying about what she didn't have she was forgetting to appreciate what she did have. She was questioning herself again too. She'd thought she was past that now.

Sarah stood up and moved closer to the pasture fence, leaning against a tree trunk. She wiggled her bare toes in the wet grass. The sound of a door opening and closing behind her sounded clearly in the quiet morning. She turned around, one hand on the tree.

It was Charles.

Charles breathed a sigh of relief when he saw Sarah down by the fence. When he'd woken up and found her gone he hadn't known what to think. He'd panicked and thrown on some clothes as quietly as he could to search for her. He hadn't wanted to awaken Gideon and worry him. The first place he'd thought to look was here. Sarah spent a great deal of time here.

He started to walk down the hill and she took a step forward just as the sun started to peek over the horizon. The light set her hair ablaze and outlined her long legs through the thin material of her gown. Charles just stopped and stared. She was beautiful. Truly, amazingly beautiful. He had caught a glimpse of this woman the first day she'd come here, when she had whipped off that god-awful bonnet in Gideon's study and confronted him. But Sarah had hidden that woman behind conservative gowns and a starchy demeanor. She had been a little sparrow, pretty in it's way but unremarkable. Now she was a songbird in flight. Beautiful, courageous, bringing the wonder of her song to all who met her. She brought it to Gideon. She was there for him in every way, giving him so much. It was no wonder she was everything to him. And she gave her song to Charles as well. In return, Charles wanted to be there for her. Gideon was, he knew that, but Charles wanted it too. He wanted her to turn to him in times of trouble, when she needed a strong back or a soft shoulder. He wanted her to rely on him the way Gideon had always relied on him.

He took a step and almost stumbled. Over the last few weeks his feelings for her had grown until he couldn't separate them from his feelings for Gideon anymore. They were intertwined, inseparable. He was in love with her, as he had only ever been in love with Gideon.

When he moved again his steps seemed to quicken of their own accord. Soon he was running toward her, his open shirt blowing back along his sides, his strides eating up the distance between them. He felt an urgency that made him desperate. He had to get to her. Sarah picked up her skirts and ran to meet him. They almost collided, but Charles stopped just in time and caught her against his chest, spinning them around.

"What's wrong?" she cried out distress. "Gideon?"

Charles cupped her face in his palms and ran his thumbs along her beloved cheeks as he shook his head. "No, no, nothing's wrong. I just had to see you. I had to touch you." He was breathless from more than his sprint down the hill. It was need, desire that wrung him out and left him in tatters. He couldn't. He shouldn't. She was Gideon's.

Sarah wrapped her arms around his waist, her breathing, her expression, everything about her screaming of a desperation that matched his own. "Charles," she whispered.

His lips pressed down on hers in an effort to appease them both. She was eager and welcoming, but it wasn't enough. He tore his mouth away from the kiss and pressed his cheek to hers, both hands now cupped around the back of her head. He held them both prisoner like that, so close to what they wanted and yet so far. Why did he deny himself? Gideon had told him time and again that he wanted Charles to have Sarah, that he would not be upset if she and Charles became that intimate. But Charles had played the martyr. Why?

Because he was afraid.

Sarah broke free of his hold and brought her mouth back to his, kissing him roughly. He loved that about her. In the bedroom was where Sarah had learned to spread her wings. She never hesitated to take what she needed from them in the intimacy of their bed. She had asked him to take her many times. With kisses like this, and with words.

He held back, letting her kiss him, not wanting to push her away. But that's what he was doing. By refusing her he was pushing her away. He'd been too much of a coward these last weeks to take that last step. Because he was afraid of letting down his defenses enough to let someone else in. Someone who might turn away as Gideon had. But Sarah would never turn away. Sarah was…Sarah.

Charles broke the kiss again and pressed his forehead to hers, breathing heavily as if he'd run a race. He was tired of sacrificing. He wanted to take something for himself. He hadn't had anything for himself in so long.

"Charles," she murmured again and pressed her hand to his racing heart.

He backed her against the tree trunk and she went willingly, trusting him enough to not even turn her head to see where he was pushing her. He reached down and began to slowly pull her skirts up, giving her the chance to push him away, to say no.

She wrapped her hand around the back of his neck and pulled him close, spreading her legs so he could move between them. With her other hand she reached down and began to undo the fall on his trousers.

He couldn't speak. If he said anything it would shatter the perfection of this moment. It would make it too real, and then he'd have to think about what he was doing. What it would mean to all of them. So he kept his silence and shuddered at the delicate touch of her hands on him.

When she touched him and pulled him free of his trousers, he pressed against her closer and rested his forearms on the tree trunk on either side of her head. The bark scratched his skin and it only made him more aware of the many sensations bombarding him. He turned and buried his face in her soft, sweet-smelling hair. He could feel the weak warmth of the sun on his back as he listened to Sarah's panting breaths. The birds were beginning to greet the morning, and he heard a horse nicker faintly from the barn.

She knew. She understood that she must do this. He could not take her. She had to invite him in, she had to be the one. And so it was Sarah who slid her arm around his neck and wrapped her leg around his waist. It was Sarah who brought his cock, hard and aching, to her warm entrance, and he had to choke off a gasp at his first touch of sex against sex. She pressed down on him, taking the tip of him inside her, and Charles couldn't take a deep breath. He tried to pull in air and only managed short, sharp inhalations. It felt so good. So goddamned good to be inside someone again. To be inside someone he loved.

He slammed inside her then. He wanted to take it slow, he wanted to savor her, savor the moment and the feelings, but he couldn't. He needed to get as deep inside her as possible. He needed to bury himself there and never come out. Sarah cried out softly and wrapped both arms around his neck. She pulled herself up and wrapped both legs around his waist and Charles was gone. He rammed her back against the tree, grabbed her hands in his and pressed them into the tree over her head and fucked her. Fucked her as he'd wanted to for so long, as she'd been asking him to. Fucked her as a man desperate for his woman needs to fuck.

His mouth slanted over hers and he swallowed her cries and her moans. He shared her breath, her taste, her heat, not letting her come up for air until she turned her face away with a gasp. He buried his lips in the curve of her neck then and sucked on the salty skin he found. Sarah's hips were pushing against his, keeping up with his rough, wild rhythm, matching his passion. He had known she would be a match for him, that she could take his rough handling. Gideon fucked her so gently, as if she'd break. But Sarah couldn't be broken. Not by this. Not by them.

Sarah yanked one hand out of his grip and buried it in his hair, pulling it sharply as she made a fist and held his mouth to her. Her legs tightened and she wriggled down so that the angle of Charles' thrusts changed. "Yes," she hissed, and Charles growled against her neck, biting her. He placed his free hand under her bottom and pulled her into him.

Sarah came. Her passage clamped down on his cock so hard he shouted at the pleasure, so sharp it was almost pain. She pulsed around him, pulling him in, not letting him go. Charles let her ride his cock. He let her writhe on him and moan, her nails biting into his scalp. He began to come. The aching pleasure was pulled from his balls in a spine-tingling rush of ecstasy and he had to lean hard into her, the tree at her back holding them both up. His fingers twined with hers against the rough bark and some small part of his mind wondered if he was hurting her. But she held his hand as tightly.

"Sarah," he finally whispered in a rough, broken voice. A small sob escaped her. He cupped her cheek and raised her face so he could look at her. Her eyes were swimming with tears, a few having already fallen. She smiled at him then, and he knew she was feeling the same things he was right now. This was right. She was as much his as she was Gideon's.

"Sarah," he whispered again, unable to put it all into words. So he bent to kiss her instead.

"Get off her." Gideon's voice was guttural. He was mad enough to kill. He couldn't believe that Charles would take her like this, so roughly, like a whore against a tree where anyone could catch them. What if Gideon hadn't woken to find them both missing? What if someone else had come out?

Charles froze and Sarah cast frightened eyes over his shoulder to Gideon. She was crying.

"By God, if you've hurt her..." Gideon snarled. He stalked closer and Charles pulled out of her as she lowered her legs to the ground. Gideon knew one painful moment of regret. He would never be able to fuck Sarah like that. He simply couldn't anymore.

Charles adjusted his trousers and then stepped back. Sarah's skirt had fallen, covering her legs. She leaned heavily on the tree. She could barely stand. Her hair was a tangled mess, some strands caught in the tree bark. Gideon choked on his anger when he saw the bruise on her neck. There were teeth marks. Sarah's hand flew up to cover it and Gideon's gaze shot to her face. She looked frightened. He whirled to face Charles.

"You did this to her."

Charles glared at him. "Yes, just as you—"

Gideon didn't let him finish. He lashed out and backhanded Charles across the face. Charles stumbled back a step, caught off guard. Gideon dropped his crutches at the same time he threw himself at Charles. When he hit Charles in the chest they both toppled over and fell to the ground, rolling down the slight hill. Gideon rolled again so he came out on top of Charles, but Charles was recovering quickly. He tried to push Gideon off, but Gideon grabbed the collar of his shirt, pressed his forearm to Charles' throat and planted his foot on the ground to hold his place.

"How could you? After everything? After I gave her to you? This is what you do? This is how you treat her? Have you no decency?" The questions were ripped from Gideon's heart, leaving an open wound.

"Gideon!" Sarah cried out. She was sobbing now. "Don't! It wasn't like that, it wasn't."

Charles finally succeeded in shoving him off and Gideon rolled onto his back. Sarah ran over and fell to her knees next to Charles. "Are you all right?" she asked him, frantic.

Charles sat up, supporting his weight on one hand. He rubbed his neck gingerly and nodded.

"What happened here?" Gideon asked. The question was almost as hard to ask as the ones he'd thrown at Charles accusingly.

"If you knew your wife at all, Gideon," Charles told him is disgust, "or me, you'd know that what just happened was what she wanted." Charles refused to look at him.

Gideon could not believe that. "Sarah is a lady. That sort of rough fucking may have been fine for whores, but not for Sarah."

Charles laughed with bitter humor. "Because only whores like me like a good, rough fuck?"

"I didn't say that."

"You didn't have to." Charles was standing now too. "You never meant a word of it, did you? You never meant for me to have her. You thought I wouldn't, that I'd continue to play the martyr and leave her alone. Well, I won't. She's as much mine as yours now, and you can't keep me from her."

"If you think I'll let you abuse my wife, you're wrong," Gideon told him. He realized then what a vulnerable position he was in, lying there with no crutches, no defenses.

"I can't believe you could even think that of me," Charles choked out. He looked sick.

"I wanted it." Sarah's voice was firm, though Gideon could still hear her tears in it. He looked at her and she met his gaze unflinchingly. "I encouraged him. I wanted him to take me, and I wanted it rough. I wanted him to take me against the tree and I wanted him to bite me." A sob ruined the effect of her confession and she pressed the back of her hand to her mouth as if to hold any more emotional outbursts inside.

"Sarah…" Gideon said in astonished confusion. He had not known. He'd had no idea that she wanted to be fucked like that. He didn't know if he could do it.

Sarah stood clumsily. Charles reached out a hand to her which she caught as she rose to her feet. Then she let go and backed away from both men.

"I wanted it. I'm sorry, Gideon. I didn't mean to…" She hiccupped on a sob again. "I thought…" She looked at Charles and, bursting into tears, she turned and ran back to the house.

Chapter Fourteen

ဆ

"You have to go to her." Charles bent down and grabbed Gideon's crutches. He stood and tossed them on the ground next to Gideon. "She thinks we did something wrong. You have to tell her we didn't."

Gideon hesitated to pick up his crutches. He had just made the biggest mistake of his life and wasn't sure how to fix it. Yes, he needed to go see Sarah. But he had to mend fences with Charles first.

"I'm sorry." He looked right at Charles as he said it, letting every ounce of regret he felt show on his face.

Charles sighed and leaned against the tree, his hands on his hips as he looked over his shoulder at the pasture. "I know you are." He turned back and Gideon flinched at the pain he saw in Charles' expression. "Is that truly what you think of me? That I could hurt Sarah that way?"

Gideon shook his head. "No. In my saner moments I know that you would never do that. That you would do everything in your power to make sure no one ever hurt her, including you or me." Instead of taking his crutches and getting up Gideon covered his face with his hands and rolled onto his back in the grass once again. "I don't know what I was thinking. You were both gone when I awoke, and I came searching and saw you together. The closer I got the more apparent what you were doing. It was rough and I jumped to conclusions."

"You have a talent for that." Charles sounded bitter rather than amused.

"I said I was sorry." Gideon hadn't meant to say it like that, as if he were the offended one.

"How many times am I going to have to forgive you, Gideon?" Charles asked quietly. "Five? A hundred? A thousand times? I feel as if I've already reached my limit."

"God, don't say that," Gideon replied fervently. "I'm quite sure I've got a great many more offenses yet to be committed waiting inside me."

"Gideon." Charles voice was tired, his reprimand weak.

"I mean it. You know I'm not easy, Charles."

"No, you are not," Charles agreed a little too quickly.

"You told me that a few weeks ago. But I don't try to be that way."

Charles straightened and moved away from the tree. "Sometimes I wonder." He shook his head when Gideon started to reply. "No, no more. Go to Sarah."

"Does this mean I am forgiven?" Gideon asked as he finally grabbed his crutches and stood up awkwardly. Charles did not offer to help.

"No. But I suppose you will be eventually."

It was more than Gideon had hoped for. Things were not right by any means, but at least they were not quite so wrong.

"Don't forget we leave for Suter's today." Neutral ground. Gideon almost sighed with relief as Charles brought up the horse-buying trip. They were walking up the hill together silently. Hills were never easy for Gideon, though he had mastered the ability to traverse them without falling down.

"Can't you go without me?" Gideon asked. He didn't want to anger Charles again, but he hated going anywhere. It was thoroughly unpleasant to watch people's reaction to him.

"No, I can't." Charles was exasperated. "I've told you, most of these gentlemen don't wish to deal with me. They consider me your lowly servant. They won't negotiate price with me or talk about bloodlines. They want you for that. And

I don't want to risk losing this Arabian. He's from von Fechtig's stables."

Gideon's lips thinned. Charles had told him what was happening after several unsuccessful trips. Gideon tried to take care of the problem through his correspondence with several buyers, but it was a futile effort. And Charles was right. They needed the Arabian.

"I'm sorry." He winced as the words escaped again.

"Yes, I know," Charles answered wryly. "So you've told me."

* * * * *

"Come in." Sarah kept her voice level by sheer force of will. She knew as soon as she heard the knock it was Gideon. It was well past dawn now. She'd been waiting for him for what seemed like hours.

The door opened and Gideon stepped in. He didn't look at her where she stood beside the bed as he shut the door behind him quietly.

"I'm sorry." He stood by the door, leaning on his crutches as he apologized, as if afraid to come any farther into the room. "I was an idiot and I came to beg your forgiveness."

Sarah let out a watery chuckle, on the verge of tears again. "Yes, you were." She licked her lips nervously. "But you were shocked. I know you were. We should not have done that there, without you."

"Nonsense." Gideon moved over to the chair in the corner and lowered himself into it. "You two have every right to do that whenever you please." He looked at her with an eyebrow cocked. "Although try not to do it in front of the entire neighborhood next time, please."

Sarah laughed again. "Oh, Gideon. Everyone was asleep."

"You hope," Gideon muttered loud enough for her to hear. She blushed. Gideon cleared his throat. "I want you to know, Sarah, that I was not upset at the fact that you and Charles have finally become intimate."

"We were rather intimate before this morning," she answered drily, sitting on the edge of the bed with her hands folded in her lap.

It was Gideon's turn to laugh quietly. "Yes, quite. But you know what I'm talking about. I always expected that Charles would have you that way one day. I'm not sure why he hesitated so long. You both knew. I've told you enough times that I would not deny you that."

"But you do not like it." Sarah finished the sentence for him, but he shook his head.

"You are wrong." Gideon took a deep breath and looked away. "I think you know how much I do like it."

Yes, she knew. At least, she knew he liked to watch her and Charles when they were together. "You didn't get to watch us this morning." The words were spoken without thought, and Sarah's eyes grew wide with dismay as she realized what she'd said.

Gideon nodded. "Ah, then you do know. Yes, I would have liked that." He clasped his hands in his lap, staring at the floor. "Does that bother you?"

Sarah shook her head and then realized Gideon couldn't see it. "No, it doesn't. I suppose it should."

Gideon's head jerked up. "Why?"

Sarah was taken aback at his question. "Why? Well, I guess because it would certainly bother everyone else to know what we do with Charles."

Gideon waved away her concerns with a snort of disgust. "Bah, who cares what they think? They can mind their own business. I certainly do."

Sarah laughed. "Yes, you certainly do." She sighed. "I could have said no that first night you came with Charles. He didn't want to be here." She wondered if he still felt that way. He'd sought her out today. But was this really what he wanted? Or did he feel compelled to consummate their relationship because of Gideon? "I never even thought to say no that night. I suppose part of me wanted him there. What does that make me, I wonder?"

"My kind of woman, apparently," Gideon responded drily. She laughed and he smiled that lopsided grimace of his that she loved. "Why?"

She didn't understand his question. "Why what?"

"Why did you want him there? Because of me? This?" He ran his bent fingers down his scarred face.

Sarah gasped. "No! I knew you wanted him there. I could see that his being there eased your concerns. I wanted you to stay and I didn't think you would if I refused to allow Charles to stay with us."

"You know me so well," Gideon murmured, leaning back in the chair. "You have from the moment we met, I think. And I thought I knew you. But today I realized that I do not know you at all."

Sarah had known this was coming. She turned her face to the wall. "I heard what you said to Charles. I'm sorry I'm not what you thought I was. I'm not a lady, not really."

"I spoke out of turn. That is not what I meant." Gideon's response was sharp. Sarah looked at him and he seemed angry.

"Wasn't it? It's clear you wanted a lady for a wife. You said as much in our first interview. You have treated me as if I were. But I failed a test today, I think."

"No, you did not. There was no test. To me you are every inch a lady. I failed the test." Gideon was furious with himself for putting Sarah in this position. That she could question herself this way was his fault entirely. Now that he'd started his confession, he felt compelled to finish it. He owed it to Sarah to risk his pride. "I panicked, you see. You and Charles were gone and I thought you had left me."

Sarah gasped and jumped to her feet. "Gideon, I would never. We would never… Surely you know that."

Gideon leaned his head against the wall behind him and blew out a breath. They said confession was good for the soul. He didn't feel good but he did feel a certain lightness at revealing his deepest fear.

"Yes, I do. But what I know and what I feel are two entirely different things, aren't they?" His mind flashed back to when he awoke this morning, to the second he realized they both were gone. He never wanted to feel that way again.

"Gideon…" Sarah sounded as if she wanted to cry. He definitely did not want that. So he sat up and went back to the point he'd been trying make.

"I did not know that you would like it so rough."

Sarah blushed so hard it seemed as if her entire body turned red. Gideon found her blushes charming. "Neither did I."

"I should have known." Gideon had berated himself repeatedly before he gathered enough courage to knock on Sarah's door. "I should have at least asked you what you wanted. I should have noticed that you were not satisfied with what we were doing."

Sarah glared at him indignantly. "Of course I was satisfied. What we have been doing is equally as satisfying as what Charles and I did this morning. I certainly would have said something if I had been unhappy. I am not such a ninny as that."

"How could you have known?" Gideon asked incredulously. "I am well aware, madam, that prior to our wedding night you had no carnal experience. I was the experienced one who should have seen what you needed."

"Are you so much a rake, then?" Sarah asked curiously. "I did not think you had much experience, particularly since coming back from the war."

Gideon could have kissed her then, if she were closer. She had spoken of the war and his injuries with mild curiosity, not morbid, reluctant fascination. As if it were commonplace to discuss it and not as if the mere mention of it would send him screaming from the room. There were a handful of people who spoke to him like that. He was eternally grateful his wife was one of them. "Come here."

Sarah did not question his command at all. She simply walked over to him and stood before him, waiting. After the way he acted this morning, her trust in him was humbling. He reached for her hand and pulled her down to sit in his lap.

"Gideon, surely I am too heavy," she protested, resisting. "I don't think your leg can hold me."

Gideon was affronted. "Nonsense. It carries me around, doesn't it? And I weigh a great deal more than you do, even without half a leg."

Sarah gingerly lowered herself onto his lap. Gideon jostled her around until he was satisfied with her position. He very much enjoyed the feel of her delicious derriere against his crotch. The thin material of her gown and wrapper were more a tease between them than a barrier. He squeezed her gently and she laid her head on his shoulder. He wore only a shirt with no waistcoat or jacket. Not even a cravat. He could feel her soft breasts pressed against him, and her hair tickled his exposed chest.

"You did not answer my question," she said quietly a few moments later.

"Hmm, did I not?" Gideon murmured. "Do you suppose other married couples discuss these things?"

"I certainly hope so," Sarah responded. "How else are people supposed to figure out what they're doing? Now answer the question."

Gideon chuckled. "I see I shall have no pride left by the time I leave your room." He sighed. "I have never had someone like you before."

Sarah hit him lightly in the chest. "That is not an answer. What do you mean, someone like me?"

Gideon was completely honest with her. "A lady. Innocent, honest, passionate. Free."

"Free?" Sarah asked. "You mean free with her favors?"

Gideon shook his head. "No. I mean free as in I didn't have to pay you for it."

"Oh." Sarah sounded completely shocked. "I...I...oh."

She felt incredibly good in his arms. Gideon ran his hand up her back into the loose, thick fall of her hair. He stroked the warm strands that flowed beneath his fingers like silk. She smelled like those flowers again. He nuzzled his nose against her temple and kissed his way down her cheek. She didn't hesitate to turn her face up for a more thorough kiss. It was a gentle exploration rather than a passionate prelude, but his ardor rose, just the same. Based on her response Sarah was not unaffected either.

"What do you want?" Gideon whispered in her ear. He bit her lobe and she squirmed pleasantly in his lap. He wrapped a hand around her hip and rubbed her against his erection. "Tell me."

"You." Her reply was breathless.

"How?"

"I...however you want." She answered in between soft, wet kisses. "I love it with you however we do it."

Gideon groaned. There were so many things he wanted to do with Sarah. Only some of them were possible, but he was now determined to try all that he could. "Are you sure? After this morning with Charles I'm afraid you might be too sore."

Sarah pulled back reluctantly. "Charles didn't hurt me. I told you that."

He pulled her back with the hand buried in her hair. "I didn't mean that. But sometimes when a man is rough, even if the woman wants it that way, she could be sore afterwards."

Their faces were mere inches apart, so close he could feel her breath on his lips. He leaned closer and ran his nose over her cheek and then rubbed her nose with his. Every part of him craved a touch of her.

She shook her head slightly, careful not to break their contact. "No, I feel fine."

"I want to be inside you." Gideon was hoarse, his desire growing each time she moved in his lap against his hardening cock.

"Yes," she said with a sigh. "Please, Gideon."

"Turn around."

"What?" Sarah was obviously confused by his command. Her eyes had gone unfocused as they kissed and he watched her try to regain her composure.

"Turn around. I want to take you from behind."

Sarah's eyes grew wide and she blushed. "How?" she whispered.

Gideon smiled. "Let me show you. Turn around."

"In your lap?"

Gideon tried not to laugh at her consternation. "Yes, in my lap," he told her patiently. "Turn around, straddle my thighs and sit back down. With your gown pulled up."

Sarah did as directed, but before she could sit down he told her, "Take the wrap off first, please."

When she sat back down Gideon ran his hands under the gown pooled around her hips. He slid them up, taking the gown with them. "Let's take this off too, shall we?" he murmured in her ear. He let his hands detour to cup her breasts, the weight of them warm and heavy in his palms. He was getting overheated, and sweat trickled down his back. He pushed the gown up and over her head and then sat back to enjoy the view.

Sarah shivered. Her legs were spread wide, her bottom a perfect heart where it rested against him. Her back was beautiful, long and graceful, arched as she held herself in his lap with her hands braced on his thighs. He brushed her long hair over her shoulder. "You are hurt," he murmured, running his fingers over the bruises and scratches on her back.

"Am I?" Sarah asked with surprise. "From the tree?"

Gideon closed his eyes as the image of Sarah and Charles fucking against the tree flashed through his mind. His first reaction when he'd seen them was a rush of desire so strong it nearly unbalanced him. Sarah pinned to the tree, helpless and moaning as Charles fucked her fast and hard, the muscles in his powerful arms flexing as he held her there, his hips pumping. He had not confessed to Sarah that part of his anger had been his reaction to them. Sarah had aroused him, but Charles had too, just as much as Sarah. He'd thought those feelings for Charles would go away now that he had Sarah. They had not. If anything, watching him with Sarah had intensified Gideon's desire for him.

"I assume so," he finally answered. He rested his hands on her shoulders and then slid them down her back, molding his hands to her skin, feeling the movement of her muscles under his palms and the delicate bones of her spine with his thumbs. He traced her ribs with his fingertips and she shivered again.

"Gideon, please," she begged sweetly.

"Please what?" He knew he was pushing her. But he wanted to see that side of her he'd seen this morning. She always welcomed him into her body with passion and enthusiasm but not the wild abandon he'd seen earlier. He needed to discover how to bring her to that point.

"Please, I need you." Her voice trembled.

"I'm right here." He punctuated his reassurance with kisses to some of the bruises on her back as he cupped her breasts.

"Inside me," she pleaded.

Gideon pulled her back a little more on his thighs and found her mound with his hand. Her curls were thick and rough on his palm, damp with arousal. He loved the way they felt against him when he was fucking her. He pressed his finger into her entrance, teasing her with gentle thrusts, rubbing around the edges of her opening. "Like that?"

Sarah shook her head as her breathing became irregular. "That feels marvelous, but no."

"No?" Gideon teased. He pushed his finger in all the way, cupping her sex so his palm pressed on her clitoris. "Like that, then?"

Sarah made a sound halfway between a gasp and a hiccup and moved her hips, her inner muscles gripping his finger as her nails dug into his legs through his trousers. Oh yes, she liked that.

"Mmm," she murmured. "Yes, like that."

"Is that all you need?" he asked, injecting a tiny bit of his own desperation into the question.

Sarah laughed. It was the low, sensual laugh she used when they were in bed. The one that only he and Charles had ever heard. "Oh no. I'm going to need much more."

Gideon smiled behind her. It had become a bit of a joke between the three of them, the notion of more, going back to their wedding night. "I still have more to give you," he assured her with as much innuendo in his tone as he could produce.

Sarah laughed again, and he felt it on the finger inside her. Felt her laughter from the inside out. God, he adored her. He worshipped everything about her. It was frightening. He didn't like being as vulnerable as he'd proven to be this morning.

He undid the fall on his trousers and shoved it down. When he pulled his cock out from his underclothes it was a relief to be free of the restriction of clothing. "I want to fuck." He was deliberately crude. Sarah shuddered and a rush of wetness coated his finger. She liked that. He suspected as much. Charles could be rather crude when they were in bed, and though Sarah tried to hide it he had noticed that it aroused her.

"Oh, good," Sarah purred. Gideon laughed. He couldn't help it. She was so different than when they'd first met.

He tried to position her so that he could get inside but it was awkward. *Damn, damn, damn,* he thought. "Can you bring your legs in between mine? This isn't working," he admitted reluctantly.

Sarah did as he told her, laughing as she almost fell off his lap. "I'm afraid I'm not as nimble as you think," she jested.

It eased Gideon's tension, as he was sure she meant it to. He gripped her hips and pulled her in close and his cock brushed against her plump bottom. He jerked as if he'd been burned. "Damn, I love your derriere," he muttered.

"What?" Sarah asked in astonishment. "My...my bottom?" She sounded so affronted that Gideon laughed again.

"Yes, your bottom," he said, imitating her horrified tones. "It's a plump, soft handful." He demonstrated by cupping one cheek in his good hand and squeezing. Sarah jumped a bit in his lap. "One reason I want to fuck you this way is so I can look at this," he squeezed again, "while we do it."

"Do men like that sort of thing?" she asked in tones equally offended and fascinated.

"This man does," Gideon growled in her ear and she shivered. He let his fingers caress the crease between her cheeks and Sarah caught her breath. "I've heard a man and a woman can fuck here too," Gideon whispered suggestively.

"What?" Sarah practically screeched. Gideon winced. "Well, this man and woman most definitely are not."

She was indignant, but Gideon didn't miss that fact that her breathing was ragged and she gave a telltale squirm in his lap. "Charles told me about it," he added nonchalantly. "He said two men can have a woman at the same time that way."

Sarah sat stock-still in his lap. "Have you two ever done that?" she whispered.

"No," Gideon whispered back. "But I'm of a mind to try it someday."

"Someday," Sarah said primly, "is not today."

"No, it isn't," Gideon agreed. He wrapped his arm around her waist and raised her up a bit. He guided his member into place with the other and then sat Sarah down on it. He slid inside and Sarah adjusted her position and took over. She pulled off him and then pushed back, her beautiful bottom pressing against him as she took him as deep as he could go.

Chapter Fifteen

❧

"Oh, Gideon," she said in a thready, quivering voice. "It feels so good. Better, even, than before."

Gideon couldn't answer. With her legs pressed together between his, she was incredibly tight. She was small to begin with, and this position caused her sweet little sheath to nearly choke him with pleasure.

They began to move in complementary rhythm, Sarah pulling off as he pulled out, sliding down as he flexed his hips upward. They were both straining, moving fast within a matter of minutes. But suddenly Sarah's hand slipped off his thigh and Gideon had to catch her before she fell.

"Oh damn," Sarah muttered.

"Sarah," Gideon chided breathlessly. He laughed as she tried to get back into position.

"My legs are mush," Sarah told him helplessly. "Help me."

So far Sarah had been doing as much work as Gideon. Gideon wanted to fuck her. He wanted to be in control. He wasn't sure he was physically able to do it anymore, but he needed to try.

"Get on your hands and knees on the floor. Can you do that?" he asked roughly.

Sarah nodded. She held his hand for balance as she knelt on the floor. She went down on all fours, presenting her bottom to him with a saucy little grin over her shoulder. "Hurry, Gideon."

She was like a mare in heat presenting herself to a stallion. And that was how Gideon wanted to take her. He wanted to mount her and fuck her hard and fast until she cried out. He could see the lips of her sex peeking through her curls, red and swollen and wet. She looked like a woman who had already been fucked today. And she had. Twice.

Gideon's heart raced as he braced his hands on the edge of the chair seat and lowered himself to the floor. He let his arms absorb most of his weight. First his stump and then his knee met the floorboards. It didn't hurt. He slid over to where Sarah waited for him.

"Are you all right?" she asked in concern.

"I'm fine." He forced himself not to be too abrupt. He came up against Sarah and she sighed with pleasure. His eyes nearly crossed. He could feel the plump heat of that bottom even better this way. But he couldn't see it. He pulled his shirt off over his head and threw it aside. That was better. He didn't bother with preliminaries. He just pulled his hips back and thrust. Although his stance was slightly uneven, she was still at the perfect height. He held on to her generous hips and pumped into her.

"Gideon," she moaned. He slid closer, his legs almost under her, and she gave a cry. "Yes! Oh Gideon, right there," she cried out. "Is your leg all right?" she asked after a moment as she panted. "Does it hurt?"

Gideon laughed. "All the feeling in my body is concentrated in one spot. *Nothing* hurts."

Sarah laughed back breathlessly. "Good. Then fuck me hard."

Gideon responded by pounding into her, and their legs and hands slipped on the slick wood floor. Sarah sank lower and lower to the ground, and Gideon followed. Soon they were splayed on the floor, Gideon still fucking her as hard as he could. Sarah was crying out with each thrust, whimpering as he pulled back. He'd found something inside her, something that was clearly giving her a great deal of pleasure.

"You like it like this, don't you?" he asked in a low voice, whispering right in her ear. He had his hands braced on the floor and Sarah kept sliding with each hard thrust and Gideon followed her, not letting up.

"Yes," she cried out. She threw her hands out and Gideon saw that he'd fucked her right up to the wall. She braced her hands on the wall and pressed back, not a passive recipient. She couldn't move much between Gideon and the floor, but her inner muscles squeezed him as she pushed her hips back in short, shallow bursts. And Gideon realized that it was better that way. It was better when they worked together. But he could do it, couldn't he? He could still take her in a hard, very physical way. His leg was holding up, and she was very nearly delirious with pleasure.

Gideon rested more of his weight on her, lowering his hips even more, and Sarah began to shake and moan. Then she fisted her hands against the wall and threw her head back and Gideon felt her coming around his shaft. It was amazing. He had been inside Sarah for many climaxes before, but none as intense as this one. One long, wordless sound came from her throat, half cry and half moan. He joined her. He couldn't hold back any longer. He felt his climax begin somewhere in the top of his head and work its way down his back before being released deep inside her. The hard jerks of his shaft inside her were a blessed relief from the tension that had held him in its grip as he fucked her.

When it was over he collapsed on top of her and their ragged breaths filled the air. It took him a moment or two to realize she was struggling a bit underneath him.

"Sorry," he mumbled and rolled off to lie on his back at her side.

Sarah laughed weakly. "You're right, even missing half a leg you weigh twice as much as me," she teased.

"What I'm missing in leg I make up for in prick," Gideon responded drily. "At least when you're around."

"Gideon!" she exclaimed with a scandalized laugh. "I cannot believe you just said that."

He rolled over onto his side to gaze at her. His head was still on the floor, so their faces were closely aligned. "I can't either," he told her seriously. "I do not believe I have ever made a lighthearted joke about my leg before."

Sarah just smiled sweetly at him.

"I have no desire to get up from the floor," Gideon confessed ruefully. "I may perhaps be a tad sore from our exertions."

Sarah bit her lip and looked distressed. "I'm sorry I like things like that."

She was being quite serious, Gideon could see that, but he couldn't stop the burst of laughter that came from him in response. She frowned at him. "Sarah, darling, I am *not* sorry," he reassured her emphatically. "Believe me when I say you are a dream come true." He reached over and hauled her close. Her bare skin squeaked a little on the wood floor. He winced. "Sorry."

She wrapped her arm around his neck and snuggled into him. "I am *not* sorry," she said, smiling.

He leaned in to kiss her just as the bedroom door opened behind them. Gideon had no time to shield Sarah, though he did wrap his arm around her protectively. He sighed with relief when he saw Charles in the doorway. Charles looked surprised for a second and then his face went blank. "Excuse me," he muttered before he backed out and closed the door.

Gideon sighed. He had no idea how to make this work.

Sarah pushed up onto one hand and glanced over her shoulder at the closed door. She turned a puzzled face to Gideon. "Why didn't he come in?" Then she looked alarmed. "You two aren't still fighting, are you?"

Gideon shook his head as he sat up. "No. I suppose he was here to tell me to hurry up. We have to leave soon and if he came in it would have delayed our departure, I'm afraid."

He covered up his unease with a smile. There was more behind Charles' rapid departure than expediency. But now was not the time to address it.

"I forgot about your trip today." Sarah looked so forlorn that Gideon leaned over and kissed her on the nose. She did not brighten up at the attention.

"We'll be back tomorrow," he assured her. "Suter's is only half a day's ride. I'm not willing to buy the Arabian without seeing him first."

"I know," Sarah said glumly. "But I shall miss you both terribly."

Gideon crawled over to his crutches, grabbing his shirt on the way. At Sarah's words he stopped and looked at her. "Good," he said. That got a smile out of her.

Charles watched Gideon kiss Sarah on the cheek before he pulled himself up onto his horse. The kiss was like a knife to Charles' gut. This morning it had been clear they didn't need him any longer. For the first time that he knew of, Gideon had been with Sarah by himself. And from the looks of it they had both been more than satisfied with the experience. Although why they were on the floor was a mystery.

He had known it would happen eventually. He'd been encouraging it. Gideon was her husband and was now intimate with her as a husband should be. So why was he desolate now that it had happened? And where did that leave him?

Gideon adjusted his seat in the saddle. He hated to ride. He hadn't always, of course. As a former cavalry officer he had once practically lived atop a horse. Charles watched him fit his stump into the special pocket sewn into the side of the saddle for just that purpose. Gideon's cheeks were flushed and his lips thinned. He was embarrassed. Charles almost snorted in disgust at him. There was nothing to be ashamed of, but Gideon couldn't see that.

Sarah was staring at him now. Charles recognized the longing in her eyes. He'd like to kiss her goodbye too. But they couldn't, could they? They would never be able to do that like she and Gideon. He spun his horse away and started toward the end of the drive. "Come along, then," he said gruffly to Gideon. He tried to ignore the hurt he saw on Sarah's face. She'd better get used to it. This was how it was going to be. They had no choice.

"Goodbye, Mr. Borden," she called out in a wavering voice.

Charles stopped his horse with a sigh. He capitulated and turned around, walking the horse back to her side. Gideon had not moved and sat there watching him. Sarah rested her hand on his Bay's side when he stopped. "Goodbye, Mrs. North," he said formally. He reached down and took her hand, carrying it to his lips. He made sure to keep the kiss chaste as the grooms were still about. But her hand tightened on his and he returned the pressure. It was all he could do. It wasn't enough.

* * * * *

"Well, that was an all but useless trip," Gideon commented angrily two days later as they neared Blakely Farm. "No Arabian to show for it and a day late getting home. Damn Suter and damn his bloody, shoddy roads."

Charles smiled grimly. "Yes, I believe you may have said that. Several times to him. And possibly five hundred times to me." He patted his Bay's neck soothingly as it became skittish from Gideon's tone.

"He's damn lucky I didn't call him out after Granger stumbled in that hole. Who leaves a bloody hole in the middle of the road? Particularly idiotic for a man who trades in horses." Gideon's horse was used to his tirades. He'd had Granger in the war. The horse had grown lazy the last several years, standing around waiting for Gideon's infrequent, reluctant rides. The grooms took him out, but Charles had seen how happy Granger was to have Gideon on his back again.

And Gideon had been glad too, after he'd gotten over his initial bout of self-consciousness.

Charles had indeed feared that Gideon would call Suter out. Gideon had been livid. First the unkempt road, Granger's stumble, and then Suter had set an outrageous price for an Arabian that was almost past his prime. They had to stay an extra day to make sure Granger was all right. Gideon didn't want to ride him and do more damage. But Granger had seen much worse in the war and he was fine. As Gideon had grumbled, it was definitely not worth leaving Sarah at home alone.

They had both been in a horrible temper for the last two days. The trip home had been spent in almost complete silence broken only by Gideon's grumbling. It was an awkward silence. That was unusual for them. Their silences were normally enjoyable. But today there was too much unsaid between them to make the silence restful.

Charles was dreading the night. He knew that Gideon would want to be with Sarah tonight. He'd talked of little else besides her the last two days and the agony of being apart. And Charles would have to concede the night to him. He, not Charles, was Sarah's husband, after all. And he no longer needed Charles with them. Knowing what awaited him did not make Charles less eager to get home and see Sarah. He had been silent on the subject, but he missed her as much as Gideon. He sighed with pained resignation. He'd thought he could handle this much better. He'd known going in that he would play third to Gideon and Sarah's marriage. But it was hard. Hard because he didn't like being pushed aside in Gideon's life, and hard because he was barred from all but Sarah's very private life.

"We're here," Gideon remarked excitedly as the drive to Blakely Farm came into view. He spurred Granger and the horse gave a surprised snort before breaking into a canter. Charles' heart gave a lurch and then he followed Gideon down the drive.

Sarah paced past the window again. She'd been watching the drive for hours. Where were they? They'd not sent a note. She'd heard nothing. They should have been back yesterday. What if they'd been set upon by brigands on the road? Had Gideon fallen? Was he injured? Or was it Charles? Gideon would not leave his side if he were ill.

She turned to the window and rubbed her arms from the chill of uncertainty that had her in its grip. It could be something simple. A horse had thrown a shoe. The negotiations for the Arabian had taken longer than planned. *Or they were dead on the road,* she thought in despair. She covered her face with her shaking hands. When had she become such a ninny? And what would she do if something had happened? She couldn't catch her breath as she fought the tears.

Then she heard it. The sound of a horse coming up the drive. She pressed her palms to the window as she looked out hopefully. It was Gideon. Thank God, it was Gideon.

Sarah flew out of the front parlor and out the door. She had to grab the stair railing to keep from tripping over her feet as she ran down to the drive. She lifted her skirts and kept running. She could see Charles now too, and she sobbed with relief as she rushed to meet them.

"Sarah!" Gideon cried out as he pulled his horse to a stop next to her. She reached a hand up to him as he bent over, concern on his face. "What is it? Are you all right?"

She could only reach his hand, and she pressed her face to his leg. "You're back," she cried. She could feel the silly tears falling, and she sniffed. Her nose was running. They'd been gone two days and she was acting like a fool.

Charles came to a stop behind her and she turned to him with a watery smile. He slid from the horse's back immediately and came to her. He hesitated when she thought he would reach for her. She took the final step and wrapped her arms around him. "I was so worried," she told them both. "I didn't know what happened. You didn't send a note. I thought..." Another sob escaped and she bit her lip. She back stepped, pulling Charles with her, not letting go. Her back touched Gideon's horse and then she reached out and wrapped an arm around his leg again while clinging to Charles with the other. "I was so worried," she said again lamely.

"Help me off this damn horse," Gideon growled. He gently extricated his leg from Sarah's arm. Charles kept one arm wrapped around Sarah's waist, hugging her close as he reached up and gave Gideon a hand down. It was awkward, and when Gideon's foot touched the ground he buckled slightly. Charles held him up. Sarah quickly went to his other side and put her arm around his waist so that he held on to both her and Charles with his arms around their shoulders. He pulled them in closer until they were all huddled there together in the lane. "Sarah," he whispered, kissing her temple. "I'm sorry. Suter said he sent a servant with a message. I'm not surprised to hear it didn't arrive." He snorted. "The man is an imbecile."

Charles chuckled. "Yes, he is." He kissed Sarah's cheek. "I should have made sure the message was sent. But things were so unorganized there, and Granger had stepped in a hole—"

"Oh," Sarah said with complete understanding. She peered over Gideon's shoulder. "Is he all right?"

"The bloody horse if fine. I, however, am in a state of extreme discomfort," Gideon grumbled.

"Oh, Gideon, I'm so sorry." Sarah started for the horse to get the crutches strapped to his side. Gideon held tight and didn't let her move.

"No, Sarah. I don't need them. I need you." She looked at him quizzically and he glanced down. Sarah followed his gaze and gasped in shocked understanding. He was hard as a pike.

"Gideon," she whispered glancing around nervously. The grooms had run over from the stable and were nearly upon them.

Charles pulled back from their embrace. "I'll get your crutches, Gideon. I need to wash and change my clothes, anyway." He gave them a polite smile. "I shall see you both at supper."

Gideon didn't release Charles either. He looked at him with growing dismay. "I thought you were angry. But that's not it at all. You've been feeling sorry for yourself. Bloody hell." He frowned fiercely. "You will accompany us."

Charles got a mulish look on his face. "Oh, I will?" He straightened his shoulders belligerently. "And I do not feel sorry for myself. What rubbish is that?" He scoffed. "About what, I ask you?"

"I want you."

Sarah's eyes grew round at Gideon's statement. He wasn't speaking to Sarah this time. She found she was holding her breath. Did he mean what she thought he meant? Which, of course, she had suspected all along.

Charles regarded him with suspicion. "I did not think you needed me there anymore."

"Need has everything to do with it," Gideon replied coolly. He glanced tellingly at the grooms now waiting to take the horses. "We shall discuss it inside." He motioned the grooms over. "Harry, hand me my crutches. Mrs. North and Mr. Borden are getting tired of holding me up." The groom looked surprised at Gideon's comment but quickly recovered and brought Gideon's crutches to him. "Please see to the horses," Gideon asked politely, earning another odd look from the grooms. "And Harry, Granger stepped in a hole. I believe he is fine, he showed no ill effects on the ride home. But keep an eye on the right foreleg."

"Yes sir," Harry replied respectfully as he led Granger away. The horse nickered as Gideon patted his side.

Gideon turned to her and Charles. "And now, inside, both of you. This discussion is long overdue."

Chapter Sixteen

ഔ

Charles entered the bedroom reluctantly. He wasn't sure what Gideon had to say to them, and he wasn't sure he wanted to hear it. He'd dreamed of hearing Gideon say he wanted him for so long, and yet now that he'd said it Charles was afraid. What if it didn't mean the same to Gideon that it did to Charles? What if Sarah didn't want to hear any of it?

Sarah sat on the edge of the bed watching them with wide eyes. She'd been characteristically quiet since Gideon's pronouncement. What exactly did she think of this situation?

"Don't mind me," Sarah said. She smiled encouragingly at Charles. "I have a feeling this has been coming for a while."

Well, that answered some questions. Charles saw Gideon smile back at Sarah in a shared exchange and he felt oddly out of place. "I—"

"Be quiet."

Gideon interrupted him rudely and Charles jerked back, his temper flaring. "I most certainly will not. Do you think I don't have a few things to say as well?"

"I'm sure you do. But you have done little more than talk at me for almost seven years. For a change why don't you listen?" He held up a hand, stopping Charles' retort. "Yes, I know. I have done very little talking for seven years. Well, isn't it time? Isn't this what you've been haranguing me about?"

Charles had no response to that. It was true. "I do not harangue," he told Gideon calmly.

Sarah snorted from the bed.

Gideon slid into a chair that sat by the wall. Charles' mouth dried up as he remembered sitting there letting Sarah suck his cock while Gideon watched. Gideon was watching him now, knowingly, as if he could read Charles' mind. "I was not angry when I found you with Sarah the other morning."

Charles nodded in acknowledgment. Gideon had said as much before and Charles believed him.

"I was jealous."

Gideon's calm statement had Charles reeling in shock. "What?"

Gideon nodded. "I can't fuck Sarah like that. You looked so...strong. So male and forceful and all the things I didn't think I could be anymore."

"Of course you can fuck her like that," Charles shot back roughly.

"I know I can." Again, Gideon had Charles confused. He laughed. "I did that same morning. When you walked in I had just fucked her across the floor."

"Ah," Charles said. That explained the floor. He shook his head. No, it didn't.

"I needed to know I could do that. I needed to know that I could still be that forceful. Because that's what you need."

Charles looked back at Sarah. She shook her head. "He's not talking to me. Although I do like that too."

Charles slowly turned back to Gideon. Gideon was smiling at him. A smirk, really, that was promising things he'd never thought to have from Gideon.

"Charles and I were intimate during the war."

At Gideon's revelation Charles backed up to the wall so he could see both Gideon and Sarah. Sarah looked relatively calm after receiving that rather shocking news.

"I suspected as much," she surprised them both by saying. "You were too comfortable with each other in our intimacies not to have a history there." She cocked her head to the side. "What happened?"

Gideon took a deep breath. "I thought he'd been shot. I saw him go down and..." He stopped for a moment. "I thought I'd lost him."

Sarah looked like she wanted to cry. "I'm sorry," she said sincerely. "I'm sorry for all you went through together."

Gideon looked down at the floor. "When it was over I dragged him off and ravished him." Sarah did look surprised at that. "What?" Gideon asked with a frown.

Sarah blushed. "I rather thought Charles would have been the one to..." She seemed at a loss for words. Charles finally laughed.

"I was. I'd been throwing myself at him for months. He was only responding to my overtures. And the stress of battle." He shook his head. "It didn't mean anything, not really. It happened more often than people think. You do awful things in the heat of battle, and afterwards...you just want to reaffirm that you're human, I think."

Gideon was shaking his head. "No. That was the only time it happened for me, and you were the only person it happened with. It was you. I wanted you."

"Gideon—"

"I'm supposed to be talking. You are listening." At Gideon's interruption Charles waved his hand, granting Gideon permission to speak.

"I wanted you desperately. But you were my charge, under my command. It was wrong. I couldn't let myself touch you. But that day all I could think...well, I told you before. I couldn't die, or let you die, without having that with you. And my feelings have never changed, never faltered. I still feel the same way about you as I did then. More, as a matter of fact."

Charles slid down the wall to sit on the floor. His legs wouldn't hold him anymore. "You what?"

Gideon continued as if Charles hadn't spoken. "But I didn't think you were mine for the taking anymore. When we were together, and the times we shared women after that, you were so physical, so commanding. You need a lover who can do that for you. I wasn't that lover. Not anymore."

"Not anymore, not anymore," Charles said angrily. "That's what I keep hearing from you. What about now? Tell me about now."

"Now, because of Sarah, I know I can."

Gideon seemed to expect something of Charles then. But all Charles had was anger. "And that's it? I'm supposed to be happy that now you think you can fuck me the way I need to be fucked so we can be together? Because obviously that's all I care about." He looked at Sarah. "Is that what you think as well?"

Sarah shook her head. "No. But Gideon is an idiot."

"I beg your pardon?" Gideon responded icily.

"You are an idiot," Charles agreed. He came to his feet. "Yes, I've stayed here all these years because I was waiting and hoping for the day when you could fuck me like a man again. You have it exactly right." He rubbed his hands together and looked around. "All right, then. How do you want me? Shall I strip? Or would you just like me to bend over the bed with my breeches down?"

"Watch yourself," Gideon growled.

"Or what?" Charles asked challengingly. "You'll turn away from me again? You'll deny my feelings for you, and yours for me? Too late." He turned to face the wall. "You'll make me love you, then you'll make me love your wife and you'll make me feel like the lowliest bastard for it? Fit for nothing but fucking?"

Soft arms slid around his waist and he felt Sarah against his back. "Don't," she whispered. "Don't run away because you're afraid. We're all afraid. I'm afraid. Do you want to know of what?" He tried to turn to her but she held him tightly and he stayed where he was. "I'm afraid that with your feelings out in the open, I will fade into the background. I am the one who will not be needed anymore."

"Never," Gideon told her. Charles held her hands where they rested on his stomach. She was trembling. He heard Gideon rise and the thump of his crutches across the floor. "Know this, Sarah, until you arrived I *had* cut Charles out of my life." This time Sarah let Charles turn as she dropped her arms and also turned to face Gideon. "I had resolved that he should leave here. That he should make a real life for himself, a normal life. I considered myself less than a man.

"I wouldn't marry any of the others because I couldn't stand the pity in their eyes. I couldn't stand the expectations in Charles'. But you, Sarah, you had hope and defiance in your eyes. You actually thought you were the unworthy one. And right then I became more than I had been."

"I showed you every day that you were still a man to me," Charles protested.

Gideon shook his head. "No. What you showed me every day was that you were the strong one. You were the one I had to rely on. You pushed me to be more, it's true. But Charles, that only made me feel less."

Charles felt as if he'd been shot. He actually rubbed his chest at the pain. "I never meant..." he whispered. "That isn't what I felt. I didn't mean to make you feel that way. I just wanted you to be..." He stopped and closed his eyes in shame. He'd wanted Gideon to be the way he was before.

"Exactly." Gideon spoke softly with no recrimination in his voice. "You've treated me differently since Sarah has been here. I think you've realized I'm not the man I was, and I can never be again."

Charles opened his eyes then and took a step toward Gideon. He had never seen Gideon look so vulnerable. "You're right." Gideon looked surprised at Charles' agreement. "Sarah has made me see you differently. Before she came I treated you as if you might break. I thought I was the key to your happiness, your future. But I'm not and I never was. You had more to give than I would let you. I wanted to be the one to give, because I thought you could only take." He shook his head. "I'm not making sense. What I'm trying to say is that you have always been the same man to me, but what that man was capable of changed, or at least I thought it had. And I'm trying to say I'm sorry. I've been blinded by my own selfishness. I stifled you with my feelings and my desires. When Sarah came I couldn't do that anymore. She needed you to be more, and you wanted that for her as well."

"I wanted it for you too." Gideon took a hesitant step toward him. "But I didn't know what you needed me to be. You wanted the old Gideon, but you also seemed to need to take care of this Gideon." He waved a hand down in front of himself.

Charles smiled. "I still want to take care of you. The same way I've always wanted to." He took that last step that brought them together, cupped Gideon's face and kissed him. It was awkward—Gideon was too shocked to respond and Charles wasn't sure how to proceed. But as chaste as it was, it was still one of the most satisfying kisses of his life. He broke the kiss and let a small fraction of the frustration he'd felt over the last few years show. "Can I touch now? Is it allowed?"

Gideon looked at Sarah. She nodded. "I may not completely understand what is happening, but I do know that it's got to involve touching." She smiled wryly. "I'm a fast learner, you see."

Gideon chuckled, a barely there burst of breath and noise that brought Charles' attention back to him. Charles traced Gideon's lower lip with his thumb, following the downward curve, loving the permanent scowl. He couldn't imagine Gideon without it now. But he wouldn't let him hide behind it anymore. Sarah had taught him that. Gideon might be stuck with it, but it wasn't whom he was inside.

"Yes," Gideon whispered. "Touch me."

In a very deliberate move Charles slid his arms around Gideon's chest, under his arms. Gideon was forced to lift his crutches from the ground, and after a moment's hesitation he let them fall to the floor. He wrapped his arms around Charles' neck tightly. "I'm not sure—"Charles didn't let him finish. He leaned in and kissed Gideon again, harder this time. When Gideon didn't respond he traced the seam of his lips with his tongue. Gideon inhaled sharply and then to Charles' utter gratification he opened his mouth and let him inside.

Charles didn't know whether to shout for joy or cry as Gideon filled his senses. To finally be able to touch, to taste, to hold him as he'd been wanting to for so long. He smelled like Gideon, of course, that French scent by Pinaud and horse. With a sense of wonder Charles realized something was missing. Sarah's scent of lavender, which normally clung to Gideon. He missed it.

Charles was tempted to devour Gideon, to shove him down and take all he could before Gideon pushed him away. But he forced himself to go slow, to savor this moment. He pressed his tongue into Gideon's willing mouth and swept it through the warm, wet cavern. He tasted so good, so unique. Charles knew that he would never be able to describe it in words but he would never forget it and always crave the flavor of Gideon. He turned his head slightly and the rough scratch of Gideon's cheek against his caused a shiver of awareness to skitter down his spine. All those years ago they had not kissed. He had never kissed a man, never felt that rough caress.

Gideon moaned and slid a hand into the hair on the back of Charles' head, gripping him and holding him tightly against his seeking, hungry mouth as Gideon's tongue tangled with his. Charles lost his restraint. The kiss turned hard and desperate, as if they both sought to make up for lost time. It became a delicious battle for control that Charles wasn't sure he wanted to win. But the contest itself was glorious. He had never been kissed in such an almost violent, thorough fashion. Holding Gideon so tightly he wasn't sure where he stopped and the other man started, Charles tried to take a step toward the bed. Gideon stumbled and suddenly they were falling. Charles caught them both with a hand on the edge of the bed, Gideon clinging to him.

They were both breathing hard, and the look in Gideon's eyes was hot and challenging. It sent a thrill straight to Charles' cock.

"What now?" Gideon rasped. The challenge was there in his voice too.

"More touching," Charles told him as he dropped Gideon on the mattress. Gideon caught himself this time and pulled himself up until he was sitting on the edge of the bed. "And tasting." At that Gideon's head snapped up and he grinned in response to the look Charles was giving him.

Charles shoved Gideon onto his back and proceeded to take his boot off. At the same time Gideon eagerly began to undo the fall of his trousers. He had barely finished before Charles was yanking them down and off. He threw them aside as he gave an admiring look to Gideon's cock. It was heavy and full, the tip wet. He wanted to taste that.

Charles dropped to his knees between Gideon's legs and Gideon sat up. Charles gazed at his mangled leg. And it was mangled. Gideon had hardly let him see it in the last few years. He'd forgotten how bad it was. Burn scars much worse than those on his face covered half his thigh, and the end was rough and uneven. Charles felt a stab of regret at his hasty amputation. He hadn't been thinking about how it would look when he'd done it. He hadn't really been thinking at all. His breathing hitched and his eyes blurred as he ruthlessly tamped down the memories. "I'm sorry," he whispered. He ran his hand along Gideon's thigh and kissed the rough skin there.

"No." Gideon put his fist beneath Charles' chin and raised his face to meet his eyes. "I'm sorry. I'm sorry you had to do that. I'm sorry I put you in that position. I wish it had not been you. I would not have you remember that."

"I think we have all said I'm sorry enough." Sarah's voice was crisp, a definite contrast to the whispered conversation of the two men. "No more talking. Get on with the touching and tasting."

Charles chuckled and Gideon laughed outright. "My wife is, as usual, correct. And I heartily approve of her suggestion."

As he moved in to take Gideon in his mouth, Charles hesitated. He'd never done this. He'd let Gideon fuck him, had truly enjoyed it. But that had been fast and furious, a rough pleasure lost in the haze of shock and desperation. This experience was so far removed from that the two were not even comparable. Then Gideon's hand was in his hair again, pulling him forward, and it seemed the most natural thing in the world to open his mouth and take him in. The heat of his shaft surprised a moan from Charles. It felt good in his mouth. The skin of Gideon's cock was so soft it was like silk on his tongue. It was the sweetest thing he'd ever tasted next to Sarah. He wrapped his lips around it, sucked it in and swirled his tongue up and down.

"Dammit," Gideon ground out. His hand tightened in Charles' hair. Charles glanced up to see Gideon watching him. He sucked a little harder and Gideon's eyes closed and his head fell back as he moaned.

Charles loved Gideon's cock with his mouth the same way he'd eaten Sarah. With slow deliberation, letting Gideon's reactions guide him. He quickly learned that Gideon liked it a little rough. Didn't they all? The thought made Charles smile around the thick rod filling his mouth.

"What?" Sarah asked quietly.

Her voice startled Charles. He'd known she was there, of course, but suddenly he felt awkward, as if he were leaving her out. He pulled away, fighting Gideon's hold.

"What made you smile?" Sarah asked him with a seductive grin.

"I was thinking that we all like it a little rough," Charles answered honestly. The gravel in his voice was a shock. Was it from having Gideon in there? He shivered a little at the thought. He tipped his head and rubbed his cheek against the soft skin on the side of Gideon's cock.

"Christ," Gideon gasped. He doubled over as if in pain, but Charles knew it was pleasure. He liked the sensation of Charles' beard rubbing on his cock. Charles felt his own prick jerk in sympathy. He wanted to feel it too. But one thing at a time.

"He does," Sarah answered. "He likes you to suck hard, to take him deep."

Discussing this with Sarah drove Charles arousal higher. He hadn't considered this. He hadn't thought about the pleasure of sharing these things with Sarah.

"Do you like watching?" Gideon asked her breathlessly. "As much as I do?" When he added the last, Charles wrapped a fist around his cock and squeezed. He nearly came at the feel of his own saliva there, slick under his hand. Gideon groaned and thrust into his grip.

"Yes," Sarah answered. She sounded as aroused as they were. "I like when you both watch as the other one pleasures me. But I find I like to watch you please each other just as much. To see you kiss and do this."

"Do you like this? You've always seemed to enjoy our cocks in your mouth." Charles kept talking with Sarah partly because he could feel how hard Gideon was becoming at their conversation. He liked it. He liked to hear them talk about pleasuring him. His hips jerked and a drop of liquid spilled from the slit in the dark pink head of his cock.

"I do." Sarah's answer was spoken quietly. He could hear the truth of it not just in her words but also in her voice.

"Join me." Charles wasn't sure what made him say it. He'd thought this would be his moment with Gideon. But he wanted more. He wanted Sarah here. He wanted to taste her, kiss her, with Gideon's cock between them.

Gideon fell back completely on the bed, his hands rammed in his hair. "God, yes." His voice was desperate. "To have you both... That would be... God..." He seemed incapable of speech then.

Charles laughed. This was perfect. Suddenly the possibilities were endless. He waited but Sarah didn't move. Finally he looked at her, a question in his expression.

She sighed and smoothed her skirts. "That's sweet, really it is, that you want to include me. But I know that this is your time. You've both waited so long, and I don't want to intrude upon it. Perhaps I should leave altogether?" The last was a hesitant question and Charles knew she was hoping the answer would be no, as he had hoped in the past.

"No." Gideon's response was immediate and harsh. "I told you I wanted you. I want you both. Here. Like this. On your knees in front of me."

"Gideon," Sarah began in shocked protest, but Charles didn't let her finish.

"We both want you. We always want you. Do you want one more than the other? If I had walked in the other day before you and Gideon were done, would you have wanted me to join you?"

Sarah blinked rapidly as she thought about his question. "Yes." Her answer was simple and straightforward, just as he'd expected it would be. "I wanted you to join us when we were done too." She smiled wryly. "I am very selfish, aren't I? I want you both loving me all the time."

"That's how we feel too, Sarah." He stripped all pretenses away, hoping she would see the truth in his face. He had never felt so vulnerable. He had never wanted to. But today was the day for it, wasn't it?

Chapter Seventeen

ജ

When Sarah took a step toward Gideon and Charles, she saw Gideon grab a fistful of blanket. It was the only sign of his agitation. He wore a fiercer scowl than usual. Perhaps he always looked like that when he was terribly aroused. Sarah couldn't be sure. They usually did this in the dark.

His eyes were locked on her and she suddenly saw his jaw flex and a muscle in his good cheek twitched. She looked down and Charles had leaned over to lick a shiny drop of Gideon's fluid from the soft head of his cock. Sarah loved to lick them both there. It was soft and salty on her tongue and drove them mad. To see Charles doing it to Gideon made Sarah's heart race, and her sex swelled and throbbed until she thought just the act of walking over to them would cause her to climax.

She dropped to her knees in front of Gideon. "Is this what you want?" she asked. She thought perhaps he liked that, the talking. She was still learning about him. She knew from their last time together that Gideon had held back with her. She didn't want him to hold back. She wanted him to be free with her, to do what he wanted, what pleased him. Watching him as he enjoyed their physical intimacies gave her as much pleasure as the acts. She wanted to see him out of control. She had a feeling today would push him to that extreme.

"Yes," he growled. How she loved his voice. It gave her shivers of desire.

"Over here," Charles murmured. He gently moved Sarah to Gideon's right. He placed the back of Gideon's left thigh against his shoulder and she watched in amazement as Gideon shuddered on the bed and his cock jerked and leaked some more. He truly loved this. She wondered how long he would last. Charles reached around her and maneuvered Gideon's right leg so that his foot rested on the ledge of the bed beneath the mattress, his leg turned out. He was fully exposed. She'd never seen him like this. His crotch was a nest of tight, dark curls, his sac heavy and full hanging down beneath the rigid length of his cock. His right thigh was thick with muscles, his left was thinner, weaker. She had almost cried when Charles kissed that leg.

She couldn't wait anymore. She placed a hand on Gideon's trembling right thigh and leaned over to lick a path from his root to his tip. Her tongue traced a heavy vein there and Gideon groaned as if he were dying.

"Closer," he whispered. He reached out blindly and Sarah scooted closer, until she was pressed to Charles' side, Gideon's cock a standard between their faces. Gideon latched on to her hair and pulled her in, and from the corner of her eye she could see him do the same to Charles. Charles smiled and then he followed her lead, licking Gideon on the other side. On his next pass Sarah joined him, so that her tongue actually met Charles' as they swirled them around the shaft. Gideon made a noise halfway between a sob and a shout. Sarah cupped his sac and rubbed the stones inside with her thumb and Gideon cried out again. "I'm not going to last," he gasped. Sarah knew he spoke the truth. She'd done this to him enough times to recognize the signs of his impending orgasm.

"Good," Charles said, his voice dark with satisfaction. "I don't want you to. Not this time. I want to taste it—taste you."

Sarah sucked the side of Gideon's cock as Charles engulfed the head in his mouth. Gideon was gasping for air, his hips thrusting. With a kiss to Charles' cheek Sarah pulled away, her hand still massaging Gideon's sac. Gideon grabbed Charles' head with both hands and pulled him down.

"Yes," Sarah whispered, amazed at her boldness but gratified at Gideon and Charles' ardent response. They both groaned and Charles moved his head up and down in counterpoint to Gideon's hips. Sarah laid her cheek against Gideon's thigh to watch her two men love each other and Gideon stilled, letting Charles do the work. She was more aroused than she'd ever been. How could that be? Neither man had touched her in passion, not really. Yet she felt as if she might explode with Gideon at any second.

"Charles," Gideon groaned and Sarah moaned at the sound of the other man's name on Gideon's lips. She hadn't realized until this moment how much she wanted this. How much she wanted them to feel for each other what she felt for them. She wanted them to want each other. She wanted them all to be able to do anything—everything—when they were together this way. Without thought Sarah turned and bit down on Gideon's thigh, so full of emotion and desire she couldn't stand it. Her hands were trembling, her sex was clenching and suddenly Gideon was coming.

"Charles!" he shouted. He curled up from the bed, holding Charles' face pressed to him, his cock buried in Charles' mouth. Charles coughed but he reached out and gripped Gideon's hip when Gideon tried to push him away. Sarah watched in wonder as Charles' throat moved, swallowing Gideon's release. Gideon whimpered, his body locked in place, his chest heaving as he came and came. Sarah clutched his good leg, pressed her breasts against it and ached for her own release.

When Gideon was done he collapsed on the bed, his cock pulling from Charles' mouth. Charles gasped and fell back to sit on his heels, his hands on his thighs. He was panting and his hair was plastered to the sides of his head with sweat. Sarah ran her fingers lightly through his damp hair. He turned and gave her a half-smile, a sensual quirk of his lips that made her hold her breath, waiting and wondering what he planned to do next.

Charles stood up and made a great show of unbuttoning his trousers. He glanced at Sarah. "Do you mind?" he asked. She thought she understood what he was asking. She shook her head with a smile. "Good," Charles replied. Then he climbed on the bed and straddled Gideon.

"And what am I supposed to do with that?" Gideon asked drily as Charles situated himself so that his cock was poised right over Gideon's mouth.

"You are supposed to want it." Charles' answer was very quiet and what had started out playful became quite serious.

When Gideon didn't say anything Charles began to pull back but Gideon stopped him with a hand wrapped around his bottom. Without a word Gideon rose onto his elbows and took Charles in his mouth. Charles gasped and gripped Gideon's shoulder so hard Sarah could see the tips of his fingers turn white with the force of his hold.

"Gideon," Charles said with an uneven sigh. His hips moved languorously as he fucked in and out of Gideon's mouth. Gideon was awkward and uncharacteristically passive. It took Charles a moment to notice but Sarah saw right away that Gideon didn't know what to do.

"For heaven's sake, Gideon," she said with exasperation, "it isn't complicated mathematics. You simply need to suck it."

Charles burst out laughing as Gideon raised his eyebrow at her. Charles stopped laughing abruptly when Gideon sucked hard enough to pull his cheeks in.

"More," Charles said, groaning as his hips flexed.

Sarah clambered onto the bed, her skirts twisting and impeding her movement. Through the haze of his desire Charles reached out a hand to help her up. When she took it he suddenly squeezed tight enough to hurt her a little. She gasped and her head jerked up. Gideon had slipped his hand between Charles' legs and his mouth rested at the very base of Charles' cock, completely engulfing his length.

As soon as she was on the bed Charles let go of her and put his fist down to support him. He was breathing raggedly as Gideon slid down and then back up his cock. Instead of grabbing Gideon and fucking him as she was sure he wanted to do, as he had done to her in the past, he ran a shaking hand through Gideon's short hair.

"I'm not going to last, Gideon," he said softly. "When you take me like that, you have to know…" His voice trailed off and he bit his lip.

Gideon let Charles slip from his mouth. "I know." He lay back and ran his hands up the back of Charles thighs. "Come fuck my mouth, then, like this. I want to take you, Charles."

Sarah sat right next to them, her skirts bunched around her, fascinated by the play between them. Gideon was rougher with Charles than with her, while Charles seemed to be afraid of being too rough. He hesitated even after Gideon issued the invitation. "He means it, Charles. You must stop worrying. You won't break him. You haven't broken me yet, have you? And didn't you just say we all liked it a little rough?"

Gideon jerked on Charles' thighs and Charles fell forward. He leaned over Gideon, dominating him, his hard cock inches from Gideon's mouth. "She's right. I like it rough. Fuck me." Gideon never thought he'd say those words to another man. Not even Charles. And he wouldn't have, not even a year ago. Before Sarah he had felt too weak. If he'd been the one taking Charles he would have been crippled by doubts about his manhood. Sarah left no room for doubt. She wanted him, he pleased her, he satisfied her in bed and she begged for more. She had made him man enough to take Charles like this without worry.

"I'm the same man who threw you down and fucked you in those woods, Charles," he whispered. "I can take it as well as I can give it."

It must have been the right thing to say. With a growl Charles thrust against Gideon's mouth, demanding entrance. Gideon obliged. It was strange, the taste and feel of Charles in his mouth. But he liked it. He liked the salty tang of him and the velvet softness of his cock as he ran his tongue along the vein pulsing there. It was different and yet not. It was Charles. And he could admit this was what he wanted. He wanted to take and be taken by this man.

Charles gave him no quarter, and he wanted none. When Charles fucked in and out of his mouth he reveled in it. Charles was rough and hard on him, forcing him to take his cock deeper with each thrust. Gideon sucked him down and demanded more. He had longed for this from Charles, to be treated as an equal, a man, a lover, not an invalid or a shell of his former self. He wanted Charles to remember him not as the broken man on the battlements who had begged and screamed, but the man who could do this to him.

Gideon dug his fingers into the flexing muscles of Charles bottom, loving the hard feel of him beneath his hands. For years he'd wanted the freedom to explore Charles' hard, muscled body with his hands and mouth. He would do it today. He would roll around on this bed with Charles and Sarah until he had his fill of them or collapsed from exhaustion.

"God, yes, Gideon," Charles rasped. "Take it, suck me like that."

At his words Gideon sucked harder. His own cock was filling again. Charles knew how to drive him mad, how to arouse him. Gideon had suppressed his desires for too long. Now the words alone were almost enough to push him over the edge. Charles continued to fuck his mouth, growing rougher by the second. And then he was pushing inside as the hot, salty taste of his release washed over Gideon's tongue, filling his mouth, spilling from his lips. He swallowed hungrily and gripped Charles harder, holding him in his mouth until the last drop of his climax fell to Gideon's tongue.

Charles was unsteady as he backed down Gideon's body until he could lie next to him. Without a word he leaned over and kissed Gideon. They tasted like semen, both of them. Gideon could taste himself in Charles' mouth, and when Charles licked the corner of his mouth Gideon knew he was licking his own semen from Gideon's lips. His stomach clenched in need at the carnality of it.

"Sarah." His voice was rough from the mouth fuck he'd just received. He smiled. He liked it.

"Gideon?" Sarah sounded desperate. He understood. When he watched her and Charles fuck he became desperate too.

"I want to fuck you now." He looked between her and Charles. "I'm hard as a pike again from sucking him."

Sarah laughed. "Well, that's convenient, then."

Gideon crawled over Charles who laughed and nipped his hip as he went past. "I'll join you two as soon as I recover. I think Gideon may have sucked my spleen out." He tried to untie his cravat with fumbling fingers. "And by then perhaps we'll all be ready to undress for the occasion."

Gideon dragged himself over Sarah as she lay down laughing. He shoved her skirts to her waist and without preamble slid inside her hot, wet sheath. He shuddered at how perfect she felt wrapped around him. She gasped and her legs went around his waist, pulling him deeper moments before she burst into climax. She moaned and trembled in his arms, and he drove into her again and again as she continued to climax.

"Sarah," he said again. She nodded as her walls pulsed around him. She understood that this was perfect. He kissed her temple as she sighed tremulously. Sarah always understood.

* * * * *

A few weeks later Sarah had her first inkling of unease. The night before Charles had asked yet again if she and Gideon would prefer he not come inside her in order to prevent his getting her with child. They had both vehemently denied having any worry about Sarah's bearing Charles' child. She believed Gideon when he said he would claim it and raise it as his own so no stigma would attach to the child. But his answer had not satisfied Charles, she could tell.

The next morning when she walked into the breakfast room she kissed Gideon's cheek and smiled at Charles. He did not smile back. She couldn't go to him or ask him what was wrong because Anders was in the room with them. They had not eaten silently for quite some time. This morning they did so. It was painful for Sarah, as if the last few weeks of happiness had never happened.

"I wish to have a dinner party."

Gideon's announcement startled Sarah and her teacup made an audible clink as she abruptly set it back down in the saucer.

"What?" she asked.

"Why?" Charles asked at the same time, a scowl on his face.

Gideon seemed unperturbed by their less than enthusiastic responses. He waved Anders away. "Leave us."

Anders immediately bowed politely and left, closing the door behind him. He had become very good at rapid exits in the last few weeks. Sarah often wondered if he knew what was going on. It was hard to keep secrets from family retainers, after all.

"It is high time we entertained," Gideon continued blithely. "Sarah and I have been married for almost two months. I know that Anne and her two will be wearing themselves ragged at this point, their rabid curiosity over our marriage driving them insane. Freddy and Brett are as bad as Anne with their managing ways and uninvited advice." He shared a smile between Sarah and Charles. "So we shall assuage their curiosity and soothe their fears with a glimpse of our blissful married existence."

Sarah's look was doubtful. Gideon cocked his head inquiringly. "Are we not blissful?"

Her look turned exasperated and she tapped the back of his hand. "Of course we are. Bliss follows me around like a devoted puppy." Gideon laughed. Charles did not. Sarah turned worried eyes to him. "Charles? Are we not blissful?"

Charles sighed. "I didn't consider what this would mean for you, Sarah."

"What do you mean? Inviting people over? It is hardly something I have longed to do, let me assure you."

Charles rested his arms on the table and twirled his table knife between his hands. "No. I mean people knowing. About us."

Sarah was taken aback. "I hadn't planned on announcing it at dinner. Were you?"

Gideon chuckled, but Charles' frown was fierce. "This is not a joke. You know that people will figure out we are all lovers. It is in every look we share, the way we touch. Anders knows."

"How do you know?" Sarah was aghast, although she had suspected.

"You see?" Charles said, waving his hand at her. "You do not want them to know." He moved his hand in a circular motion. "This is not normal and is certainly not approved of."

"I gave you the choice of normal. You denied wanting normal, very forcefully if I remember correctly." Gideon had turned cool again, his voice sharp and cutting.

"Perhaps I was wrong."

At Charles' response Sarah's hand involuntarily went to her heart. He was thinking about leaving. She couldn't breathe for a moment.

Charles shook his head. "No, I wasn't. I'm sorry. I don't want normal. I want this. But perhaps that's wrong of me. They will hurt Sarah, ostracize her."

"Who? Anne? Freddy? Brett?" Gideon scoffed. "Think, Charles. They have no room to criticize since they have the same sort of relationship we do. I hardly think they will have the temerity to cast stones."

"No. But others will. I could not stand it if my presence here caused either of you trouble."

Sarah rose and went to Charles, pulling out the chair next to him and sitting down facing him. "I'm sorry. My initial reaction was a negative one. But I do not care. Let them scorn me." She took Charles' hand in both of hers. "I care about us three, and only us. I am happier than I have ever been, Charles. You both make me so happy I feel as if I'm living in a dream. Here at the farm we needn't worry about what others think."

"One day we will leave the farm, Sarah," Charles told her. "We will go to London or some other place, where strangers will judge you harshly for our relationship."

"London?" Sarah laughed to cover her unease. "What use have I for London?" She shook her head. "I would not like to be the object of pity or, worse, aversion because of my mark, Charles. No, for many reasons I will not go to London."

Now Gideon was scowling. "Your birthmark is not hideous, Sarah. It is hardly noticeable when one knows you."

She smiled wryly at Gideon. "I could say the same of your scars."

Gideon waved aside her observation dismissively. "Nonsense, they are in no way comparable. You are a beautiful woman, and a small discoloration on your cheek cannot change the configuration of your features or the voluptuous curves of your form."

Sarah was overwhelmed. "Gideon...I...I don't know what to say. No one has ever said something like that to me before."

"He is right." Charles placed his hand over hers. "You are beautiful. I told you that on your wedding night."

"Our wedding night." Gideon spoke quietly but with an intensity that said more than his words. "I knew that night. I knew then that we would all be together like this. At least, I knew that's what I wanted." He took a deep breath and his voice and posture were relaxed when he continued. "I want them to know. I want the world to know."

"Yes, but..." Sarah couldn't voice it. She loved Charles, truly, but could she handle the consequences of their arrangement?

"I know," Gideon said rather sadly. He sat back in his chair, his shoulders drooping. "I can't tell them. But surely letting our friends know of our happiness is not dangerous to Sarah's reputation?"

"What of yours?" Charles asked, as dejected as Gideon. "I know the last few weeks I have not done a very good job of hiding my feelings for you either. I grin like a fool when you're around, and Lord knows that has not been the case for the last several years."

"Look at us," Sarah said sharply. "What a sorry lot we are." She stood up and brushed out her skirts. "Of course we shall have our acquaintances to dinner. I dare any of them to cast a disparaging eye on us." She made a fist and stuck her thumb out, swinging her arm like a pugilist. "I shall poke them in the eye if they try."

Charles leaned forward and rested his cheek on his fist with a silly grin as he watched her.

Gideon laughed outright. "Ah, Sarah. What would we do without you to defend us?"

Chapter Eighteen

ഇ

"How are you this evening, Mr. Haversham?"

Sarah was extremely nervous. She hadn't seen the Duke and Duchess of Ashland and Mr. Haversham since the wedding day. The knowledge that the three were lovers like her and Gideon and Charles did not quell her unease. She simply was not good around people. Perhaps eventually she would grow accustomed to them. Presumably she would be seeing a great deal of them since they spent most of their time at the ducal seat at Ashton Park. And from what the duke said, with the birth of their child the time they spent in the country would increase. Gideon had drily noted that their absence from Blakely Farm for the past two months was the longest he had been relieved of their company since his arrival in Ashton on the Green. Sarah had tried to hush him, but the duchess, Anne, had only laughed and assured him that she would resume her frequent visits if he continued to be so entertaining.

The vicar, Mr. Matthews, was also here. Gideon and Charles had told her he knew of the relationship between the ducal couple and Mr. Haversham. There was something about Mr. Matthews that set her at ease. She feared him far less than the others.

The presence of near strangers in what she now thought of as her home did indeed overset her nerves a little. But it was this conversation with Mr. Haversham that had her shaking with trepidation. She'd planned what she wanted to say very carefully over the last week, since the invitations had been sent and accepted. Now she could hardly think of the speech she had prepared.

"I am quite well, Mrs. North, thank you," he answered politely. "And you? Married life seems to agree with you. Even married life with North." He raised his brow and smiled, and the twinkle in his eye took the sting from his remark.

Sarah gave him a mock reprimanding look. "Do you not like my husband, Mr. Haversham?"

He laughed. "Much more tonight than before." He looked around the drawing room, which Sarah had redone in Chinese red and light blue, a mixture of the masculine and feminine, which had pleased her very much. "You have changed things here."

"Do you like it?" she asked. She'd been a little nervous about that too. She'd redecorated without any real knowledge of how to proceed. Mr. Howard at the store in the village had gone through pattern books with her and ordered what she needed, but his was the only advice she had sought. The house was very much hers now, her stamp on every room. There was still some work to be done, but she was pleased with the outcome so far. She hoped it wasn't too ordinary or plebeian for Gideon's friends' tastes.

Mr. Haversham smiled warmly. "I like the room very much. But that wasn't what I was referring to."

He set his glass of wine down on the table beside him and turned a gimlet-eyed gaze on her. They stood in the corner of the room, set apart from the others who sat in the center of the room conversing. Sarah had deliberately led Mr. Haversham over here. She did not want anyone else to hear them. She blushed now at his scrutiny.

"I am assuming you did not separate me from the crowd to discover my opinion of your decorating," he said. "So I am going to take a stab in the dark and suggest that you wish to talk about North."

"No." She could see her answer surprised him. "I wish to talk about Mr. Borden."

Understanding dawned in his eyes. "Ah, I see."

Now that the moment was at hand, Sarah found words escaped her. She licked her dry lips. "Actually, I would like to talk about you. If that is all right?" She glanced nervously at him from the corner of her eye and then turned her attention to the hunting print on the wall as if they were discussing it.

"By all means," Mr. Haversham said with extreme politeness. "I am always happy to have the conversation revolve around me."

Sarah couldn't stop her burst of quiet laughter. "I believe that sounds like something the duke would say, sir, rather than you."

"We spend a great deal of time together. Perhaps he has undue influence over me."

Sarah blushed as the thought of how much time the two men did spend together, and what they did with that time, lent a new meaning to his offhand remark.

Mr. Haversham chuckled quietly beside her. "Ah, I see you are aware of our relationship."

Sarah bit her lip and nodded, looking at the floor.

"Is that what you wish to talk about? My relationship with the duke and duchess?" His voice was quiet, the question spoken gently. She nodded again. "What would you like to know? I'm afraid I can't discuss too much about it. We like to maintain our privacy as much as possible, you understand. But living in such close proximity, and Anne being Anne, we will see a great deal of one another. It was inevitable that you should learn of our...situation. But why me? Wouldn't it be easier to speak to Anne?"

Sarah shook her head. "No. I need your unique perspective." She forced herself to turn and face him. "Are you happy?"

He looked puzzled. "Yes. I am content, if that is what you mean."

Sarah looked away. She was frustrated. She needed to know how Mr. Haversham felt about his role in the duke and duchess' lives. He was the third, the outsider. She feared Charles was not content in that role. Was it possible for any man to be? "Mr. Borden is…" She paused, not sure how much to reveal to this virtual stranger. "I cannot show affection for him. I believe he is hurt by it. I know I am. But what are we to do?" She sighed tremulously and turned back to see him watching her with sympathy. "Are you happy?" she asked again.

"Yes." This time his answer was firm and unequivocal. "I could not be happier. That is what you really want to know, isn't it? If I would be happier in a more traditional relationship? If I wish I was married with a house and family of my own?" Sarah nodded. "The answer is no." He shook his head. "No, the answer is I have a house and family of my own. I am married. I am married to Freddy and to Anne, and Ashton Park is my home. They are my family. This child is mine. I am far happier in this life than I could ever be with someone else, someone I did not love as I love Anne and Freddy. Perhaps my life might be easier, but no, Mrs. North, it would not be better."

Sarah blinked rapidly, her eyes filling with tears. Mr. Haversham gallantly handed over his handkerchief and she wiped at her cheeks. "I needed to hear that," she whispered.

"Then you need to ask Charles, because he is the one you should hear it from." Mr. Haversham spoke kindly but firmly. "We have all known for quite a long time that he and North were entangled. Anne worried endlessly about this marriage. She shall be extremely relieved to hear she can stop worrying." Sarah gave a watery chuckle as she sniffed. "I know that Borden feels as I do, Mrs. North. He made his choices long ago. That his choices have led to a happiness few men find in their lifetime is a joy to him, I am sure, as it is to me."

"But…are there not times when you long for more?" she asked quietly, twisting the handkerchief she held. "I see Charles' face when Gideon and I are affectionate in public. I know he feels hurt, left out."

"When you are with us, Mrs. North, you may show affection to whomever you wish." Mr. Haversham smiled and his good humor was irresistible. "And you may trust that we shall do the same." He sobered slightly. "Yes, there are times when the constraints of society are onerous for us. When I want to proclaim that they are mine and I am theirs. But as I said, we all made a choice and we live with the consequences. We understand that. It does not make me feel as if I mean less to them. Rather, my silence and my discretion are just one more way I show my devotion to them and I take care of them."

"Sarah?" Charles' voice coming directly over her shoulder startled her and she jumped guiltily. "Are you all right?"

Sarah realized the rest of the room had gone quiet and she turned to see Gideon standing with his crutches watching them, the duke and duchess turned on the settee and giving Mr. Haversham identical inquiring looks.

"I'm fine," she rushed to assure them. "Mr. Haversham simply said something that made me very happy. I'm afraid I'm being overly emotional. I was quite nervous, you know, about this evening." She forced herself to stop babbling. Then she did something that took every ounce of courage she possessed. She leaned forward and kissed Charles lightly on the lips, in front of everyone. "Thank you, Charles, for coming to my rescue. But I am only being a ninny."

Charles was too shocked to respond. His eyes were wide as saucers and he looked around as he took a step back. Sarah followed him and slid her hand around his arm.

"What did you say to my wife, Haversham?" Gideon drawled. "That you have to leave early?"

Anne's trill of laughter broke the tension. "Oh, Gideon, you are endlessly amusing. Really, you are. You have missed us, admit it." She stepped over next to Gideon and reached back for the duke's arm. They turned toward the door to head into the dining room. "If we did not come to visit, who would you sharpen your tongue on if not my poor men?"

"Poor indeed," Gideon murmured loud enough for all to hear. "When you and the duke are visiting I shall curb my considerable wit." He glanced over his shoulder. "Haversham can hold the horses on the ducal carriage while we make our bows in order to protect his delicate sensibilities."

"You try to wound me, North," Mr. Haversham said with a wink at Sarah. He offered her his arm so that she walked with a very quiet Charles on one side and Mr. Haversham on the other, mimicking Gideon, Anne and the duke ahead of them. "If I were not so secure in my place, I would tremble at your censure." He peeked around Sarah to look at Charles. "But the stones you throw no longer crush me, since you have proven to be more man and less paragon of suffering virtue."

"More man than you?" Gideon rejoined as he let Anne and the duke precede him into the dining room. "That hardly requires a Herculean effort."

"I wouldn't be so sure about that," the duke drawled as he passed Gideon. "You haven't slept in his sheets."

"Frederick Thorne," Anne chided in a shocked voice. "You shall upset Mrs. North."

"What about the vicar?" Mr. Matthews said with a grin. "Isn't anyone worried about upsetting the vicar?" He looked at the two groups of three. "I feel like the proverbial leper."

Mr. Haversham stuck out his other elbow and Mr. Matthews locked arms with him as he laughed.

"Don't read anything into it," Mr. Haversham told him with a disdainful look.

"In this company?" Mr. Matthews replied. "I fear for my virtue."

Anne's laughter drifted out the dining room door as Sarah blushed and laughed at the same time.

The clink of silverware against china was subdued, the candles burning in the candelabrum in the middle of the table casting artful shadows around the room. The conversation had been light throughout dinner, for which Gideon was grateful. He had not liked seeing Sarah upset earlier. He'd wanted to hit Haversham, but he knew it was irrational. He knew Sarah had initiated the conversation, and he had some idea of what it had been about. But all parties seemed to be over the tension that had momentarily gripped them and even Charles had smiled and laughed a time or two.

Like Sarah, Gideon was worried about Charles. He'd thought that once they became lovers Charles would be happy. He wasn't. Why? He claimed he was worried about Sarah. Gideon believed that was part of the reason for his discontent. He wondered if he was the other part. He had clearly failed to live up to Charles' expectations, as usual. He sighed inwardly. He didn't know what else to do. He didn't think Charles' feelings for him or Sarah had changed. Charles was the very soul of loyalty and fidelity. But Gideon's affections had not been enough to make up for the daily evidence of the sacrifices Charles had made for him. Every time Charles looked at him he must be thrown back into the war and that horrific night at Badajoz.

"I met a man in London recently, Mrs. North, who might interest you," Mr. Matthews said. "A doctor. He claims to be able to remove marks such as yours through a revolutionary new treatment."

Charles slammed his fork down on his plate. "What?" Anger made the word more bark than anything else.

Mr. Matthews was taken aback by Charles' anger. "I meant nothing by it, Borden. I mentioned it simply because I thought it was interesting and believed Mrs. North might as well. I meant no disrespect." He bowed in Sarah's direction.

Gideon could feel his scowl tightening the skin on his cheeks and nose and forehead. "My wife is not in need of such a doctor," he said coldly.

"Gideon, Charles," Sarah said mildly. She smiled at Mr. Matthews. "No offense taken, sir. There have been charlatans making such claims for as long as I can remember. It is impossible, I assure you."

Gideon couldn't believe how calm she was. She was so aware of her mark, so afraid of what everyone thought. How could Matthews bring it up like that at dinner?

Sarah took a sip of her wine and then set the glass down. She motioned for everyone to continue eating. "I wonder, Mr. Matthews, how did this doctor claim to perform such a miracle?"

She was blushing. Her calm demeanor was a mask. Gideon almost cursed out loud. He looked at Charles and he seemed as angry as Gideon.

"It doesn't matter how," Charles ground out. "It is foolishness. Sarah does not need to remove the mark. She is beautiful as she is."

"Of course she is," Anne replied, as calm as Sarah. "But what if it's true? Would you do it?"

All eyes turned to Sarah. She was painfully red and Gideon could see her clutching her napkin in a white-knuckled fist.

"I would forbid it," Gideon declared. "I'll not have her risking her health for such a stupid thing. Her birthmark? It is hardly noticeable! How dare you even bring it up."

"Gideon, please, you insult the duchess with your tone," Sarah said quietly. "She is your friend, as are all our guests. They meant no harm."

Anne looked on the verge of tears. "I'm so sorry, Sarah! I assumed that you would be used to people asking about it. I did not mean to ruin your evening. Truly. I agree with North and Borden. You are beautiful. You have no need of such treatment. Forgive me."

There were murmurs of assent around the table, but they did not soothe Gideon's anger.

Sarah smiled kindly at Anne and her color faded. "I know, Your Grace. I am not offended. And yes, many people ask about the mark. But it does not make me immune to self-consciousness."

"Then let us not speak of it again," Ashland said graciously. "We would not make our hostess uncomfortable. It is not well done of a guest."

Mr. Matthews was now blushing a crimson red. "I'm sorry, ma'am. I should take my leave."

Sarah rolled her eyes in exasperation and Gideon relaxed. "Nonsense, Mr. Matthews. It is of interest to me, you were right. As I said, I have had many people ask, and several doctors have claimed to be able to cure me of it. A curious choice of words, I always thought. It is not a disease that weakens me. It is as much a part of me as my arm or my leg, and I certainly do not wish to be cured of those. Do I, Gideon?"

He smiled proudly at her. She was turning the tables to put her guests at ease again. "No, my dear. I do not recommend the cure for leg."

Haversham laughed. "No, I must agree with you there, North, as much as it pains me. The cure for leg is definitely worse than what may ail you."

Charles did not laugh. His face was grim. "I am thankful, Sarah, that your father did not give any credence to these doctors."

Sarah looked surprised. "Oh, but he did. When I was very young one of them tried to cure me with a noxious draught that made me violently ill. They feared I would not survive the cure. They dared not risk such treatment again. Though when I was younger I begged them to."

"Why?" Ashland asked. He truly seemed puzzled. But he wouldn't have any idea, would he? He was gorgeous, even Gideon could see that. His life was a charmed one. He'd never had people turn away at the sight of him—spurn him because of a disfigurement. Yes, Haversham had been injured in the war, but he'd kept his leg. He had nothing more than a limp. And whatever scars he bore were out of sight. Gideon felt a surge of irrational anger at Ashland's perfection and his intrusive question.

Sarah just laughed. "I was a young girl with no suitors. Perhaps present company does not see my mark as a disfigurement," at her statement she smiled and nodded in appreciation to those around the table and they nodded back congenially, "but offers were not forthcoming prior to Gideon."

"I'm sorry, Mrs. North." Ashland's contrition was genuine. "I didn't realize. I must say that the gentlemen of your previous acquaintance must be extraordinarily stupid." He paused a moment before asking a hesitant question. "So you would change it, then, if you could?"

Sarah shook her head. "No, not now. What difference could it possibly make now?" She gestured around them. "I have a husband, a home, I am quite content. None of these things would change were I to suddenly, magically be relieved of my birthmark." She looked between Charles and Gideon as she spoke and he felt the sincerity in her words. "The mark is a part of me, it made me who I am. It brought me here, in a roundabout way. I have no memories without it. It is all I know." She shook her head again. "No, I would not change it. And that surprises me too." She laughed wryly. "There are many times I despair of going out among strangers because the mark is the first thing they see." She tipped her head thoughtfully. "But here at the farm, and in the village, what they see first is that I am Mrs. Gideon North of Blakely Farm. What I look like matters not compared to who I am. This is a relatively new lesson, of course." She laughed again. "I seem to be the last person to grow accustomed to my birthmark."

Sarah's comments cut Gideon to the quick. That he had done this for her, made her accept herself in such a way, made her life easier on such a fundamental level, meant the world to him. He glanced at Charles. But he did have memories of his life before his own disfigurement. And so did Charles. And that was what Charles couldn't forget. Gideon was fighting a losing battle for Charles with a ghost of himself.

Chapter Nineteen

ℬ

"I contacted that London doctor, Dr. Phinneas Jones. He will be arriving here at the end of this week," Gideon announced at breakfast.

"Who?" Sarah asked, clearly confused.

Charles put down his tea as he stared at Gideon. It had been almost three weeks since the dinner party where Stephen Matthews had mentioned the doctor, but Charles remembered the conversation clearly. He knew instantly whom Gideon referred to. "Why?" He tried to keep the anger out of his tone. He had to believe that Gideon had done it for the right reasons. But dammit, Sarah didn't need the doctor. She was fine. No, better than fine—beautiful. Gideon had said so himself at dinner. And nothing since. Nothing about contacting this doctor.

Gideon was watching Charles, not Sarah. "I did not contact him for Sarah."

Charles eyes widened in disbelief. "For you?" Gideon nodded. "Dammit, Gideon," Charles burst out. He stopped when Gideon looked over at Anders, who had frozen by the sideboard.

"That will be all right now, Anders," Gideon told him. "We shall let you know when we are finished." Anders bowed blandly and left the room and Gideon turned back to Charles. "You may now continue your tirade."

"No, he may not. Not until this is explained to me." Sarah spoke firmly from across the table, looking between the two of them. "Who is Dr. Phinneas Jones?" She broke with a tremulous little sigh and reached for Gideon's hand. "And what is wrong with you, Gideon, that you need a doctor?"

Gideon let her clutch his hand. He had become blasé about Sarah's touches. He let her handle his scarred hands and face all the time without pulling away anymore. Which made his decision to contact this charlatan doctor all the more confounding.

"Dr. Jones is the man Mr. Matthews met in London who claimed he could rid people of their birthmarks, my dear." Gideon still spoke calmly. "I contacted him about my scars."

Sarah recoiled. "Gideon, you mustn't! These doctors do not know what they're doing. It's a trick, a lie." She entreated him earnestly, leaning forward on the table now. "Don't let him touch you, Gideon. He will kill you as soon as cure you. I know it."

"Sarah—" Gideon began in a placating tone.

Charles cut him off. "Listen to her. And listen to me. You are being an idiot again. We do not mind your scars, Gideon. No one does. For whom do you wish to remove them?"

"Can I not wish to remove them for myself?" Gideon inquired. "Is it not enough that I wish to be free of them?"

Sarah looked stricken. "I did not think they bothered you to that extent. Gideon, what Charles says is true. The scars do not affect me. You are Gideon, just the way you are. And I adore you." She grabbed his hand again and kissed his palm. "If removing the scars will take you away from me, I do not wish it."

"Do you not wonder what I looked like without them?" Gideon asked quietly. The question was directed at Sarah, but Charles answered.

"I know what you looked like without them. And I am your lover today with them." Charles was stricken as well. No matter what this doctor did, Gideon would not be the same no matter how much he wished to be. And it tore Charles up inside. Every day he tried to show Gideon that the man he was now was all Charles could wish for. And every day he felt as if he failed Gideon in some way.

The past was the past. The dreams came less frequently. If Gideon did this Charles was afraid it would dredge up the old memories again. He was through with them. He had moved on, into this life with Gideon and Sarah. A life he would not trade for anything—not even to have Gideon hale and hearty again. And that made Charles feel immeasurably guilty. There was a time that he would have given everything to make Gideon the man he was. But that time was past. Now they had Sarah, and what the three of them had together was better than what he and Gideon could have had alone.

"Perhaps this is not about you, Charles." Gideon spoke coolly.

"Well perhaps it should be," Charles snapped. "Perhaps it should be about me and Sarah. What does this treatment consist of?"

Gideon averted his eyes and that told Charles more than any words could. "I thought so. How ill will you be, Gideon? Is it going to kill you, as Sarah warned?"

"Don't be overly dramatic," Gideon said. "Yes, I will be ill for a time, during the treatment. It involves minuscule amounts of poison administered in a draught as well as in a cream rubbed into the scars. Not enough to kill, but enough to putrefy the skin so that it heals properly."

"Putrefy the skin?" Sarah whispered in horror. She slid her chair back from the table so quickly it toppled over as she stood, her hand over her mouth, the blood draining from her face.

Charles rose angrily and went to her side, wrapping an arm around her shoulders. She was shaking. "Look what you are doing to her!" he barked at Gideon. "Just the thought has her shaking like a leaf. Can you imagine what she will be like during the treatment? Did you think of us at all when you made this decision?"

Gideon carefully placed his napkin on the table, picked up his crutches and rose from his chair. "I thought of nothing else. You are correct, Charles, this should be about you and Sarah and it is. You both deserve some level of normalcy in our arrangement. I can provide that if I look more like a man and less like an abomination."

"Gideon, we love you just as you are. How many times must we say it before you believe it?" Sarah's voice wavered and Charles saw her bite her trembling lip. Tears filled her eyes. "We have a wonderful life. I don't want to change it. We all decided we didn't want a normal life, not what passes for normal. We want to be together, all three of us. And we're happy, aren't we?"

Gideon reached his hand out beseechingly. "We can be happier, Sarah. Charles once told me that I wanted to be more for you than I was. He was right. He is right. I want to be the man I was for both of you."

"What you want cannot be, Gideon," Charles told him in a tired voice. "Sarah told them at that dinner that she would not change her life, she would not remove her birthmark because she had all she could want and removing it would not change her life in any way. That her mark had brought us all together."

"I said it then, but it is not the way I have always felt." Sarah's voice was quiet and sad. "There was a time when I would have given anything to get rid of it." Charles turned to her only to see her staring at Gideon as if her heart were breaking. "That was when I had nothing of my own. I feel that way now because what I have is enough. Both of you and the farm are enough for me. I cannot envision being any happier than I am right now."

"Then this has to be enough, Gideon. It is enough for Sarah and me. Why can't it be enough for you?" What he really wanted to ask was why he couldn't be enough. He had never been enough for Gideon.

Gideon's face hardened. "You say that but you don't mean it. You know, Charles, you know what I was like before. How can you say the man before you now is enough?" He gave Charles no time to answer. "I am happy with the two of you, happier than I ever thought I would be, after the war. But we can be happier still. If I remove the scars, all the unhappiness associated with them will be gone too."

"I have no unhappiness associated with them." Sarah's voice was gaining strength again. "I have never known you any differently than you are now." She reached down and straightened her chair with Charles' help. When it was upright she held on to the back tightly. "If you did not have your scars would you have married me? If you were the man you were before?"

Gideon hesitated a moment and Charles wanted to strangle him. "Yes, I would have," he finally answered. "But the chances of our meeting in those circumstances would have been very slim. I was planning on a life with Charles."

"With no wife," Sarah added woodenly. "And now you are stuck with one."

"Don't be ridiculous," Gideon snapped. "I would have fallen in love with you then as I have now. I do not want to change what we have, Sarah. I only want to change what I am, what I look like. Why is that so wrong?"

Sarah sat back down wearily. "It is not wrong, Gideon. I'm sorry. I just..." She shook her head. "I will support you whatever you do, you know that."

Charles stared at her aghast. "What are you saying? You'll sit by and blithely watch him throw his life away on an impossible dream? You know it won't work! And if it does, it won't matter." He turned to glare at Gideon. "Do you hear me? It won't matter. It doesn't matter what you look like to me." He stalked over to Gideon and nearly overset him when he grabbed his shoulders and kissed him. The first time he'd kissed him anywhere but in the privacy of the bedroom. Gideon kissed him back, reaching around and clutching a fistful of his jacket as he let Charles ravage his mouth. Gideon moaned when Charles pulled back. "I want you, scars and all. I want you because of who you are, not what you look like."

Gideon laughed wryly and shoved him away. "You can say that because you're perfect, Charles. You're strong and virile and handsome. You are the honey to the bee. But for the rest of us, we are what we look like. It affects everything we do and the way the world perceives us." He cast a baleful eye on Charles. "You said it yourself—you treated me differently after my injuries. You believed I was capable of less. And that was because of the way I look."

"He's right." Sarah spoke calmly from the table, where she was pouring herself a fresh cup of tea. It was no longer steaming. Her shaking hands belied her steady tone. "My whole life has been defined by my birthmark. Even this marriage occurred because of it." She looked up and met Charles' eyes. He could see how hard this was for her. "I cannot blame Gideon for what he wants, Charles. I have no recollection of being perfect as he does. This is all I have known and at one time I dreamed of being rid of my deformity. It must be worse for Gideon. This is not enough for him. I'm sorry for that. I'm sorry we weren't enough. But I cannot be angry with him for it."

"It is not about whether or not this is enough." Gideon's hand slashed the air. "Of course it is enough. I love you both. I am happy with you both. I want no others. This is about me not being enough for *you*. I know what you say," he told Charles as he started to say something, "but I also know that deep inside you wish for it. And I have the chance to give it to you, Charles. Let me give you the man you first fell in love with."

Sarah covered her face with her hands at his words and Charles cursed. "If you are referring to Captain North, I don't want him! I thought I loved him. I realize now I didn't know what love was." He paced to the window and shoved a hand through his hair and then turned to face Gideon again. "You are different now, Gideon. And I like it. No, I love it. You're not afraid to admit that you love me, to be with me. You were afraid then." It was his turn to shush Gideon with a slash of his hand. "We fought all the time, Gideon. Perhaps you don't remember that, perhaps you don't want to. But I do. Without Sarah...I found it increasingly hard to be with you, Gideon. I cared for you, but I couldn't live with you." He looked at Sarah then and she was watching him with wide, startled eyes. "What happened to you, Gideon, and Sarah's influence, have made you the man I can love today." He licked his lips. "I don't want him back, the other Gideon," he whispered. "The one who thought more about duty and honor and sacrifice than he did of me." He put both hands on his hips and blew out a breath, fighting tears. "I want the man in front of me, scars and all."

"I don't believe that." Gideon sounded angry. Charles had had enough of Gideon's anger.

"You only believe what you want to, what suits your ends!" Charles cried out. "I'm tired of our life revolving around your needs, Gideon." Gideon looked as if Charles had struck him. "For once I want you to do what I want, what I need. And I want you to forget this idiocy. I want you to think of Sarah and me and what this will do to us." For a moment Gideon appeared unsure, his resolve wavering. Charles pushed his advantage. "Every day I look at you Gideon and I see how close I came to losing you. I remember what we went through, what I had to do to save you. Don't throw away those sacrifices."

Gideon's face hardened once more. "We will meet with the doctor and then I will make a final decision," he said, ending the discussion. "Anders!" he called out. The butler returned immediately. Gideon bowed and took his leave. "I shall see you both later." When the door shut behind him Charles closed his eyes in despair. He knew Gideon well enough to know he'd lost this battle.

* * * * *

When Charles came to them that night Gideon was surprised. He had not ended their conversation well this morning. But Charles had only confirmed his deepest fears. He couldn't look at Gideon without remembering. And Gideon hated that.

Sarah had been so quiet all day. Gideon had assured her over and over tonight of his love, his devotion, his need for her. Surely she didn't think this would change the way he felt about her? He knew he was taking a risk, taking Sarah's affections for granted by doing this. It wasn't for Sarah. She cared for him as he was. But wasn't that part of what being one of three meant? He had to think of each of them, Sarah and Charles, and weigh his decisions on what was best for all. And in this situation Sarah would still love him as much without scars, and Charles would be able to leave those awful memories behind.

"What are you thinking about?" Charles murmured as he leaned down and kissed Gideon's shoulder. "You stopped. Sarah is getting impatient." There was humor in his voice.

Gideon opened his eyes and met Charles' warm brown gaze. They were in bed and Sarah was riding Gideon slowly. They were taking it slowly tonight. He and Charles had lazily licked and nipped and sucked Sarah until she was writhing on the bed, pausing frequently to kiss each other much to Sarah's delight. She truly loved to see them touch and kiss. She had actually come the other night just from watching Charles suck his cock. Gideon blinked, surprised by his emotional response. Was there any other woman as perfect for them? He didn't think so.

Now he lay on his back with Sarah atop him, and Charles lay beside them, resting on one elbow with his cheek cradled in the palm of his hand. He was caressing and fondling each of them, leaning in to steal kisses. He slid his hand between their legs to feel Gideon's cock slipping in and out of her. Gideon loved that. He loved having Charles touch him while he fucked Sarah, just as he loved having Sarah touch him when he sucked or was sucked by Charles.

For the hundredth time he wondered what it would be like to fuck Charles again while Sarah watched. They hadn't done it, not yet. He wasn't sure Sarah was ready for that. She'd been so opposed to the idea of being fucked in the bottom, he didn't think she'd like watching them do it to each other. But God, he wanted to. And that new part of himself that could take Charles in his mouth without flinching, with joy and desire, wanted to experience Charles that way too.

Sarah leaned down and pressed her breasts to his chest as she nibbled his ear. "I am impatient," she whispered. "Fuck me, Gideon."

He shuddered with desire at her crass words. He loved the earthiness of them. Loved that she'd picked up Charles' language in the bedroom. He thrust his hips up shallowly, teasing her with his cock.

She laughed quietly. "You know that's not enough for me." She ground her sex down on him, swallowing him and squeezing him tightly with her warm, wet sheath and Gideon groaned.

"Roll over and show her who's in charge, Gideon," Charles suggested with a seductive smile that was no more than a little curve in the corner of his lips. He slid down to lie next to Gideon and scooted so close he was pressed to Gideon's side. Then he pushed a hand beneath Gideon's back and started to turn him. Gideon let him. He held Sarah close and rolled with her, Charles following as if attached to Gideon's back with string. Sarah cried out in pleasure as she came to rest on her back and Gideon snuggled in closer, driving his cock in deeper. Charles stopped above him, straddling his hips, his cock a brand on Gideon's back as he nuzzled Gideon's nape. "Tell me what you were thinking about," he whispered.

"You," Gideon answered, bowing his neck to give Charles more access to it as he braced his arms beside Sarah's shoulders and fucked in and out of her, feeling her breathy sighs against his lips.

"I was thinking about you too," Charles told him quietly. He licked his shoulder and pressed light kisses down his spine before he gently bit the cheek of Gideon's arse. "I was thinking how much I'd like to fuck you while you fuck Sarah," he whispered. "Would you both like that?"

Gideon froze and beneath him Sarah's sex clenched then a rush of liquid heat surrounded him as she came with a deep moan.

"Yes," Gideon said a bit breathlessly, not at all surprised that he and Charles had been thinking about the same thing. "I think we would both like that very much."

Chapter Twenty

ॐ

Charles moved slightly, nestling his cock in the crease between Gideon's cheeks. "Are you sure?" he murmured, rubbing up and down in a very small rocking motion. He was barely moving, the tip of his cock leaving a cool wet spot where it teased him. Gideon broke out in goose bumps.

"Yes." He put every ounce of desire and conviction he could breathlessly muster into that one word and hoped it was enough. The feel of Charles' cock so close to its ultimate destination had him practically speechless with lust. Then Sarah made a delicious noise below him, tightened her walls around him again and said, "Yes," in a voice as full of anticipation as his, and Gideon couldn't have said another word if they had demanded it of him.

Gideon kissed her. He had to. He needed to feel her passion, to know that she didn't think less of him because he wanted Charles that way. And Sarah didn't disappoint. She never had and he knew somehow that she never would. Instead she kissed him as if he were the air she breathed, as if she would wither and die without the passion he returned to her, as strong and deep and abiding as the gifts she gave to him.

When Charles pulled away from him the cool air against his heated skin was a shock. Even more shocking was Charles' finger circling his entrance. "I need to put something here, to get inside. I don't want to hurt you."

Gideon jerked away from Sarah's kiss with a gasp. "I didn't... Did I hurt you? When I took you?" He'd never considered it before. Charles had not protested at the time. He'd seemed to enjoy their coupling as much as Gideon.

Charles laughed. "Yes, it hurt. But the pain was overshadowed by finally having you inside me. And it was fresh after a battle, in the middle of the woods. I hardly expected you to have a courtesan's oils handy."

Gideon shook his head and Sarah kissed the corner of his mouth. "I handled that badly. I waited too long to be with you and couldn't control myself when I finally was. I'm sorry." He felt a drop of something cool and slick drip onto his behind and slither down his crease. He shivered.

"I'm not," Charles answered as his finger followed the drop and circled Gideon's entrance again.

"What is that?" Gideon asked in a rough voice.

"Oil," Charles told him. He leaned forward, pressing the finger harder against that small hole and Gideon arched a little into the unfamiliar feeling. Charles held the small bottle out for him to see.

"Where did you get it?" Sarah asked, perplexed. "That's not mine."

"I brought it in here earlier today. Here, hold it." Charles passed the bottle to Sarah.

"You've been planning this all day?" Gideon asked in a choked voice.

"I've been planning this for six years," Charles told him with smug satisfaction. "And now the day, or night, has finally arrived. I finally get to plunder this gorgeous arse." He accompanied his words with a firm squeeze of a flexed cheek, and Gideon found himself relaxing into Charles' hands.

"Do what you will," he said with mock resignation.

Charles laughed. "Oh, I plan on it. Don't worry."

Sarah played with the hair at Gideon's temple. "Could you perhaps tell me exactly what you're doing?" she asked shyly. "I don't really know how men fuck each other."

Gideon groaned. Sarah could turn an innocent question into a sensual tease.

"Do you remember how I told you that a man could fuck a woman in the bottom?" Gideon asked. The last word hitched as Charles dipped the end of his finger inside Gideon. Christ, that was the first time Charles had been inside him in any way. It was foreign and erotic and it was all Gideon could do not to arch back and jam that finger as deep into him as it would go. He had to breathe deeply to fight the urge. He hadn't known he'd feel this way. He'd thought it would be an intense experience, that he'd enjoy the knowledge of Charles inside him more than the actual act. He was beginning to understand, however, that the fuck itself was going to be beyond his wildest imaginings.

"Oh!" Sarah exclaimed with a breathy hiccup of shock. "I didn't realize. How stupid of me. Of course." She bit her lip and Gideon followed suit as Charles' finger entered him and pressed a little deeper than before. "Are you all right?" Sarah asked quietly with a worried expression.

Gideon nodded. He licked his suddenly dry lips before answering. "Better than all right. It feels very, very good."

Charles chuckled behind him. "Excellent. I was beginning to wonder."

"Wonder no more." Gideon groaned as Charles twisted his finger inside rather than pull it out right away.

"Sarah," Charles murmured as he leaned over Gideon's back, "would you let one of us do this to you?" He kissed the blades of Gideon's shoulders, then bit the tendon between his shoulder and neck lightly, his finger working its way into Gideon more with each breath he took. Gideon turned his head to see Charles watching Sarah closely.

Sarah slid her hand down to Gideon's chest to toy with the hair there, not looking at either of them. "I don't know. I'd like to see how this goes first, if that's all right." Her voice was unsure, but her sex tightened again and grew wetter and Gideon smiled. Soon they would both be inside Sarah.

Gideon took a deep breath through his nose as Charles rubbed a second finger on the edge of his hole. He knew Charles was going to put it in next to the first. He was surprised by how much he wanted it. "I think it's going to go very well," he assured Sarah in a gravelly voice. His reward was that finger working its way inside. He grunted slightly and spread his thighs wider.

Sarah bit her lip and her hips thrust up just a little. Gideon was still inside her, just barely now. He wasn't as hard as he'd been before. Charles' invasion was taking too much concentration. But he knew that would pass and he'd be hard as stone and ready to fuck again by the time Charles was inside him. His cock twitched just thinking about it. "You like this, don't you?" he asked Sarah. "You like knowing that Charles is getting ready to fuck me on top of you."

Sarah nodded, still staring at his chest. "How is he getting ready to fuck you?" she whispered.

"God, I love when she says that word," Charles said fervently from behind him. "She makes it sound innocent and decadent at the same time."

Gideon agreed silently. Charles was doing something painfully pleasurable with his fingers that had robbed him of speech again. He could feel the sweat dripping down his temple and beading in the small of his back.

"I've got my fingers inside him, Sarah, like what I do to you, except back here." Charles answered her question for him.

"Oh." Her voice trembled and she squirmed beneath him. "Does he get wet, like I do?"

Gideon snorted a breathless laugh. "No," he managed to rasp.

Charles laughed as well. "No, that's what the oil is for."

Sarah seemed to think about it for a second or two. "Would you have to use oil on me there too?"

Gideon groaned at the image that produced. He leaned down and captured her lips in a rough kiss. When he pulled back he growled out, "Yes."

Charles began to pull his fingers out slowly and Gideon hissed out a breath. He felt stretched and aching back there and Charles hadn't even started yet, not really. For a moment he felt trepidation. Then Charles smacked him on the arse and demanded, "Give me the oil," and Gideon laughed as Sarah quickly held out the bottle.

Charles sighed and hummed a little as he massaged the oil onto his cock. Gideon could hear the wet sound of his strokes and his back end clenched in response.

"Gideon?" Sarah whispered.

He opened his eyes to meet her stare. He hadn't even realized he'd shut his eyes. "Hmmm?"

"Are you scared?" she asked in a small voice. "I think I'd be a little scared." He knew what she meant was *she* was a little scared.

"Of Charles?" He shook his head with a grin. "No, he stopped scaring me long ago."

"I heard that," Charles said with a sticky caress of his arse. "You were never scared of me."

Sarah gave him a tentative smile.

"I'm not scared, Sarah. I know Charles wants to do this because he knows it will feel good. Everything we do here is about feeling good, isn't it?" She nodded. "And I want him inside me. You understand that, don't you? You've told us both many times that you want us inside you. That's how I feel right now." He closed his eyes, anticipation coursing through his veins. All trepidation was gone and exhilaration had taken its place. Finally, finally after these years he was going to have Charles inside him. "I've waited so long, Sarah..."

"Gideon." When Charles spoke his name like that, Gideon felt ten feet tall, as if he could move mountains. It was the way Charles said it when he was about to come.

"Yes," he answered the unspoken question. "God, yes."

Sarah ran her hand through his hair and then pulled his lips to hers. "Make me feel it too, Gideon," she whispered.

Gideon bit her lower lip softly and then let it go with a lick. "I plan to sometime in the near future."

Sarah let out a panicked gasp. "I didn't mean…"

Gideon hushed her and kissed her tenderly. "Not today, Sarah. Not now." He arched his back. Charles was there. The wet, slick end of his prick was pressing against Gideon's entrance.

"Relax, Gideon," Charles murmured. "Take a deep breath and then push back."

"How do you know how to do this?" Gideon asked breathlessly. He wondered with a sharp pang of jealousy if Charles had done this with another man while waiting for Gideon.

"Years ago when I was in London I went to a brothel that offers male companionship," Charles said, rubbing the tip around and around Gideon's sensitive hole. Gideon found himself relaxing. He could feel that dark passage blooming under Charles' sensual caress, preparing to take him.

"I see," Gideon choked out, his disappointment and hurt at Charles' admission almost drowning out the pleasure.

Charles stopped and sighed. "No, you don't. I picked a fellow who looked and acted quite knowledgeable and then shocked the hell out him by asking him how it should be done. I had no desire to fuck him even when he was clearly trying to entice me with his lurid descriptions. I have not wanted to do this with any man but you, Gideon, since I met you." He began that gentle, insistent rub again and the jealous tension that had Gideon in its grip faded. "But I must say, he knew what he was talking about, apparently. And the same method works for women too, he said."

"Oh, good," Sarah commented drily from below Gideon. "I was quite worried."

Gideon laughed and Charles chose that moment to press inside. Gideon gasped.

"No, Gideon," Charles said. It sounded as if he were speaking through clenched teeth. "Don't tense up. Relax. Take a deep breath. Now."

The burn was sharp where Charles kept up a relentless pressure. Gideon forced himself to relax, focusing on Sarah's hand smoothing gently up and down his arm. He took a deep breath and pressed back and suddenly Charles slipped inside and then glided home. Gideon was stretched and felt an aching fullness, but whatever pain he'd felt was gone. He started to move but Charles stopped him with a firm grip on his hip.

"Don't," Charles ground out. "Don't move yet. You're not ready."

"I'm fine," Gideon told him. "It doesn't hurt."

"I just want to sit here for a minute." Charles sounded raspy. He leaned over Gideon's back and kissed his neck tenderly and then laid his forehead on Gideon's shoulder. Gideon felt something wet drop on his shoulder.

"Oh, Charles," Sarah whispered. She wrapped her arms around both of them and kissed the top of Charles' head.

"Are you crying?" Gideon asked in wonder.

"Be quiet," Charles told him with a sniff. "You are going to ruin this moment for me." He rested his lips against Gideon's shoulder, not kissing him, just resting them there. "I've waited so long, Gideon," he whispered in a broken voice. "This is…" he shook his head and sat up. The move caused his cock to slip around inside Gideon a little and he groaned at the feeling.

"I can't believe you're inside me," Gideon told him with disbelief. "It's…" He laughed. "I don't have words for it. It just is. God, Charles, if I had known…"

Charles re-situated himself on the bed and Gideon groaned and pressed back, seeking more. His cock began to revive in Sarah's wet heat. "I think he liked that," she murmured, sliding her hand down his back. "He's getting harder."

"I have no secrets from either of you," he said roughly, forcing his hips to stay still.

Charles slid out just a little and then pressed back in, as if testing the waters.

"More," Gideon ground out and Sarah grinned as Charles laughed behind him.

"I have more to give you," Charles answered with the familiar words and Gideon's cheeks heated because he hadn't realized he'd sounded like Sarah.

Charles pulled out and thrust back in harder than before and Gideon cursed. "That feels so damn good," he told Charles.

"Tell me," Charles demanded. "Tell us how it feels. Describe it for Sarah."

Charles began to fuck him in a slow, steady rhythm that had Gideon fearing for his sanity. "I'm full of him, Sarah," he whispered. She moaned beneath him and bent her legs, tipping up her hips to take him deeper. He was hard now and ready to fuck and be fucked. "He's so hot inside me, slick and hard. I never knew he would feel so good."

"Fuck her, Gideon," Charles ordered him. "With me. Like this." Charles pulled out of Gideon and pressed Gideon into Sarah with his hands on Gideon's hips. Then he thrust inside pulling Gideon's hips back. It was lesson enough. Gideon picked up the cadence immediately and Sarah clutched his shoulders, her head thrown back on the pillow.

"Listen, Sarah," he whispered. He could see how his words were affecting her, feel it in the vise of her sex around his shaft. "You can hear his prick tunneling into me through all that oil. So slick and hard."

Sarah groaned. "You said that already," she told him in a shaky voice.

"Do you like it?" Charles asked roughly. "Tell me you like it. You like to be fucked, don't you, Gideon?"

Gideon liked it more than he'd thought possible. Having Charles' cock parting him, fucking him, possessing him—he knew he'd crave it from this day on. But all he said was a low-voiced "Yes."

Then the rhythm and the fuck took over and there was no more talk. Just the sights and sounds and feeling of being owned and taken by the two most important people in the world to him. His arms grew weak and began to tremble and Gideon had to lower his weight onto Sarah, who took it gladly and fucked him rough and as hard as Charles. He let Charles take over completely, fucking Gideon into Sarah with each stroke. She was a match for them. Her nails dug into his back and he grunted at the bite of them, but the pain grounded him so he could savor Charles' possession and Sarah's enjoyment of them. His new position drove Charles into a point that sent shards of white-hot pleasure shooting from his arse to his prick. And Sarah swallowed that heat and gave it back to him as her walls trembled around him.

He felt his orgasm coming. His back tensed and so did his balls. He felt the tightening of his passage around Charles' prick and Charles groaned as he fucked Gideon a little harder. He needed something to hold on to. He felt as if he were going to fly apart. He wrapped his arms around Sarah and she held him to her. "Yes, Gideon," she whispered in his ear. "Give it to me. Give me your pleasure. Show me how good Charles makes you feel."

"Sarah," he whispered brokenly. Charles didn't stop. He kept fucking in and out in an oiled glide that caused Gideon to start shivering uncontrollably. Sarah moaned and tensed and he felt her begin to come, not a frantic climax but a deep, steady throb of pleasure, and Charles pushed deep and hit that spot and Gideon was gone. The heat of his release raced through him and out into Sarah as Gideon gave a strangled cry. He could feel his passage clenching tight around Charles.

Charles groaned and Gideon felt a rush of heat fill him and he knew that he'd come inside him. Gideon jerked between him and Sarah, surrounded by a pleasure more intense than any he'd ever felt.

When it was over none of them moved for a minute or two. Their breaths were ragged in the still night air as a breeze cooled the sweat on their skin. After a short while Gideon felt Charles' spent cock slip from him with a sense of loss. Finally Sarah spoke.

"Gideon, I love you. But I can't breathe."

He and Charles burst into weak laughter and Charles helped him roll off Sarah. "I'm sorry, my sweet." He cleared his throat because his voice was raspy. "I may never walk again."

Sarah looked at him with concern. "Are you all right?"

He smiled at her and then at Charles. "I'm perfectly exhausted. You have both fucked me into near unconsciousness."

"Ah," Charles said as he lay down next to Gideon and nuzzled his cheek. "Should I say I'm sorry?"

"No." Gideon raised a brow as he turned to look at him. "You should get something to clean us all up, and then we can figure out how soon we can do that again."

Sarah laughed. "I have so many different possible combinations for *that* going through my mind."

Charles reached over Gideon's chest and grabbed Sarah's hand to kiss her palm while Gideon leaned over and kissed her cheek. "It isn't complicated mathematics, Sarah," Gideon teased. "All you have to do is fuck."

Sarah groaned as he used almost the same words she had used weeks ago while Charles climbed from the bed laughing and headed into the small bathing chamber attached to the room. "Make her say it, Gideon," he called out quietly over his shoulder. "The more she says it the sooner I can do it again."

Sarah and Gideon shared a look and Sarah began to chant under her breath, "Fuck, fuck, fuck, fuck—"

Gideon laughed and put a hand over her mouth. "Give me some recovery time, my dear, please." Sarah grinned behind his hand and Gideon's heart swelled. This is what he wanted all the time. The three of them together like this with no horrific memories coming between them.

He could hear Charles whistling softly in the other room as water splashed into a basin. Sarah turned her smiling face toward the sound. Gideon felt the ache in his arse, bathed in the slippery feel of oil and Charles. He could make it happen. He could make their lives all about now and erase the past. It was best for all of them.

Chapter Twenty-One

❧

"When Dr. Jones arrives we shall have to have Anne and her two to dinner again. She will never forgive me if I leave her out of my personal affairs." Gideon was being sarcastic, but the affection in his voice was unmistakable.

Sarah put her teacup down very slowly. They were sitting in the gazebo. It was a beautiful summer day, the sun shining as a slight breeze kept the air from becoming stifling. Charles had come up from the paddock to join them for tea.

She was watching Charles' reaction to Gideon's statement. For all that Charles had known Gideon longer than her, she often felt that she understood Gideon better. And she understood Charles better than Gideon did without a doubt. She inwardly sighed. How could two men have lived together and loved each other for so long and still not know each other?

Charles was not as careful with his cup as Sarah. He slammed his down on the table rattling the teapot and other dishes, his tea spilling over. "What do mean when Dr. Jones arrives? Surely you've changed your mind!" He sounded incredulous, which just made Sarah shake her head. In all the time she'd known Gideon she had yet to see him change his mind, except about Charles. And that had apparently taken over six years.

"Why would I change my mind?" Gideon asked, genuinely perplexed.

Charles looked as if Gideon had slapped him across the face. "After last night you can ask me that?"

Gideon blushed, which Sarah would have found endearing under different circumstances. "Last night was…too long in coming," Gideon said awkwardly. "It had nothing to do with present circumstances." His look turned guarded. "Are you telling me it was all about making me change my mind?"

"No," Charles ground out angrily. "You know it wasn't. I wasn't lying last night. I've wanted to fuck you for six long years."

Sarah looked around frantically and breathed a sigh of relief when she saw that no one was near enough to hear them. Neither Gideon nor Charles was paying any attention to their surroundings.

"But as usual, you thought a good fuck would solve all my problems, is that right?" Gideon grabbed his crutches and stood up and Charles rose from his chair to face him.

"Please," Sarah implored, surprised by how quickly the fight had escalated. Their emotions had been running so high the last few days. Sarah was exhausted, both physically and emotionally. "Sit down, both of you, and let's discuss this civilly."

"I think I could fuck you morning, noon and night," Charles answered Gideon, ignoring Sarah, "and it wouldn't solve all your problems."

"Please," Sarah said again more vehemently. She put a hand to her head. They were giving her a headache.

Charles gestured at her. "Do you see what you're doing to Sarah?"

"What I'm doing to Sarah?" Gideon said incredulously. "You began this argument, Charles, not I."

"No," Charles disagreed, pointing a finger at Gideon accusingly, "you started it. You started it with your asinine ideas about this London doctor."

"You have decided they are asinine and that's that?" Gideon barked. "Let me reiterate what I have said a thousand times, Charles. You are not in charge of me, my past, my decisions or my future."

Charles paled. "And that's that?" he asked sharply. "Whatever Gideon wants, damn the consequences to Charles or Sarah? Let them accept your decisions or not, you don't care? It's all about Gideon?"

"Of course not," Gideon snapped back. "I told you yesterday that I made this decision for all of us. If you would stop your theatrics you would see that this could only be good for us. You are oversimplifying the situation."

Charles crossed his arms mulishly. "Well, I'm just a simple farm boy, Gideon. It's what I do, oversimplify. I see you trying to commit suicide for some reason I cannot comprehend, breaking Sarah's heart and ignoring my pleas. What part am I missing?"

"Charles, please," Sarah whispered. There wasn't much conviction in it. Unlike Charles she had known that last night would not change Gideon's plans. She'd hoped to try a more subtle approach over the next few days, but Charles' frontal assault today had thrown up Gideon's defenses and she despaired of breaching them now. He would dig in and hold his ground on the issue.

"I am doing this for you," Gideon replied stoically. "You may not see it yet, but in the end you will understand."

"Make me understand it now," Charles demanded. "Don't ask me to watch you kill yourself if you can't explain why to me."

"When the scars are gone, Charles, you'll be able to look at me without remembering."

Sarah froze and so did Charles. She hadn't understood, then, either. This was for Charles. *Oh, Gideon,* she thought sadly. Did he really think Charles needed or wanted this from him? Did he really think this dangerous path would lead to a future with no past?

"If you are doing this for me, then I should have the right to put a stop to it." Charles spoke with barely controlled anger. "Are you the same man I fucked last night? You can't be. If you were, you would remember that I didn't give a damn about the scars or the past. All I cared about was fucking you, Gideon. Being inside you, part of you, holding you. Sharing you with the woman we both love. Making a future together. Is that all you were thinking about last night? Your bloody damn scars?"

"You were behind me." Gideon spoke bitterly.

It took Charles a moment to comprehend what he meant. "It was a hell of lot easier to fuck you that way when you were fucking Sarah!" Charles exclaimed in exasperation. "If you can think of a better way then please share it with me."

"Could we please stop talking about fucking at the top of our voices?" Sarah asked shrilly.

"Sarah," Charles said, clenching his teeth as he fought to keep his voice down, "you were facing Gideon. Were you thinking about his scars while we fucked?"

"We've been over this," Gideon barked, moving to stand at the railing, turning his back to them. "Sarah has no memories of me before."

"Am I supposed to feel guilty that I do?" Charles cried out. "Apologize because I knew you before this? Apologize again for saving your life?"

"I am repaying that debt," Gideon said coolly, staring out at the pasture.

Charles growled and in a fit of frustrated temper swept his arm out and knocked the tea service from the table. The teacups shattered on the floor and Sarah gasped. Gideon's head snapped around at the crash. "What are you doing?" he demanded.

"You wish to destroy everything we have here? Well, then, I will help you." Charles stalked over to the steps. "Better yet, I'll let you do it all on your own, you're doing such a good job of it. I'm leaving. I refuse to stay here and watch you make the biggest mistake of your life. Of all our lives." He turned and leapt down the stairs, walking briskly toward the house.

When he was gone silence descended on the gazebo.

"Are you going to leave me too?" Gideon asked calmly.

Sarah raised a shaking hand and smoothed her hair over her aching head. Her eyes stung with unshed tears. "No." She looked at Gideon, refusing to hide her distress just to make him feel better. "I'll stay. I'll stay because I love you and because you need me, whether you admit it or not. And I'll stay because I agree with Charles. I think this is a mistake. But unlike Charles I understand why you are doing it and that only you can stop this madness."

"Madness?" Gideon inquired in a politely bored tone.

Sarah stood up. "Yes, madness. For surely it is madness to risk what we have." She couldn't stop herself from making one last effort. "So few people have this, Gideon. This house is filled with love, and you are at the center of it. If you would only forgive yourself, you would see that."

"It is not forgiveness I seek," Gideon said in genuine surprise.

"Isn't it?" Sarah replied as she walked gingerly toward the steps, avoiding the smashed china. She turned and faced him at the top step. "Charles does not blame you, Gideon. He does not blame himself anymore either. He accepted your forgiveness. Can you not accept his?"

"I—"

Sarah held up a hand and he stopped obediently. "No, no more. My head aches and my heart is breaking. Charles is right." She turned with a sigh and took the steps down. She saw a groom bringing Charles' mount from the stables and her heart constricted. If Gideon had finally driven Charles away, could she forgive him? Her uncertainty over the answer to that question was more dreadful than any harsh words spoken this morning.

* * * * *

"Madam." Dr. Jones bowed deeply to her with an ingratiating smile. She hated him already and he'd just walked in the door.

"Dr. Jones." She held out hand and he grasped her fingertips weakly. Ugh, he was insipid. A short, rotund little man with beady eyes and thinning gray hair. If he could remove disfiguring birthmarks and scars, why couldn't he stop his own hair loss? *Doctor, heal thyself,* Sarah thought snidely.

"Come in, doctor," Gideon asked politely from the drawing room door. He turned and moved on his crutches over to the settee and Sarah watched Dr. Jones follow his progress. She didn't like the calculating gleam in his eye as he stared at Gideon.

Dr. Jones took a seat with a great deal of pomp as he fluffed out his coattails before sitting. To add insult to injury he was a popinjay. He wore a bright yellow coat with a glaring red waistcoat and a neckcloth that combined the two. Really, he was an eyesore from head to toe.

Sarah sighed at her thoughts. She didn't recall being such a mean-spirited woman before. But Dr. Jones seemed to bring out the worst in her. At least she hadn't voiced her feelings aloud. She looked at Gideon and winced. Apparently she didn't have to. From the censorious look on his face he knew exactly what she was thinking.

"When shall we begin the treatment?" Gideon asked immediately.

The doctor seemed surprised at Gideon's forthright manner but recovered quickly. "Immediately if that is your wish. So I shall be treating both of you? You did not make that clear in your letters." His smile was unctuous and made Sarah want to wash her hands.

"No," she replied. She gave the doctor a look she had learned from Gideon and he gulped like a fish out of water. She raised her eyebrow in a superior way. "I am not in need of your treatment." She paused for effect. "Doctor." Scorn dripped from her tone.

"Sarah." Gideon's voice had a warning in it. She disregarded it. She knew he would do nothing to her no matter how she treated this so-called doctor.

"You mustn't disparage those who try to better their situation through the miracles of modern medicine, Mrs. North," Dr. Jones said, sounding alarmingly like her father when he was preparing to give a sermon. "Mr. North has been burdened by the scars of his heroic war service. It is our Christian duty to help him be free of their taint."

Sarah was so outraged at his comments she had no response for a moment. She looked at Gideon in consternation. Surely he wasn't going to let this idiot masquerading as a man of medicine touch him? Gideon sat there with a pained expression on his face, his eyes closed. She turned back to Dr. Jones, who looked smug, as if he'd put her in her place.

"Yes," she agreed with an exaggerated nod of her head. "Gideon is shockingly reticent about his feelings." She clasped her hands together and brought them to her chest. "Locked inside his maimed and scarred body." She fluttered her eyelashes as if overwhelmed and heaved a great, tremulous sigh.

"Thank you, Mrs. Siddons, that will be quite enough," Gideon said drily.

There was slow clapping from the drawing room doorway and Sarah turned to see a stranger standing there grinning broadly while he showed his appreciation of her performance. He looked exhausted and rumpled, as if he'd traveled all night. "Perhaps not the caliber of Mrs. Siddons, whom I had the honor of seeing on the stage in Bath, but a fine performance just the same."

Gideon had stiffened across from her and Dr. Jones was frowning darkly. She cast an inquiring glance at Anders who stood holding the door open. "Dr. Peters to see you, Mr.

North," Anders said blandly. The name was familiar but Sarah couldn't place it.

Gideon must have sensed her confusion. "Let me introduce you to Dr. Thomas Peters, Sarah. The man who saved my life at Badajoz."

"I was not aware you were under the care of another physician, Mr. North," Dr. Jones said disapprovingly.

Dr. Peters sauntered into the room, gazing around with avid curiosity. Sarah was not immune from his scrutiny. Indeed, she seemed to receive the bulk of it. "Under my care?" he said in astonishment. "Why, doctor, he owes me his life! The ancient Chinese believe that he now belongs to me."

"God bless his Britannic Majesty George," Gideon intoned, "and my supreme luck to be his subject and not an ancient Chinaman."

Dr. Peters laughed as he came to a stop in front of Sarah. He bowed low before her. "Mrs. North, it is a pleasure to make your acquaintance." He stood up and took a step back, perusing her with a puzzled look on his face. "From Borden's drunken description I expected you to reside permanently atop a marble pedestal, a golden halo floating above your head."

Sarah's laughter burst out in unabashed glee. "You've seen him, then?" she asked eagerly. "Is he all right?"

For two days she had worried, waiting for some word from Charles. He had stormed off with his satchel not long after he and Gideon had their argument in the gazebo. He'd left with a passionate goodbye for Sarah and a terse "I'm going to London."

"Compared to what?" Dr. Peters answered noncommittally.

"I see," Gideon drawled as he leaned back in his chair. "Charles has sent reinforcements."

"Hardly," Dr. Peters grunted as he fell onto the other end of the settee where Sarah sat and laid his head against the back with a sigh. He really was exhausted. "If I am the cavalry come to save the day, you really are a lost cause, North." He opened one eye and looked at Sarah. "I apologize, ma'am. But Borden poured me into a carriage and I've been jostled nonstop from London. I am tired, thirsty, dusty and weary beyond comprehension. The last before I even entered the carriage, truth be told. I'm afraid my manners were left on the roadside."

Sarah turned to Anders. "Send us some tea, Anders, and some food for Dr. Peters." Anders nodded and closed the door.

Dr. Jones frowned harder as the implications of refreshments being ordered for Dr. Peters and not for him sank in. He stood abruptly. "I shall leave you to greet your old friend properly, Mr. North," he said with a slight bow. "If you would have someone show me to my room?"

Sarah did not need him to ask twice. Before Gideon could answer she rang for a footman.

After Dr. Jones had made his irritated exit, Dr. Peters turned to her. "Again, excuse my rudeness, Mrs. North, but may I speak to your husband alone?"

Sarah hastily rose. "Of course, Dr. Peters. I hope you will join us for dinner? And of course you shall stay with us."

"You are indeed the angel Borden made you out to be," he said sincerely.

Sarah smiled at him. "Nonsense," she scoffed. "How absolutely boring that would be."

The doctor laughed and she gave Gideon a saucy grin over her shoulder. His return smile was genuine if reluctant. "Be nice," she admonished him before she closed the door.

"I am not an angel either," he muttered, "thanks to Dr. Peters."

She was still chuckling at Dr. Peters' fervent "Truer words were never spoken" as she walked away.

* * * * *

Gideon wasn't sure whether to be angry or amused. Charles really had been desperate to send Peters. He was uneasy, however, at the fact that Charles had not returned.

"What in the bloody hell do you think you're doing, North?" Peters asked in annoyance. "I was unaware that along with your other infirmities you had become feeble in the head."

"You are still as droll as you were before, I see," Gideon told him. "And I am hardly infirm."

Peters glared at him. "If Borden brandishes another sharp object at me in order to force me to save your life one more time, I will not be responsible for the consequences."

"Dare I hope the consequences will be your failure to appear?"

"It won't work."

Gideon sighed. He'd attribute Peters' haphazard conversational style to exhaustion, but the fact was the doctor always talked like this. One minute he was talking about one topic, and the next he'd moved on to another. And he was always starting his conversations in the middle, as if he'd been carrying on the conversation in his head and suddenly decided to make it public. "I assume you are talking about Dr. Jones' treatment?"

"No, Faraday's experiments with electrical currents. Of course I mean Jones' treatment." Peters sounded disgusted with him, which was not unexpected. Peters had always sounded disgusted with him.

Gideon sighed again. He had always done that in response to Peters' disgust too. How odd to fall back onto old habits. "I know it won't work. One look at him and I could see he was not to be trusted." Peters rubbed his hands over his face and then gave Gideon a sympathetic look. It shocked Gideon and increased his unease. "What?"

"Even if Jones' treatment managed to get rid of the scars, it wouldn't erase the past, Gideon. I know." He laughed bitterly. "Trust me, I know. There is no erasing the past no matter how we try."

Chapter Twenty-Two

෬

Gideon said nothing. He just clenched his jaw and refused to look at Peters. The doctor fell back wearily in his seat again. There was a knock on the door and they both sat silently as Anders came in with the tea tray and poured them each a cup. He left and it took a moment for Peters to resume their conversation.

"How many men do you think I saved in the war, Gideon?" he asked quietly.

Gideon shot him a wary look. "I don't know. A great many I would think."

Peters was nodding. "Yes, a great many." He sat slumped on the settee, staring at his hands as he rubbed one thumb repeatedly with the other. It was clearly an unconscious gesture. "And how many do you think I failed to save?"

Gideon was uncomfortable with the turn in the conversation. "Just as many."

Peters was still nodding. "At least, yes." Then he looked at Gideon and Gideon noticed how bloodshot his eyes were, and how bleak. "I remember them all, Gideon. Each and every one." He stood, his weariness palpable, so heavy that Gideon began to feel it himself. He walked over to the window and stared down at the paddock where the grooms were walking some of the newer horses yet to be trained. They pulled at the leads, pawing the ground. "I've stared at the bottom of too many empty bottles since the war. And not one of them helped me forget."

"They were not your responsibility, Peters," Gideon told him gruffly. "Just as I was not and am not now."

Peters barked out a laugh and turned to face Gideon. He leaned against the window frame and crossed his legs casually, though Gideon knew it for a lie. "You all were. I played God, Gideon. I made the decision who would live and who would die. And some I helped along their way."

"To ease their suffering," Gideon said. "There was no malice in it."

"You screamed at me to let you die. I didn't."

Gideon winced at the reminder. "You were right not to. I didn't mean it."

"Maybe they didn't either." Peters turned away again. "I don't want to remember them, Gideon. But part of me won't give them up." He shoved his hands into the pockets on his bottle green jacket. "If I don't remember them, who will?"

Gideon had no answer. "Why didn't you let me die?"

Peters laughed and this time it was a genuine laugh. "I had nothing to do with it after my initial involvement on the field at Badajoz. Charles refused to let you go." He shook his head. "No, that's not true. I could have let you die. I could have kept Charles from you. It would have killed you fast enough. But it would have killed him too." He turned and walked over to the nearest chair, sinking into it. "Every doctor—every good doctor—has an instinct that tells him what treatments will help and what treatments will harm each individual patient. And my instinct told me that if I separated you and Charles you'd die. So I let him stay and take care of you, and you both lived."

"Charles was not injured, at least not to my knowledge."

"I'm a doctor, not a fool." Gideon snorted and Peters ignored him. "I knew what was going on. It was written on Charles' face for all to see, and it was in your voice when you called for him in your delirium." Peters reached for his teacup but he didn't take a drink, just stared at it in his hand. "If you had died he would have walked right out on the next battlefield into a bullet or a bayonet. Or he would have put a bullet in his own brain."

Gideon had a sick feeling at the thought and rubbed his chest. "I hate that he remembers," he whispered. He was shocked as soon as the words were out. He hadn't meant to say them.

"You can't make him forget. Nothing will make him forget. Not even if you rid yourself of the scars, which simply isn't possible. You'll just kill yourself trying."

"I hate that he's the one who wakes up shaking and retching and crying in the night. I hate that I can't make that go away. And I hate even more that I'm the one who did that to him." Gideon covered his eyes with one hand, willing his weakness away. Willing the words away.

"Then go to him and hold him until he stops shaking, and clean him up after he retches," Peters said prosaically. "That's all you can do, and all he expects you to do. You're not God either, Gideon." Gideon pulled his hand away to glare at him and Peters put his cup down with a sigh. "What about Mrs. North?"

Gideon frowned. "What about her?"

"How does she feel about Charles? About all this?"

Gideon wasn't sure what he meant by all this. "She loves him." He shook his head. "I think she understands him more than I do."

"Well, that's not difficult," Peters said with snort of disgust. So they were back on their old footing, thank God. Peters looked around. "I need a drink."

Gideon picked up his crutches and rose from his chair. He went to the wall and slid back a panel that was all but invisible, revealing a shelf filled with bottles.

"Well, that's handy," Peters said with appreciation as he walked over.

Gideon silently handed a bottle of whiskey to Peters, who hesitated a moment and then took it. Gideon passed him a glass.

"She loves you, you know," he said over his shoulder as he walked back to the settee. He looked thin now that Gideon thought about it. Too thin and much too haggard.

"Yes," Gideon agreed, "she does. Although it hasn't done her much good."

Peters looked up, the bottle suspended over the glass, the amber liquid held just below the lip. "I think she's done all right, North."

Gideon watched him fill the glass and then take a long drink. He sighed with contentment as he lowered the glass. He raised it after a moment and drained it dry. Then he set it back on the table and refilled it. Gideon quietly left him to his whiskey, closing the door behind him.

* * * * *

Dr. Peters was slumped so far down in his chair Sarah feared he was going to slide under the table. He'd hardly eaten a thing. He was clearly drunk. Although to be fair, he was a quiet, polite drunkard. Added to his exhaustion, the drink had done him in.

Even drunk, Dr. Peters was a better dinner companion than Dr. Jones. Jones had spent most of dinner trying to piously convince her and Gideon of the importance of taking his treatment. He seemed to think it would make them more attractive, more self-confident, happier, stronger and apparently fertile. The last had finally caused Gideon to give him an ice-cold, quelling look. Sarah just laughed.

"Trust me, doctor," she said as she cut her lamb, "Mr. North has no problems pertaining to his virility."

Dr. Jones turned beet red and Dr. Peters chuckled drunkenly. "Good to know," Peters mumbled. He actually elicited a small smile from Gideon.

"Thank you, my dear," Gideon said graciously. He turned to Dr. Jones. "I'm sorry for wasting your time, doctor. I shall send a letter for my man of business with you to London and you will be duly compensated for the inconvenience."

Dr. Peters let out a quiet snore. Sarah motioned the footman over. "Please see Dr. Peters to his room. Carefully, please. He is exhausted from his travels."

As the footman gently roused Peters from his chair and led him from the room, Dr. Jones muttered, "I believe it is the drink that has affected him more than his travels."

Gideon turned an angry expression on the doctor, surprising Sarah. "You have no idea what you are talking about, doctor, and I do not like the implications of your tone."

Dr. Jones threw his napkin down on the table and stood. He bowed to both of them. "I shall retire and leave for London first thing in the morning." He looked at Gideon. "I shall attend you in your study at that time to receive the letter you spoke of."

Gideon nodded coldly and Anders opened the door to let the doctor out. When the door closed behind the doctor, Gideon slumped in his seat. "I'm sorry," he said, sheepishly looking at Sarah. "I cannot promise I won't do that again."

Sarah set her fork down and toyed with her spoon a moment before nonchalantly stirring her tea. "Seek out medical miracles?"

Gideon shook his head. "No. I believe I have received the only miracle I'm going to get in this life. I meant inflict unpleasant people on you in awkward situations." He sighed. "I'm not a very good judge of character. You and Charles are much better at that. It takes me some time to realize people are not what they seem." He sat up and took a drink of his wine. He licked his lips as he set the glass down. "I tend to avoid people rather than misjudge them. It's easier that way."

Sarah patted his hand. "You must let me take care of it then, darling. I shall protect you from unscrupulous characters."

Gideon's brow popped up as he gave her that wry look that she adored. "My lady in shining armor."

Anders came to remove the dishes. He started to pour Sarah another cup of tea, but Gideon waved him away. Sarah looked at him questioningly. "Would you care to take a walk?" he asked. "It's a beautiful evening."

Sarah smiled. "I'd love to." She got up and waited by the door for him. He seemed to be walking rather slowly tonight.

They walked down the drive and past the gazebo, meandering down the path to her favorite bench by the old tree near the pasture. They sat and she waited for Gideon to speak. There had to be a reason he'd wanted to walk. She gazed up at the sky. It was black, filled with brightly shining stars. It looked like expensive velvet and she had a vision of herself rolling around on it, her bare skin caressed by the decadent softness of it, fistfuls of stars falling from her hands like diamonds.

"What are you thinking about?" Gideon asked quietly. He turned to face her, his hands resting on his crutches in front of him. He smiled at her. "You were smiling."

"Something silly," she told him. She could feel herself blushing. Gideon liked the practical side of her. She hadn't known this fanciful side of her existed until recently. He probably didn't either.

"Tell me," he said quietly. He reached out and traced his finger over the tendons in the back of her hand where it lay in her lap. It was one of his scarred fingers. She caressed it and he covered her hand with his.

"I was thinking the sky looked like black velvet and diamonds, and I wanted to roll around on it naked and spill the stars from my hands."

Gideon stroked her hand with his thumb. "I'd like to see that. I have the means for the velvet. I'm not so sure about the diamonds, however."

Sarah laughed quietly. She peeked at him sideways. "I don't need the diamonds. Too sharp to roll around on."

He was quiet again for a few minutes. Then he set his crutches carefully down on the ground and tugged on her arm, pulling her toward him. He pulled her up on his lap and she cuddled into him, her head on his shoulder.

"I'm not very brave, am I?" he asked quietly.

Sarah pressed her nose to his neck and breathed in his beloved scent. "What do you mean?"

"Charles was right. I'm afraid to get a prosthesis, afraid to ride." He paused and hugged her tightly against his chest. "I thought that to do so meant everyone would know how weak I was, how easily broken. If I avoided those things, then I could live in the past, remembering when I could walk and ride like a normal man."

"You are a normal man in every way that matters," Sarah argued, sitting up his lap. "And you are very brave."

"I agree that I am normal in all the ways that matter." He pointed to his leg and his face. "You and Charles have helped me to see that these don't matter. You see who I am, not this shell." He shook his head. "But I am not brave, despite how the world wishes to brand me the great tragic hero."

Sarah tilted his head up with her hand cupped around his scarred cheek. She ran her fingers over it and leaned in and kissed it. "This is bravery," she whispered. "Not how you got them. But that you let me see them and touch them." She caressed his cheek again. "I know how hard that was for you. And that, to me, is bravery." She touched her own cheek. "I used to cover it, you know. Hide it as best I as I could. But you have always faced the world proudly."

"Trust me, if I could have worn a poke bonnet, I would have," Gideon told her drily.

Sarah laughed and settled against his shoulder again. "No, you wouldn't have. Your stubbornness demands the world accept you on your terms." She sighed. "Your bravery is similar to something you once told me about your carriage horses. It is not about what you did in one moment in time but about what you do day in and day out."

"I'm angry at him." Gideon spoke quietly. "I know it is irrational. But I feel as if he deserted me when I needed him most."

"Has he ever left like this before?" Sarah didn't think so.

"No. I think I was counting on that. I am a selfish coward. Marvelous."

Sarah hit him lightly on the shoulder opposite where her head rested. "Stop focusing on yourself, Gideon. Try to think like Charles. Why do you think he left this time?"

Gideon took a deep breath and was quiet for a time. Finally he answered. "Because he knew you would not leave. He left me with you."

"Yes," Sarah agreed. "I think that is certainly true. And I'm humbled by his trust." Gideon gave her a curious look. "He has never trusted anyone else to care for you, Gideon. You are the most precious thing to him and he left you in my care."

Gideon shook his head roughly. "No, Sarah. You are as precious to him."

"How does that make you feel?" She asked warily.

Gideon looked surprised. "I would have it no other way," he said simply. "We, Charles and I, have always shared the same thoughts, the same feelings, the same desires. It seems quite natural that we would both love you. For any other thing to have occurred would have been...discordant."

Sarah laughed at his choice of words. "And God forbid Charles bring disorder to your existence?"

"Charles has always been the one to bring order to the chaos of my life." There was so much more underlying those simple words and Sarah felt a lump in her throat and the pain and confusion he must feel at Charles leaving. "Although," he drew out the word, "at first I thought that your arrival meant his imminent departure."

"Why?"

"I didn't think I could have both of you. I thought it was asking too much. Of fate and of him. I thought he should leave and find a normal life somewhere without me." He looked at her. "Us."

Sarah bit her lip. "I'm not so sure he hasn't done just that." Sarah finally admitted her worst fear.

Gideon just frowned at her. "You know he wouldn't."

"He couldn't stand to see you hurting again," she told him. She hadn't brought this up before because she hadn't wanted Gideon to feel any more guilt. But he needed to understand what Charles had been thinking. "He spent years getting you to this point, Gideon. Supporting you and caring for you until you were strong enough to stand on your own again." That brow went up at her choice of words but she ignored it. "You were asking him to stand by and watch you throw all that away. To watch you willingly make yourself weak and ill, perhaps die. And he simply couldn't do it. He loves you too much and he still has too many memories. It would have finally broken him."

Gideon's hands clenched where he held her. "I didn't think about that," he murmured with disgust. "I truly am a selfish bastard. I never thought what it would to him to see me like that again."

"He tried to tell you," Sarah said soothingly, "but you didn't want to hear it then. All you could think about was the past and making it go away. You couldn't see the present."

Gideon lowered his head until his forehead rested on her shoulder. "We have to go fetch him, you know."

Sarah went stiff with shock and scrambled off his lap, nearly oversetting him. "What? To London?" Her heart was beating frantically. "Surely you can't be serious."

"It's another test."

"Charles wouldn't test us that way. He knows what it means to us. You're right, he'll come back." Her words were a quick jumble as she tried to convince them both.

"I'm not talking about a test from Charles, I'm talking about a test for us. For you and me." He reached down for his crutches and stood to face her. "We have to do it, Sarah. We're both stronger now. We have each other and we have Charles. The rest of the world doesn't matter. We need to do this if only to prove it to ourselves."

Sarah couldn't take a deep breath. Could she do it? Gideon saw her uncertainty.

"You handled Jones without any problems. You put him quite firmly in his place."

Sarah snorted. "He is an ignorant fool and hardly signifies."

Gideon laughed as he moved toward her. "My dear, most men can be described thusly."

He stopped right in front of her and she rested her hands on his chest as she looked at him anxiously. "You would disparage your sex?"

Gideon nodded in mock seriousness. "I am in a position to do so, being one myself." He nuzzled her temple. "Don't worry, Sarah. You shall conquer London as you have me."

Chapter Twenty-Three

ɕ

"Are you sure you won't come in?" Sarah asked anxiously, peering into the carriage.

Gideon turned to see Peters lean out the door with a weak smile. "No thank you. I am not up to any of Randall's sanctimonious lectures today."

Gideon's step faltered, and not because of his new prosthesis. "Perhaps we should send a note to Charles instead," he mused. He did not relish Lord Jason Randall cornering him with a heartfelt lecture today either.

Peters laughed and closed the carriage door with a snap. "Oh no, you don't," he told Gideon through the window. "You have to do a little bowing and scraping. Borden deserves as much, and in front of witnesses."

"What about me?" Sarah whined plaintively with a little grin. "Do I have to bow and scrape?"

"Never, my dear Mrs. North," Peters said gallantly. "You are here so that when Borden dismisses Gideon's abject misery he'll see that there is more to come home to than this ugly fellow."

Gideon preened as he adjusted his hat. "I though the beaver quite fetching, actually, not to mention this new block of wood." He looked down at the tip of the prosthesis poking out from under his pant leg. He still wasn't used to seeing another full leg there. It disoriented him a little each time he saw it. He looked back up at Peters and dropped his teasing tone. "I want you to know that I appreciate what you've done, Peters."

Peters waved at him dismissively. "It's my job to know the best prosthesis makers in London. But you were robbed. I didn't have the heart to tell you how much he overcharged."

"That's not all I meant and you know it."

Peters dismissed him again. "I have no idea what you are talking about. My time at Blakely Farm is a blur, I'm afraid. I was exhausted and quite, quite drunk." He pointed accusingly at Gideon. "And for that, sir, I hold you accountable." He tapped the roof of the carriage with his fist. "Driver, save me from Randall. Away!" The carriage lurched as Gideon watched Sarah wave.

Sarah turned and walked back to him, taking his arm in hers. Without a word they turned as one and faced the house. Beside him he saw Sarah straighten her shoulders and take a deep breath.

"Do I look all right?" she asked. He almost snorted at the womanly question.

"You look beautiful," he answered honestly. And she did. She wore some sort of military style hat in blue and green that made her cheeks look pink and her eyes shine. Her gorgeous blonde hair peeked out around the edges. She'd done something different with it, but he wasn't sure what. He liked it. "You look good in blue."

Sarah smiled at him. "I've been told that before." She took a deep breath. "Are you ready?"

At his nod she tugged him forward and he made his slow way to the steps. He wasn't used to the new leg yet. He was still relying heavily on a cane, but he felt freer than he had in years. He was actually walking. His hip and leg were protesting the weight. He supposed it would take some getting used to. But by God, he was going to walk in there and claim Charles. It was a heady feeling.

* * * * *

Charles' eyes nearly crossed with boredom as he listened to Tony Richards brag for the tenth—or was it twentieth?—time about the fact his son took three steps without falling today and he was only ten months old. He felt vaguely guilty for not caring one fig so he listened politely.

Peters was supposed to have sent a note after seeing Gideon and Sarah. Perhaps he didn't remember that promise? He'd been rather drunk when Charles had loaded him into the hired coach. Or it may be he was too busy trying to save Gideon's life to write. Gideon might even now be on his deathbed.

"Excuse me," a voice drawled and someone picked up Charles' arm by the wrist. Richards stopped talking and Charles turned in surprise to Simon Gantry. "Oh good," Simon said with relief. "He still has a pulse." He gestured behind him at Daniel Steinberg and Derek Knightly, who were laughing at his expense. "We were afraid you'd bored him to death, Richards." He waved across the room and called, "He's fine! Everyone can stop worrying."

Even Richards smiled reluctantly as the room burst into guffaws. "I suppose I may be talking about it a little too much?" he asked with good humor.

"Perhaps a tad," Simon agreed, nodding sagely. "We're all avoiding you until the boy leaves for Eton."

"Harrow," Richards said distinctly as he turned and walked toward his lovers, Lord and Lady Randall. "Eton," he mumbled and shuddered.

"I went to Eton," Simon said, affronted.

Charles bit his lip to keep from laughing. Simon regarded him with a jaundiced eye. "Still holding out, eh?" he asked. "How long before you go running back to Ashton on the Green?"

Charles sighed dejectedly. "That obvious, is it?" He twisted his neck, trying to relieve the tension there. "I don't like London. There's too many people, and I don't fit in here." He smiled grimly. "I'm a country boy, you know, a farm lad."

"You may have been once," Simon said as he casually gestured a footman with a tray over to them. He put his empty glass on the tray. "Another, if you would, please," he asked and then turned back to Charles. "But not anymore. You're more than that now."

"But not enough." Charles failed to keep all the bitterness out of his voice.

"Don't be a bore," Simon told him, accepting a full glass of whiskey from the footman. "Thank God Kate serves more than tea at tea," he said fervently and took a sip. "We don't look down on you, do we? Is there someone else you'd rather be socializing with who does? If we are not good enough, feel free to leave."

Charles sighed in frustration. "You're right. I'm sorry. I had to deal with some very aggravating attitudes today when negotiating for a horse. It's meant to be a surprise for North, but at this rate I'm not sure I can pull it off."

Simon merely cocked a brow at him.

Charles closed his eyes briefly in mortification. "Can I say I'm sorry again? I've fallen into a pit of self-pity and I can't seem to find my way out."

"Ah yes, my old friend the pit of self-pity," Simon drawled. "I like to crawl in there now and then. It's so dark and cozy."

"Shut up, Gantry," Knightly said, shoving the other man out of the way. "The lot of you with your self-pitying ways. Makes a man want to vomit." He turned to Charles. "No one turns away good money, Borden. Shove it in their face and they'll take it. To hell with their attitudes. I'm no gentleman either, and it's never stopped me."

Simon shook the spilled whiskey off his hand. "No, I daresay not, Knightly," he agreed sarcastically. "But then being the size of an ox helps prevents anyone from stopping you."

"Who is trying to stop Derek?" a feminine voice inquired, and the men parted to allow Knightly's lover, Mrs. Witherspoon, into their midst. She was a beauty, small and curvaceous, with auburn curls and sweet freckles on her nose. Charles ached to see Sarah's long blonde hair instead. Mrs. Witherspoon wrapped her arm around Knightly's and blinked innocently at Simon. "You've spilled your drink, Mr. Gantry."

Knightly was also the lover of Mrs. Witherspoon's husband. Charles felt a pang of homesickness like a punch to the gut. He wanted Sarah to claim him like that in front of a roomful of people. She would too. He missed her and Gideon so much. Maybe they didn't need the Arabian he was here to buy. He should be at home with Gideon. If he'd let that damn doctor pour poison down his throat Charles would kill him.

"Really, Gantry," Knightly said with disgust, handing him a handkerchief. There was a gleam of humor in his eye. "Can't you hold your liquor?" Simon stood there glaring, speechless at Knightly's effrontery.

"Good heavens, Simon, you're all wet." Miss Very Thomas, the Randalls' niece, came up and glanced in distaste at Simon's wet coat. "And you smell like a distillery. Not that I've ever been in one, but I assume they smell like you." She smiled around the group and linked arms with Mrs. Witherspoon. "Hello! How are you all? Enjoying Jason's whiskey, are you? Drink it all up. He deserves it."

"Keeping Tarrant away again, is he?" Knightly growled. "You should listen to him, Very. Tarrant is not a nice fellow."

"I like them that way, Derek," she said defensively. "You are a thoroughly abominable fellow, and I like you, don't I?"

Mrs. Witherspoon laughed. "Thoroughly abominable. Say your apologies to Simon, Derek."

"Hmm, saw that, did you?" he muttered. "Apologies, Gantry."

"I should say so," Simon said with a sniff.

Miss Thomas leaned over and kissed him on the cheek. "There, all better." Simon just looked at her and she shrugged. "Well, it works for little Anthony."

Simon groaned. "Isn't this where I entered the conversation?"

The drawing room door opened and the Randall's man announced, "Mr. and Mrs. Gideon North," and Charles' heart stopped beating for a moment as he stood there and gaped at them.

They were gorgeous. Sarah was nervous as hell. He could see it in her eyes and the set of her shoulders. But she needn't be. She was so bloody gorgeous she drew every male eye in the room. She smoothed her skirts. He didn't remember her owning a dress cut that low. He frowned. What was Gideon thinking letting her wear that in here with all these men ogling her? He grinned at the hat. It was perfect, just as Mrs. Duncan said it would be.

He frowned again. She looked shorter next to Gideon. He stumbled back a step as Gideon took a step toward him. A step. With a cane, not crutches. Charles quickly looked down. He had a prosthesis. He'd been gone three bloody days and the stubborn fool went and got a prosthesis. Charles vowed then and there to storm off in anger more often.

He glanced in disbelief at Sarah. She was watching him with pleading eyes, and a bright red blush stained her cheeks. It was then he noticed the room was unnaturally quiet. He glanced around to see everyone looking between him and Gideon and Sarah. Suddenly Lady Randall broke the silence.

"Welcome," she said as she walked toward them, her hand outstretched. Lord Randall and Richards followed her.

"Lady Randall," Gideon said formally with a small bow as he took her hand. "May I introduce my wife, Mrs. Sarah North?"

"How do you do?" Sarah murmured shyly.

"And this is my husband Lord Randall and our dear friend Mr. Anthony Richards," Lady Randall said without an ounce of embarrassment.

He could see the moment Sarah caught the implication. Her eyes widened. "How do you do?" she murmured again as first Randall and then Richards bowed over her hand.

Randall clapped Gideon on the back. "So you've finally come back to London? It's good to see you." Gideon hardly spared him a glance. He was too busy staring intently at Charles.

Richards held out his arm to Sarah. It took her a moment to realize what he'd done, and she blushed again as she took it. Richards looked over at Charles. Without a word he led Sarah over to him.

"What are you doing here?" he asked, and then could have kicked himself as she looked uncertain. "I mean...London. London?" He couldn't think straight.

Sarah looked at everyone standing around and then a resolute look came over her face. She let go of Richards and took a step that brought her quite close to Charles. Too close for public scrutiny. She reached up and toyed with a button on his coat. "We came to fetch you home."

"You did?" Charles was aware he sounded like an idiot, but he couldn't do anything about it.

Sarah nodded. "Mmm-hmm. Do you want to come?" She looked up at him with those melting brown eyes, pleading with him.

He cupped her elbows in his hands. "Yes," he said quietly.

Sarah's arms slid around his waist and he gathered her close. She sniffed into his neckcloth. "Good," she said, her voice muffled.

"Good," Gideon said from over her shoulder.

Charles looked up at him and had to close his eyes for a moment his relief was so great. "You didn't do it."

Gideon shook his head. "No." He looked down. "I got this instead. What do you think?"

Sarah wasn't letting go of him. She had a death grip on his middle, as if afraid he would disappear. Charles looked over her shoulder and down to see the tip of the prosthesis poking out of Gideon's pant leg. Charles nearly broke down and cried but he didn't want to embarrass himself. "Not very pretty," he choked out, "but it will do."

Gideon feigned mock disappointment. "But I want pretty."

Charles was stunned into speechlessness again. Gideon joking about his leg?

"Honestly, North," Gantry drawled, "don't be selfish. You've got enough pretty for one man."

Charles looked over to see the other man eyeing him and Sarah appreciatively and it was his turn to blush. He supposed they all knew now, then, didn't they? And he didn't care. He hugged Sarah with a huge grin. He could see the smile in Gideon's eyes.

"That thing really is ugly, North," Knightly said. He hunkered down next to Gideon and actually knocked on his leg. "How does it work?" He yanked up Gideon's pant leg. "Does it have a hinge of some sort?"

Gideon smacked him on the shoulder with his cane. "Leave off, Knightly," he growled. "Take offense if you like, but you are not the one I want manhandling my leg right now."

Knightly actually had the grace to blush. "Sorry," he mumbled. But he rubbed his chin contemplatively. "Come see me tomorrow. I've a few ideas rattling around about that. I'd like to show you some sketches. I think I've got a better design. You need one for riding too, correct?"

Charles could almost see the cogs turning in Knightly's head. He might be a rude bully, but he was a genius. There was no denying that. "I'll get him there," Charles promised.

"And you must bring Mrs. North too, Mr. Borden," Mrs. Witherspoon added with a smile, pulling Knightly along. Ian Witherspoon stood behind them grinning. He was as polished as Knightly was rough. "We would love to get to know her better."

Suddenly everyone was saying goodbye and they were ushered to the door before Charles was aware of what was happening. They hardly spoke as the footman hailed a hackney. Gideon eyed the horses critically.

"Just get in," Charles told him in exasperation before he could start. "You can berate the hackney drivers tomorrow." After he'd helped both Gideon and Sarah inside he asked, "Where are you staying?"

"Osborne's," Gideon told the driver.

"That's where I'm staying," Charles said in amazement.

Gideon shook his head. "Of course it is. It's where you always stay in London."

Before he could retort, Sarah grabbed his hand. "Oh, if only we were more private. I want to climb into your lap and eat you up. I missed you so much."

"And that is why we are all staying at Osborne's," Gideon replied drily. "We shall be conveniently located for lap sitting and eating up."

* * * * *

Sarah gasped as he slipped inside her. Gideon had to pause and breathe deeply for a moment. It was more amazing than he'd imagined. Charles was already filling her back passage, pressing against Gideon as he pushed fully into her. She moaned as he came to rest.

"Are you all right?" Charles asked in a rough voice. "You feel so bloody tight."

Sarah nodded jerkily. She straddled Gideon, their position mirroring what they'd done less than a week ago when Gideon was the one between them. He'd loved that, loved being inside Sarah while Charles was inside him. But he loved this too. Knowing they were sharing Sarah in the most intimate way possible, truly being together, connected in such a basic way. One, where before they were three.

"Talk to me, Sarah," Gideon growled. As wonderful as it felt, if she was uncomfortable they'd stop. They had a lifetime to work up to this. They didn't have to rush into it tonight. But it felt right. There had been no hesitation on her part. She'd wanted them both inside and had told them so.

A tear slid down her cheek and Gideon cursed and started to pull out, but she shook her head. "No, Gideon. I'm crying because it feels so good to have you both this way." She wrapped Charles' arms around her and held tightly to his hands while she rested her cheek against his chest. She pressed down slightly and the movement pushed the tip of his cock against Charles'.

Charles shuddered and Gideon could feel it inside Sarah. He could feel Charles move inside her. He gasped at the shock and wonder of it.

"Promise you won't leave us again, Charles," she whispered. "I couldn't bear it."

"I came to London to buy a horse," he said sheepishly.

Sarah's eyes flew open. "What?"

Charles looked at Gideon apologetically over her shoulder. "There's an Arabian here, another one from von Fechtig's stables. I came to buy it for you." He shook his head. "I never imagined you'd believe I'd left for good." He frowned. "I'm not happy about it, actually. Did you really think I'd give this up?" He thrust into Sarah and she and Gideon caught their breath. "I'll never willingly walk away from you two," he vowed roughly. "You'll have to kick me out."

"I've tried that," Gideon said with amusement. "It didn't work."

Charles pulled out and as he slid back in Gideon pulled out just as Charles had explained before they started. "Bloody hell," Gideon growled. It felt so good he saw stars. The press of Charles' prick sliding down his and then back up... Hell, he could feel the full lip of the head as it caught on his. He shuddered. "I'm not going to last."

"You better," Charles ground out in challenge. "You'll hold out until Sarah comes."

Sarah was shaking like a leaf. "I won't either," she said breathlessly. "To have you both inside me at the same time is the most wondrous thing I've ever felt." She looked down at Gideon. "It's like velvet and diamonds." He smiled in understanding and then arched his neck as he and Charles passed inside her again.

"What?" Charles asked. He sounded almost grim as he spoke through clenched teeth. Gideon was glad to know he wasn't the only one on the edge already.

"A fantasy," Sarah gasped. "I fantasized about rolling around in black velvet dropping diamonds from my hands. It was the most decadent thing I'd ever thought of. But this surpasses it."

Charles pressed her forward so that she fell onto her hands beside Gideon's shoulders. Gideon's angle changed, and he could tell from Sarah's groan that he was now pressing against her clitoris as Charles drove his prick more forcefully into her along Gideon's. Damn if Charles wasn't good at this. Gideon grinned. "Did you ask someone about this too?" he asked.

"Yes," Charles growled. "If we're going to do it, we're going to do it right."

Sarah couldn't catch her breath. Her face was right over his and Gideon could see the rapture of her expression, her intense concentration. She had her eyes closed. He slid out and in, keeping pace with Charles, watching her growing excitement.

"Yes, Sarah," he whispered. "Come for us, darling. Let me see it, feel it. And then we will come for you."

She nodded. He saw her shoulders relax and her walls trembled around his cock. Charles cursed. Suddenly her eyes flew open and she looked panicked. "Kiss me, Gideon," she cried out.

He reached up and grabbed a fistful of her hair and pulled her down for a kiss that was rough and all-consuming. As soon as his tongue swiped into her mouth she gave a muffled cry and began to come. Her hands moved to grip his shoulders, her nails digging in, and she groaned as her pulsing sex squeezed him so tightly he couldn't move.

"Sarah," Charles groaned. His prick started to jerk in her behind and Gideon felt Charles' release, felt the overwhelming heat blossom on the other side of the thin wall separating them.

He came. How could he not? The moment was tender, erotic, fulfilling. All the things he'd dreamed Sarah would bring to them. He broke their kiss with a gasp and buried his face in the curve of her neck, holding on tightly as he spilled inside her with Charles. He never wanted this moment to end. And it wouldn't. He would have this forever now. His head dropped back on the bed behind him and Sarah collapsed on his chest.

When his tears fell he wasn't ashamed. He lay there and felt the cool tracks of them on his temple. He felt a similar wetness on his chest where Sarah lay.

"What's this?" Charles asked quietly. He moved and Sarah squirmed on top of Gideon. Then she sighed and let out a little hiccup. "Why are you both crying?" Charles whispered.

"I never thought to have this sort of happiness," Sarah said tearfully. "To have not just one man but two love me so thoroughly. To belong to someone at last."

"Yes," Gideon said. "Yes. To belong to someone at last."

Charles climbed from the bed and returned a moment later. He cleaned Sarah with a cloth and then climbed into bed beside them. He tucked a strand of Sarah's hair behind her ear and then tweaked Gideon's earlobe. "From the moment I met you, Sarah, I knew you were the one." Gideon turned to look at him and Charles wiped a tear off his cheek with his thumb. "I knew that you would bring us together. That you would break through Gideon's defenses at last and make everything work."

Sarah slid off Gideon and he missed her warmth. But he couldn't be upset as she climbed on Charles with a sob. Charles shushed her with laughter in his voice. "I knew the minute I saw Gideon that my life would never be the same. I had the same feeling when we met you."

Gideon nodded and soothed a hand down her back. "I *had* built up my defenses. You're right, Charles. I wasn't letting you or anyone else in. But Sarah chipped away at that until I couldn't resist anymore. And suddenly the gates were open and there was no turning back."

"I want to go home," Sarah sniffed. "I came to London. I did it. But I don't like it here and I want to go home to the farm. Where we are strong together and we are building something. Something wonderful." She looked at Gideon from the shelter of Charles' arms. "You shall get a better leg and a new Arabian and then you are taking me home."

"Yes," Charles and Gideon said at the same time. All three of them laughed. "Yes," Gideon tried again. "We shall go home. You told me that our house was filled with love and I was at the center of it. But you are, Sarah, darling, and I want to watch you blossom there. I want to make a future there with you and Charles."

"A future I have waited a very long time for," Charles said quietly.

Gideon leaned over and kissed Charles' shoulder. "Your wait is over," he whispered. He could feel the twinkle in his eye. "My defenses are down and the gates are open," he added with a heavy dose of innuendo.

Charles caught the back of his head and dragged him close while keeping the other arm wrapped around Sarah. "Good," he whispered against Gideon's lips. He softly kissed him. "Because I find that I really, really like being in the back, no matter who's in the middle."

Gideon laughed softly as Sarah exclaimed "Charles!" and hit him on the chest. Then she snuggled up to him. "I'll let Gideon be in the middle next time, but then it's my turn again."

Both men laughed, but the look they exchanged was heated. "I agree," Gideon murmured, and Charles nodded.

"And when we get home, it's Charles' turn," Sarah said with a wicked smile at Gideon.

"I agree," Gideon said again, staring at Charles.

"Absolutely," Charles replied. "And about time."

Epilogue

✿

"I'm going to have a baby," Sarah told Anne without preamble.

They were in the gazebo watching Charles and Gideon down in the paddock. They were arguing over a horse, of course. Gideon was too soft on them according to Charles, and Charles was too hard on them according to Gideon. She smiled. She didn't mind the fighting. The making up was extremely enjoyable. Fights usually meant Gideon was in the middle. She liked that almost as much as Gideon.

"What?" Anne yelled in astonishment. "Why didn't you tell me?"

Sarah turned from watching her men to smile at Anne. "That's what I'm doing."

"Have you told Gideon and Charles yet?" Anne asked, coming over to give Sarah a one-armed hug while bouncing little baby Bertie in the other.

Sarah shook her head. "No. I think Charles suspects, but Gideon has no idea." She glanced over her shoulder as Gideon yelled loudly at Charles. She saw him pointing angrily to the barn and Charles glared back at him, hands on hips.

"Why?" Anne demanded. "You have to tell them."

"I plan to," she said. "Tonight." She turned and put her hands on the railing as Gideon turned and waved. She waved back. He tugged on the lead of the horse he was training and resumed walking it around the paddock. He didn't even need a cane now. She was continually amazed at the mobility Derek Knightly's prosthesis gave him. It was weighted perfectly to Gideon. He said it felt almost like his own leg. His gait was still ungainly, but he looked beautiful to Sarah.

"I am afraid that it is all too perfect," she whispered.

Down in the paddock the grooms came and took the horses. Charles ran over and put one hand on the top rung as he vaulted over the fence. He started walking backward toward the gazebo, clearly taunting Gideon who calmly walked over and used the gate. Charles stopped and waited for him on the path and threw his arm around Gideon's shoulders affectionately. They headed toward the ladies with a wave.

"I suppose because it is perfect," Sarah mused. She hadn't asked for a good day for a very long while. They came without asking now.

"Yes," Anne agreed. "Yes, it is." Anne laughed as they heard the duke hail Gideon and Charles as they walked past Sarah's bench under the tree where he was reading a book, Mr. Haversham dozing beside him.

Sarah couldn't wait for them. She turned and dashed down the stairs and ran to meet Gideon and Charles on the path, her arms flung wide.

The End

Also by *Samantha Kane*

એ

eBooks:

A Lady In Waiting
Brothers in Arms 1: The Courage to Love
Brothers in Arms 2: Love Under Siege
Brothers in Arms 3: Love's Strategy
Brothers in Arms 4: At Love's Command
Brothers in Arms 5: Retreat from Love
Brothers in Arms 6: Love in Exile
Brothers in Arms 7: Love's Fortress
Cougar Challenge: Play it Again, Sam
Ellora's Cavemen: Jewels of the Nile II *(anthology)*
Hunters for Hire: Tomorrow
Islands

Print Books:

Aged to Perfection *(anthology)*
At Love's Command
Ellora's Cavemen: Jewels of the Nile II *(anthology)*
Love in Exile
Love Under Siege
Retreat From Love
Tempt The Cougar *(anthology)*
The Courage to Love
Tomorrow

About the Author

ഇ

Samantha has a Master's Degree in History, and is a full time writer and mother. She lives in North Carolina with her husband and three children.

Samantha Kane welcomes comments from readers. You can find her website and email address on her author bio page at www.ellorascave.com.

Tell Us What You Think

We appreciate hearing reader opinions about our books. You can email us at Comments@EllorasCave.com.

Why an electronic book?

We live in the Information Age — an exciting time in the history of human civilization, in which technology rules supreme and continues to progress in leaps and bounds every minute of every day. For a multitude of reasons, more and more avid literary fans are opting to purchase e-books instead of paper books. The question from those not yet initiated into the world of electronic reading is simply: *Why?*

1. *Price.* An electronic title at Ellora's Cave Publishing and Cerridwen Press runs anywhere from 40% to 75% less than the cover price of the exact same title in paperback format. Why? Basic mathematics and cost. It is less expensive to publish an e-book (no paper and printing, no warehousing and shipping) than it is to publish a paperback, so the savings are passed along to the consumer.

2. *Space.* Running out of room in your house for your books? That is one worry you will never have with electronic books. For a low one-time cost, you can purchase a handheld device specifically designed for e-reading. Many e-readers have large, convenient screens for viewing. Better yet, hundreds of titles can be stored within your new library — on a single microchip. There are a variety of e-readers from different manufacturers. You can also read e-books on your PC or laptop computer. (Please note that Ellora's Cave does not endorse any specific brands.

You can check our websites at www.ellorascave.com or www.cerridwenpress.com for information we make available to new consumers.)

3. *Mobility.* Because your new e-library consists of only a microchip within a small, easily transportable e-reader, your entire cache of books can be taken with you wherever you go.

4. *Personal Viewing Preferences.* Are the words you are currently reading too small? Too large? Too... ANNOYING? Paperback books cannot be modified according to personal preferences, but e-books can.

5. *Instant Gratification.* Is it the middle of the night and all the bookstores near you are closed? Are you tired of waiting days, sometimes weeks, for bookstores to ship the novels you bought? Ellora's Cave Publishing sells instantaneous downloads twenty-four hours a day, seven days a week, every day of the year. Our webstore is never closed. Our e-book delivery system is 100% automated, meaning your order is filled as soon as you pay for it.

Those are a few of the top reasons why electronic books are replacing paperbacks for many avid readers.

As always, Ellora's Cave and Cerridwen Press welcome your questions and comments. We invite you to email us at Comments@ellorascave.com or write to us directly at Ellora's Cave Publishing Inc., 1056 Home Avenue, Akron, OH 44310-3502.

ELLORA'S CAVE

Romanticon

Annual convention
for women who
refuse to behave

COLUMBUS DAY WEEKEND

www.JasmineJade.com/Romanticon
For additional info contact: conventions@ellorascave.com

Discover for yourself why readers can't get enough
of the multiple award-winning publisher
Ellora's Cave.

Whether you prefer e-books or paperbacks,
be sure to visit EC on the web at
www.ellorascave.com

for an erotic reading experience that will leave you
breathless.

Made in the USA
Lexington, KY
01 December 2010